THE ALCHEMY

This Large Print Book carries the
Seal of Approval of N.A.V.H.

THE ALCHEMY

GILBERT MORRIS & LYNN MORRIS

THORNDIKE PRESS

An imprint of Thomson Gale, a part of The Thomson Corporation

LT
CF
Mor
2008

Detroit • New York • San Francisco • New Haven, Conn. • Waterville, Maine • London

THOMSON

™

GALE

LIBRARY OF CONGRESS CATALOGING-IN-PUBLICATION DATA

Morris, Gilbert.
    The alchemy / by Gilbert Morris and Lynn Morris.
        p. cm. — (Creoles series)
    ISBN-13: 978-0-7862-9838-9 (hardcover : alk. paper)
    ISBN-10: 0-7862-9838-3 (hardcover : alk. paper)
    1. Women — Louisiana — Fiction. 2. New Orleans (La.) — Fiction. 3.
Creoles — Fiction. 4. Large type books. I. Morris, Lynn. II. Title.
    PS3563.O8742A77 2007
    813'.54—dc22   2007022287

Published in 2007 by arrangement with Thomas Nelson, Inc.

Printed in the United States of America on permanent paper
10 9 8 7 6 5 4 3 2 1

To John Clark,
my beloved brother in the Lord.

THE CREOLE HERITAGE

In the early nineteenth century, the culture of New Orleans was as rich and wildly varied as the citizens' complexions. Pure Spanish families, descended from haughty dons, still dwelt in the city, and some pure French families resided there, but many were already mingled with both Spaniards and Africans. Acadians — or "Cajuns," as they came to be called — lived outside of the city. This small pocket of Frenchmen had wandered far from home, but, like many groups in New Orleans, they stubbornly kept much of their eighteenth-century heritage intact and ingrained.

Of course, there were many slaves, but there were also the *gens de couleur libres,* or free men and women of color. Some of these were pure Africans, but most of them were the mulattoes, griffes, quadroons, and ocotoroons who were the result of French and Spanish blending with slaves. There were Americans, too, though they were strictly confined to the "American district." And there were Creoles, people of French and Spanish blood who were born outside of their native countries. Creoles born in New Orleans were Louisianians, but they were not considered Americans.

All well-born Creole families sent their children to receive a classical education at the Ursuline Convent or the Jesuit schools, and both institutions accepted charity children.

This series of novels traces the history of four young women who were fellow students at the Ursuline Convent School:

- *The Exiles:* Chantel
- *The Immortelles:* Damita
- *The Alchemy:* Simone
- *The Tapestry:* Leonie

■ ■ ■ ■

PART ONE:
1832–1837
COLIN

■ ■ ■ ■

CHAPTER ONE

The Marquis Armand de Cuvier, Lord Beaufort, leaned forward with a sense of satisfaction as he touched the tip of his quill to the white parchment. Quickly the musical notes seemed to flow from his heart (which the marquis felt was the *real* producer of music!), and something close to rapture touched the composer. He continued to write as rapidly as possible, for he had discovered that when he composed his scores, when the inspiration flowed, nothing must be allowed to interfere.

The sun threw golden beams through the window to the marquis' right hand, and the warm breezes of May caressed him, stirring his hair gently. Spring had come to France in the year of 1832 almost in a bound, it seemed, bringing out the greenery and causing the flowers to burst in small explosions of color. Even now, as the marquis continued to cover the parchment with musical

11

notes, he was conscious of a sense of well-being.

The composition had not gone well for some time, and Lord Beaufort had lost sleep over it for weeks. Ordinarily the marquis was a gentle man, soft-spoken, with a ready smile, but when whatever demon it is that clogs up the inspiration in the mind of the composer gripped him, he became short-tempered and hard to live with. His beloved wife, Jeanne, had learned to recognize those times and managed to keep him from the more violent outbursts. The servants also had learned to recognize the marquis' uncreative periods and walked softly around him during those days.

An ormolu clock beat out a rhythm like soft heartbeats, and once, as the marquis scribbled furiously, from a lower story came the sound of a clock tolling off one — two — three, sprinkling the hours all through the house. The marquis paid no attention to it. When he was composing, he had the gift of closing himself off to almost anything.

A loud, angry voice from outside his window sounded suddenly, the violence of it breaking into the composer's inspiration. "Cannot I have even a moment's peace?" he cried aloud.

Anger swept through Lord Beaufort, and

with a violent gesture, he flung the quill down and saw a blob of ink obliterate his last few notations. He leaped up, knocking his chair over backwards. It fell with a crash as he moved quickly to the window. At forty-six, Armand de Cuvier was an active man of medium height with wavy brown hair and eyes that were ordinarily warm. Just now, however, they seemed to flash, sending off flecks of light. Leaning over the window and looking down, he saw his gardener, Philippe, a huge man of forty, grasping a stranger by the arm. Philippe was shouting something, and the young man he held was trying to respond.

Suddenly Philippe's massive arm moved, and his fist caught the visitor high on the forehead. He fell backwards as if poleaxed and lay without moving.

"What in the world is going on down there, Philippe?"

"This fellow insists on seeing you, my lord. He would not take no for an answer."

"Well, I think you've killed the fellow. I'll be right down."

The marquis hurried out of the room, stepping lightly down the stairs, through the hallway, and outside. He walked quickly to where Philippe was picking up the young fellow.

"Now, what's all this about?"

The young man Philippe gripped tightly by the arms was six feet tall but not strongly built like the gardener. His eyes were focused, at least, and the marquis saw that they were of a brilliant, cornflower blue. His hat had been knocked off, revealing thick hair of an auburn tint that caught the sun. He had a wedge-shaped face, a wide mouth, and his eyes were deep-set. When he saw the marquis, he tried to bow, but Philippe held him tightly. "Monsieur, I am Colin Seymour." Then he tried to speak in French, but it was so pitiful that the marquis could not understand much of it.

The marquis asked, "You are English?"

"Yes, sir," Seymour said at once. "I'm sorry I don't speak French."

"It doesn't matter," Armand said. "What do you want here?"

"I'll tell you what he wants," Philippe broke in. He shook the young man, saying, "He broke into the barn, and he's stolen some food."

"Is that right?"

"I did sleep in the barn, but I didn't steal any food."

"He's a liar!" Philippe said roughly. "He's a tramp. Look at him."

Indeed, Colin Seymour was dressed in

14

clothing that would have done dishonor to a tramp. He wore a pair of brown britches that were patched on both knees and in the seat, and the stockings that enclosed his lower legs were more runs and holes than cloth. His shirt had at one time been white but now was filthy, and the light-greenish jacket looked as if it were covered with mold. His hair was untrimmed, and his unshaven face was grimy. He was thin and had a lean and hungry look about him.

"What do you want here?" the marquis demanded.

"I was just —"

"He wanted to steal something," Philippe said loudly. "That's all these tramps want."

"I expect you're right. Hang onto him and have Merle go get the sheriff."

"Please, sir, I really am not a thief!"

"Shut your mouth!" Philippe said, shaking the young man like a rat. "You're going to jail where you belong."

At that moment the front door of the house opened, and Jeanne de Cuvier, Lady Beaufort, stepped outside and approached the trio. She was a small woman, well shaped, in her late thirties. Her hair was light with a trace of gold in it, and her eyes were hazel flecked with blue.

"What is this, Armand?"

"Oh, just a petty thief, my dear. Don't trouble yourself about it. Philippe, take him now, and hold him until Merle gets back with the sheriff."

"Just a minute, Philippe." Madam de Cuvier had her eyes fixed on the young man's features. "He doesn't look very dangerous to me."

"You don't know these tramps, my lady," Philippe grunted. "He'd slit your throat in a minute if he had the chance."

"What is your name, young man?"

"My name is Colin Seymour, Madam."

"And you are English?"

"I am American."

"That is even worse," Philippe snarled, tightening his grip. "Everyone knows the Yankees are nothing but a bunch of killers."

"Please go inside, my dear," Armand said with concern. "In your condition, you don't need this excitement."

"Just a minute, Armand. Let me talk with him."

Armand threw up his hands. "That will be the end of it, I suppose. You take in every broken-winged bird until I can't get in the house, but this fellow is not a crippled animal. He could be dangerous, as Philippe says."

"How long have you been in France, Colin?"

Young Seymour attempted to smile. "About two weeks. I was picked up by the police and put in jail."

"You see!" Philippe exclaimed triumphantly. "He's a criminal!"

"I had done nothing and committed no crime — unless having no money is a crime in France."

"You're bleeding," Jeanne said. Indeed, Philippe's massive fist had opened a cut over the young man's left eyebrow. The blood was trickling down, and Jeanne said, "Bring him inside. That must be attended to."

Philippe began to protest, but Armand interrupted. "Never mind, Philippe. All he can do is run away, and that might solve the problem."

"He'll cut our throats. You'll see!" Philippe said, glaring at Seymour. "Give me the word, and I'll have Merle go for the sheriff."

"Come inside, young man," Jeanne said.

"Go on. Do what she tells you," Armand commanded.

Colin followed the woman, aware that Philippe was glaring at him as he left. He had no intention of escaping, however.

17

When they reached the kitchen, the house-keeper, Josephine Bettencourt, stared at them. "Who is this?"

"Another one of your mistress's injured creatures."

"Sit down there, young man," Jeanne said. "Josephine, get something that we can clean this blood off with, and perhaps a plaster to put over it."

"Sit down there," Armand commanded fiercely, pointing at a stool. He stood back and studied the young man as the two women cleaned the blood off his face. He could not help but smile when he saw the tender expression in his wife's eyes. *I think she would be kind to Judas,* he thought. He watched as they carefully put a plaster over the cut, and then he stepped forward. "Now that you've saved his life, I have a few questions for him."

Jeanne went to her husband and took his arm. "He's only a boy. How old are you, Colin?"

"I'm twenty-one, ma'am."

" 'Ma'am'? What is 'ma'am'?"

"That's what we call ladies in America."

"Ma'am! What a hideous word! Everything from America is ugly," Armand said, but kindness had begun to show in his expression. "Why did you come to France?"

"I came all the way here to meet you, sir."

"To meet me!" Armand exclaimed in surprise. "But I don't know you."

"But I know you — at least, I know your music."

Armand suddenly slapped his forehead with his open palm. "Oh no, don't tell me! Not another genius who has come to let me expose his talent to the world."

"Armand, be quiet. Let him talk," Jeanne said firmly. "Tell us about yourself."

"I want to sing in the opera," Colin said simply.

Armand stared at him and shook his head, laughing cynically. "So do about one million other people the world over. It seems half the people I meet want to be in opera. What do you know about music, anyway? Have you studied?"

"Not exactly."

"Not exactly? What does that mean? You've either studied, or you haven't."

"I've never been to a singing school, but I want to learn."

Armand was amused. Indeed, he had been besieged for years by budding operatic hopefuls. He could no longer attend a party without someone saying, "I have a nephew who has great talent. If you would only take him in hand, Marquis . . ." Armand had developed a hard shell when such requests were thrown at him. Sometimes he lost his temper. One lady had produced her son with a statement: "I believe my son has a great career inside him." Armand had replied shortly: "That's a good place for it, Madam." His wife, of course, had chastised him for his rudeness.

Armand had a surefire system for eliminating such applicants as young Seymour. "Can you sing right now?" he demanded. Usually this was enough to shut down the request, for most singers required music, an instrument to accompany them, the right setting, and the right mood, and when they were challenged directly, many were simply unable to sing a note.

"Well, you say you want to be a singer. Can you sing?"

"Yes sir."

Jeanne giggled and put her hand on her stomach that was just beginning to swell with the child she was carrying. "He is a young man with much confidence."

"Confidence doesn't fill operatic houses. Voices do that," Armand said sternly. "Very well," he said, "sing."

Instantly Colin Seymour opened his mouth and began to sing. It was an aria from *The Barber of Seville,* by Gioacchino

Rossini, a rather demanding piece for any tenor. The room was filled with the sound of the song, which was a rousing piece of music.

Seymour's eyes were alight, and despite the ugly, purplish lump that was developing on his forehead, he seemed completely unconscious of anything except the song. It was not a trained voice, as both Armand and Jeanne saw at once, but it had power that most tenors never even dreamed of. At one point it practically rattled the dishes on the shelves, and Josephine Bettencourt's eyes flew open, and she covered her mouth with her hand.

Finally the song ended, and Seymour said nothing. He simply stood waiting.

"Well," Armand said slowly, "you certainly are loud."

"Oh, he's more than that, Armand!" Jeanne protested. "He has such a sweet sound in his voice."

"You speak Italian, then?"

"No, sir, I do not."

"How do you know the words?"

"I memorized them from hearing them onstage. I have some idea what they mean, but even without being sure, I love to sing them."

Armand hesitated. Jeanne reminded him,

"I've heard worse voices at the opera house in Paris."

"You never heard one as ill-trained, though. He has a thousand faults."

"Oh, I know that, sir! That's why I've come all the way to France. If you'll just teach me, I'll work. I'll do anything. I'll clean the stables. Just tell me what to do."

"I don't have time for that. I'm too busy composing. You'll have to leave."

"Are you hungry?"

Seymour looked at the mistress of the house. "I . . . am a little hungry."

"When did you eat last?" Jeanne asked.

"I think it was two days ago. I found some turnips in a field."

"Nothing but raw turnips! Josephine, quick. We must feed this young man."

Josephine laughed. "Yes, Madam, I think we must. He's skinny as a plucked chicken."

Armand, despite his harsh verbal judgment, was interested in the young man. As Josephine moved around the kitchen, he pulled Jeanne off to the side and said, "I know you, my dear. Your mind is already spinning webs in which to catch me."

"He's such a sweet young man."

"How do you know that? He may be totally depraved."

"With those innocent blue eyes? Of course

22

he's not!"

Armand suddenly laughed. "I understand that some of the most vicious criminals in the world have blue eyes and look innocent as babies."

"You just made that up. You always make up things when you don't want me to do something."

"Well, he *does* have potential, but I can't take on a student. I'm right in the middle of this opera, and it's very difficult. I keep getting interrupted." He continued to argue fervently.

Finally Jeanne pleaded, "Please, Armand, let's at least hear his story."

"All right, I'll listen, but I'm telling you now I can't help him."

They moved over to the table where the young man was eating. He obviously was ravenously hungry, but both noticed that he had at least the rudiments of good manners.

When Josephine had removed his plate, Jeanne said, "Tell us about yourself, Colin."

"Well, there's not much to tell. My parents died in an epidemic before I was six. I was raised by a distant cousin of my father, a man named Silas Winters. He was a fisherman who lived outside New Orleans."

"Was he good to you?"

"Well, ma'am, he was a hard man, and fishing is a hard job." He put out his hands, and both of them saw that they were scarred and covered with calluses. They looked strong, however, and he said, "He died about a year ago."

"Did you get any education at all?" Jeanne asked softly.

"Just what little I could pick up. I learned to read and write."

"What did you do then," Armand asked, "after your relative died?"

"I got a job cleaning the opera house in New Orleans, and oh sir, I have never heard anything like it! I stayed for all the performances. It didn't pay much, but I loved the music. I'd never heard anything like it."

"And so that's what you did? You memorized the music?"

"Yes, ma'am, I did." Colin's eyes were bright, and despite the purplish wound, he looked eager. "I don't want to beg, but if you could let me stay, and just once in a while tell me a little about singing, I can garden for you or take care of your horses. I can fix most things. I'll do anything, my lord!"

"I'm sorry. It's just impossible. I don't have the time." He expected the young man to argue, but he saw that the eager light seemed to be extinguished in the young man's eyes. "I'm sorry," he said. "But we have a room overhead in the stable. You can stay there tonight, and I'll do something about getting you back to America."

"Thank you, sir."

The young man was so meek that Armand felt terrible. He turned and walked out of the room, saying, "Come with me." When the young man followed, they went outside where Philippe was still working on the yard. "Philippe, this young man will be staying in the room over the barn tonight. See that he has a bath, and perhaps you can find some better clothes for him."

Philippe stared at the American. "He'll cut our throats, sir."

"Oh, I don't think he's dangerous. Do as I tell you."

"Yes, sir." Philippe nodded. "Come along, fellow."

Armand went at once upstairs and tried to work on his score again. He cleaned up the mess he had made and was not surprised to find that he had lost his train of thought. He struggled with it for over an hour, then finally muttered, "Blast it! Now I'll have to wait until it comes back." He heard the door open and turned to see Jeanne enter. She walked over and put her arm around him.

"Are you having difficulty with the composition?"

"Don't I always?"

"You'll do it, and it'll be magnificent."

Armand laughed. "When you're this nice, I know you want something. It makes me suspicious."

"I think you might guess what it is." She put both arms around him, and he stood up and turned to embrace her. He loved the woman with all of his heart and looked forward to the birth of their first child with great expectation. "I think I can guess all right."

"Please, Armand, let the boy stay. He'll work hard for his keep, and he's so hungry to learn."

"He's too old to learn everything an opera singer needs to know."

"No, he's not. He's only twenty-one, and he has really a fine voice — just untrained."

Armand sat down and pulled her onto his lap. She cuddled up against him and put her face on his chest. "Please, Armand."

"You know I can never refuse you anything."

"That's because you're the most wonderful husband in the world."

"I suspect you're right about that, and the handsomest too."

Jeanne laughed and straightened up. She put her hand behind his neck, pulled his head down, and kissed him. "You're a good man, the best I know."

"Before you start buttering me up, listen to my terms. He can stay, and he can help Philippe with the grounds and muck out stables for Perin and do anything else that needs doing. I'll try him out for a month. If he has the ability to learn, we'll see. But I have no time for petty talents. If I see he has no potential, he'll have to go."

Jeanne patted his cheek and smiled. "You do have wonderful ideas."

"I haven't had an idea of my own since I married you. You put them all in my head."

"It's going to be wonderful!" Jeanne laughed and threw her arms around him and put her cheek against his. "He's going to be a great singer, and one day you'll be proud to say, 'Colin Seymour was my pupil!' "

CHAPTER TWO

Philippe Gerard looked like a huge bear as he approached Colin, who was covering some young roses with dead leaves. Philippe wore a cap pulled down over his ears, and his nose was red, a certain indication that he had been sampling the cognac of which he was so fond. For a moment he watched silently, then asked, "What you do that to her for?"

Colin looked up and grinned. Philippe's English was worst when he was drunk.

The big gardener read the young man's expression. "My English is ver' good! The English language is hard. What you doing?"

"I'm covering up these roses so that storm that's coming won't freeze them."

Philippe stared at the younger man for a moment, then he leaned forward and struck Colin a blow on the arm. It was meant to be a friendly punch, but Philippe never knew his own strength, and Colin staggered backward. Catching his balance, he grinned and said, "Don't hit me because you can't learn English."

Philippe laughed, exposing his enormous teeth, and said, "Come on in the house. I have something you will like there."

"I know what it is. You're trying to get me drunk."

"Why not you get drunk? We celebrate."

"Celebrate what?"

"You don't know?" Philippe stared at Colin with astonishment. "This is your birthday."

"No, it's not. My birthday's in May."

"I mean, you come here seven months ago today. Don't you rememer nothing?"

"Has it been that long?" Colin asked softly, as if speaking to himself. He looked around the chateau grounds, which were now dead and brown, but he had seen them when they were emerald green and bright with every kind of flower that France offered. He had dug and trenched and hauled fertilizer and done the other dirty jobs that Philippe heaped on him. Now he looked up and laughed. "I remember that first month well enough, Philippe. You tried to kill me with work."

"Work never hurt nobody," Philippe said firmly. "Come on. We'll have a drink."

Colin stuck the shovel down in the frozen earth and accompanied Philippe to his house. Philippe was not married, and the house gave evidence of it: clothes thrown everywhere, dirty dishes piled up, dust enough to write one's name on any flat surface.

"Why don't you clean this place up, Philippe?"

"What for? Who's gonna see it?"

"Well, I see it, for one."

"You came here looking like a ragpicker, and now you gonna tell me my house isn't nice? She's nice enough for *me*."

Moving swiftly to the cabinet, Philippe opened the door and took out a square, brown bottle. He pulled the cork out with his teeth, and then picked up two dirty glasses and sloshed the amber liquid in both of them. "Here, you drink this. It make a man of you."

"Philippe, you know I don't like to drink."

"This is a celebration. You drink when I say so."

"All right, but just a taste." Colin took the liquor bottle, poured most of his drink back in, then took a swallow. He shivered and gasped as the fiery liquor bit his stomach. "I don't know why anyone drinks. It tastes awful, it burns your stomach, and it rots your insides eventually."

"She makes me feel good."

"Not she — *it* makes you feel good."

"What difference it make?"

"I thought you wanted to learn English."

"I never go to that country. Nothing but barbarians there. I bet the gardens there look like a pigpen."

It was an old argument between the two, Philippe maintaining that France was the only decent place for a human being to live on planet earth, and Colin trying to tell him that other countries had something to offer as well.

"Sit down. We eat some of this cake that Josephine made. She is very good."

"The cake or the woman?"

Philippe took several swallows from the bottle. Colin could see the liquor going down the thick throat of his friend. The two had indeed become friends during the period that Colin had been there. The big gardener had been a hard and demanding sort of fellow, but when he saw that Colin was not afraid of work or of asking questions, Philippe warmed up to him.

"You know, Colin, I think? I think I marry Josephine Bettencourt."

"You in love with her?"

"In love? No! She is a wealthy woman.

She will be able to take care of me in my old age."

"But you're older than she is."

"Mens lasts longer than womens."

"I think you're dreaming. Women live longer than men."

"Josephine will not dare to live longer than me. It would not be proper."

Leaning back in his chair, Colin listened as Philippe rambled on. The big man had strange ideas and was totally unreliable where liquor was concerned. But he was amusing and had been a good friend to Colin.

"You know, you look better than you did when you come here. You looked like a skinny tramp dressed in rags." Philippe stared at his friend with glassy eyes and noted with approval how the young man had filled out. He had a naturally deep chest, and now muscle had formed in the shoulders, the chest, and the arms. His face had filled out, too, so that his fair skin had been burned by the hot summer sun and still held some of that golden color.

Philippe leaned forward and said, "I like you, Colin. I am going to tell you what you should do with your life."

Colin grinned. It seemed that Philippe had a different plan for his life from week to week, sometimes from day to day. "What have you got on your mind now?"

"Forget all of that singing nonsense. You could be a fine gardener. Maybe as good as me someday."

"You've taught me a lot, Philippe. I've enjoyed working for you."

"With all this singing: la, la, la, la, la! Who care about that?"

"Well, I do for one, Philippe." Colin smiled. "It's what I want to do."

"It's no fit thing for a real man. A man should use his hands to make his living, not go tra-la-la-ing all over the place. And besides, the master treats you worse than I do."

"You're right about that. You put blisters on my hands, but he puts them on my soul."

Philippe nodded. "See what I mean? You don't have to put up with all that. Why, you could be a fine gardener, a master! Take a few more years."

"No, I don't think so, Philippe. I may never make it as a singer, but I've got to try."

Philippe argued vehemently for a time, all the while sipping from the cognac bottle. Finally Colin changed the subject by saying, "The marquis is really happy, isn't he, with this child coming on?"

"He's a foolish man about his wife. He will be foolish about the child too."

"I've never seen anyone so happy or love a woman so much."

Philippe belched, and then scratched his behind. "It's not good for a man to love a woman too much."

"Why, Philippe? Why would you say that?"

"Because someone might run off with her."

Colin suddenly grinned, his teeth looking very white against his tan. "Maybe a man should marry an ugly woman."

Philippe stared at him. "But somebody might run off with her too."

"But if she's ugly, you wouldn't care."

Philippe was a slow thinker, particularly when drunk, but the humor of Colin's remark finally got to him. He bellowed with laughter, lunged to his feet, and pounded Colin's arm. "By gar," he said, "you are one funny fellow. But I still think you should be a gardener."

Colin leaned back from Philippe's clumsy punch. "You nearly broke my arm." He hesitated, then asked, "Have you ever thought what it would be like if something happened to the Lady Beaufort?"

Philippe's eyes suddenly flew open wide, and he reached out and grabbed the lapels of Colin's coat. He lifted him off the floor and whispered, "Don't ever say that! Don't even say such things! It's bad luck."

"I guess you're right," Colin said. When Philippe put him down, he pulled his coat together and said, "We'll have to pray that she'll be all right, and the child too."

"Yes, we do that. I will say an extra rosary for her every day. You ever say a rosary?"

"No. I'm not Catholic, you know. I'm Protestant."

Philippe stared at the younger man and then shrugged. "Well," he said, "nobody's perfect."

"You sound like a braying donkey!"

Colin had never been able to accustom himself to the harshness of the marquis' words. Armand de Cuvier knew but one way to teach. "It's the hard things," he often shouted, "that teach a man! The soft ways are no good."

"What was wrong with what I did, Monsieur?"

"What was wrong with it? *Everything* was wrong with it!" Armand doubled up his fists. He struck Colin three light, rapid blows in the chest and said, "It must come from in *here.* You are trying to sing from your throat." He wrapped both hands around Colin's throat and squeezed. "There is no power in the throat." He began to pound his chest again. "From here! From here and from down here in the diaphragm!"

Colin listened silently. Armand finally quieted down enough to give him more instructions. For seven months, Colin had lived for these times when he was learning how to sing. He had been studying Italian with the help of the marchioness and had made rapid progress. Her method was quite different. She was soft and gentle and could never bring herself to rebuke him. Quite a difference from her husband!

"Am I making any progress at all, sir?" Colin asked.

The marquis turned and stared at his pupil. He saw the deep-set eyes were not as bright as usual, and the broad shoulders were slumped. He put his hand on Colin's shoulder and squeezed it. "The hard ways are best. Yes, you are making progress."

"Really?" Colin asked, his eyes widening.

"Yes, you're not as bad as you were when you first came here."

Colin laughed. "I think that's the best thing you ever said to me, sir."

"You are making progress. Now, don't seek compliments."

"Philippe says I ought to give up singing and become a gardener."

"You are a good gardener. Is that what you'd like to do?"

Instantly Colin sat taller, and determination was a thread of iron in his voice. "I want to be a singer, sir, no matter how long it takes."

"Well, you've already found out that it's not easy."

"I don't care about that, sir, and I can never thank you enough for letting me stay and for helping me."

The gratitude in the young man's eyes seemed to trouble the marquis. He waved his hand and said, "Enough of that. Now, try it again. This time, in this passage here," he put his fingers on the notes, "try to make it as sweet as a dove."

For the next hour Colin sang at the direction of the marquis. Finally the marquis said, "Well, enough for today." He hesitated, then said, "It was very good, Colin. Very good." He picked up his coat and put it on. "It's getting cold in here. We'll have to have more fires when my son is born."

"You always say 'son.' What if it is a daughter?"

"I will love her equally well. Of course, a man wants a son to take his name, but if it is a daughter, she will be like my dear wife. And what man could ask for more than that?"

"I've appreciated your teaching, sir, but one thing has meant more to me than that."

"What, Colin?"

"I've learned something about how a man should love his wife. I had never seen such a thing as the love you have for Madam Jeanne."

"When you find a woman, find one you can give your whole heart to." Armand laughed and said, "I'll tell you what, my boy. You have done well. I don't commend you much, but I have a reward for you."

"Yes, sir. What is that?"

"I'm going to take you to the opera in Paris."

"Really, sir? That would be wonderful!"

"We'll go next week. We'll have to buy you some new clothes. We'll make a holiday of it."

Colin was stunned by the opera house. His only experience had been in the rather small and somewhat dingy opera house that he had cleaned back in New Orleans. But when he entered and saw the blaze of light from the crystal chandeliers, the red plush seats, the ceiling so high above them it seemed that there could be a cloud gathering there, the elaborate dresses of the women, and the men all dressed in the finest fashions, he could not speak.

"If you don't shut your mouth, a fly might go in, Colin." Armand laughed. The two were without Jeanne, who chose to stay home because of her advanced pregnancy.

"I can't believe it. It's so beautiful!"

"Well, the building is magnificent, but it's nothing without the singing. They are doing your favorite tonight, *The Barber of Seville.* You remember? The first song you ever sang for me was from that opera."

"I remember, sir."

"Come along. We don't want to miss the overture."

Colin followed him into the box and took a seat next to him. It was raised up enough so that he had a panoramic view of the Paris Opera House. He was amazed at the beauty of the women and somewhat shocked by the low-cut dresses many of them wore. There was a humming of talk, and laughter filled the air, and then the marquis said, "Now, it begins."

Colin never forgot what followed. He missed nothing. The orchestra, as it played the overture, fascinated him. He had never heard such playing in all of his life, and he soaked it in to his very soul.

And when the singers came on and opened their mouths, he marveled at the clearness and power of their voices. He was glad that he was now able to understand at least part of what they were singing.

There was an intermission, and the marquis turned and asked, "How do you like it, Colin?"

"It's magnificent — but I'll never be able to do what those people do."

"Never take counsel of your fears, Colin." Armand smiled. "Your voice is better than anyone's on that stage. They had the advantage of early training."

All through the rest of the opera, Armand continued to point out the flaws as well as the skills of the singers. Finally, when it was over, Colin stood with the others and applauded until his hands hurt.

"Come along. We'll go meet them."

"You mean — meet the singers?"

"Why, of course." Armand smiled. "Wouldn't you like to?"

"Yes!"

Colin accompanied Armand down the stairs, and they made their way backstage. Many other visitors were there, but Colin saw that the marquis was so well known that the crowd parted before him. When they stood before the star tenor, Alex Chapelle, Colin was surprised to find that the singer was much older than he seemed on the stage.

"Alex, I would like for you to meet a friend of mine. This is Colin Seymour, a young American who has been studying with me."

Chapelle was a short, rotund man with lines in his face that had been invisible from a distance. He bowed from the waist and said, "A pupil of the maestro. I would love to hear you sing, sir."

"Oh, I'm just a beginner, Monsieur."

"You had better watch out. This young fellow will put you out of business one day, Alex."

Chapelle laughed and shook his head. "That is always the way of it. I envy this young man, and I trust he is properly grateful for the training you've given him."

"Oh yes, sir, I am. I couldn't be more grateful."

Colin stood back while the marquis greeted other singers. He seemed to know everyone. They finally left the theater and got into their coach. Colin asked, "Do you really think I could sing as well as Monsieur Chapelle some day?"

"Colin, you don't understand, do you?"

"Understand what?"

"You can already sing better than he can."

"Oh no, sir. No, not really!"

"Your voice is better than his. It's more powerful. It's smoother. It just hasn't had as much training. He has more control because he's spent practically his whole life at it, but in another year or two, you'll be better in that respect also."

Colin tried to speak but could not. Finally he whispered, "I'll do my best — my very best!"

As soon as Colin entered the kitchen and saw Philippe's face, he stopped dead. "What's wrong, Philippe?" he demanded.

Philippe shook his head. "Where have you been?" he asked.

"I went into the village to get some supplies. What's wrong?"

"It's Lady Jeanne. The child is coming."

"But that's good, isn't it?" Colin spoke hopefully, but as he stepped closer to Philippe, he saw the pain on the big man's face. "What's wrong?"

"The doctor has been here for two hours. Our lady is having a terribly hard time."

Colin stared at Philippe and could not think how to answer him. Josephine Bettencourt entered the kitchen. Her face was pale. "Is it really bad, Miss Josephine?"

"Very bad! I heard the doctors talking. They think there's —" She turned away quickly, but not before Colin saw the tears running down her cheeks.

Colin stood numbly, not knowing what to do. "It'll be all right," he whispered. "It has to be."

Philippe shook his head. There was a dark streak of pessimism in the big gardener. He went outside, and Colin followed. Philippe pulled a flat bottle from his inner pocket and drank from it. He offered it to Colin, who shook his head.

"I'm going to get drunk."

"Don't. It may be all right."

The night passed more slowly than any that Colin could remember. The seconds seemed like hours, and there was nothing to do but wait for news. Colin paced the floor in the kitchen, and Philippe continued to drink. He was so numb with alcohol that he sat against a wall, his head back, his eyes glazed. Annette, Jeanne's maid, entered the kitchen at about midnight, and Colin asked, "How is she, Annette?"

Annette shook her head and bit her lip. She could not answer, but the expression on her face told Colin the situation had not improved.

Finally Colin could not stand the stillness of the house. He poked Philippe's arm and said, "I'm going to get more wood." Philippe did not answer, and Colin went outside. He made ten trips to the wood pile, carrying in wood for all the fireplaces, until the boxes were full. After filling the box of the room next to Jeanne's, he saw one of the doctors leaving.

"Doctor," Colin said, "how is Lady Beaufort?"

The doctor, whose name Colin did not know, was a tall man with a sallow face and a thin mustache. He stroked it now with nervous fingers, and Colin read his answer in his eyes before it came to his lips. "She died fifteen minutes ago."

Colin's lips trembled, and tears came to his eyes. Jeanne de Cuvier had been more like a mother to him than any woman he had ever known. Every day he had experienced her kindness and her encouragement. Suddenly it was as if the sun had gone out. He questioned why God would allow another terrible experience in his life. He turned blindly and walked out into the night, wondering how in the world his master would handle the greatest loss that could come to a man.

■ ■ ■ ■

After the funeral of Jeanne de Cuvier, Armand de Cuvier refused to see anyone. He took his meals in his room and never left it. He received no visitors, and only his valet, a small man named Etienne, saw him.

"Philippe, what's he going to do?" Colin asked. "He can't stay in that room forever."

Philippe was chopping wood. His mighty blows were enough to demolish most things, and he seemed to be taking out his anger on the wood. "What is he going to do? He's going to grieve."

"But he can't do that forever, can he?"

"No. He may kill himself."

"Philippe, don't say a thing like that!"

"Why not? He's lost what he loved best: his wife and his child. I know how he feels. I had a wife once, and I lost her."

"You never told me that, Philippe."

"I don't like to think about it."

"I wish I could help him."

Philippe tested the ax with his thumb and was silent for a time. Finally he said, "My young friend, some things nobody on this earth can help with, and the marquis is finding out what that's like. Only the good God can help him."

CHAPTER THREE

Annette Jourdain paused outside the side door to the mansion, holding a parcel. She bent over and stroked the head of the yellow hammer-headed tomcat that pushed himself against her feet. She stroked his coarse fur, saying, "You are a no-good fellow. I heard you out yowling last night. Did you not find a lady friend?"

The big cat growled deep in his throat and butted against Annette's calf, begging for more attention. Laughing, she pushed him away. "I have no time for you. Go find another girlfriend, and try not to fight so much." Straightening up, Annette looked up at the blue sky and for a moment let her gaze follow the outlines of the gardens that surrounded the house, thinking what a beautiful place Beaufort was. The tulips in bloom were Philippe's pride and joy, and she could see the big man bending over, planting something. April had come to

France, the forerunner of a glorious spring, and for a moment Annette breathed in the deep fragrance of loamy earth and of wood burning somewhere.

With a sigh she entered the kitchen. Putting down the parcel, she said, "They did not have any fresh truffles at the market, Josephine."

Josephine had married the gardener, Philippe, and was now Josephine Gerard. Philippe had proposed a dozen times over the last two years and was refused, but he was a determined man. Finally Josephine said, "I'll have to marry you to make you leave me alone!" It had proved to be a successful marriage, however, and the two were well satisfied. At Annette's words, Josephine frowned and shook her head. "You would think they would keep a good stock. There's always a market for them. Did you get the other things?"

"Yes, but I am not very good at picking out vegetables. I was trained to be a ladies' maid. I don't know why Monsieur Armand keeps me on. His wife has been dead for two years now, and I have nothing really to do."

"I think it's for sentimental reasons. He still grieves for her."

Annette took vegetables out of the sack

and placed them on the table in front of the housekeeper. "He's much better than he used to be. I thought for the first year after Madam died that he would die also. I never saw a man grieve so much."

"Yes, you are right. You know, Annette, I think if it had not been for Colin, he might have taken his own life."

"He's grown very fond of Colin."

Josephine looked inquisitively at the younger woman. Annette was now twenty, a little plump and bright-eyed with curly auburn hair and dancing brown eyes. A beauty indeed. "What is this with 'Colin'?"

"What am I supposed to call him — Monsieur Seymour?"

"I think you have eyes for him, Annette."

"He's a handsome man, and oh, when he sings those love songs, it makes me melt inside, you know?"

"I do not melt inside," Josephine said sternly, "and I do not think it wise for you to be so familiar with him."

"Why not? We're both young. I like him a great deal, and after all, the marquis has no children. It may be he will adopt Colin. If I marry him, I would be the marchioness. I would be your employer. You would have to do what I say." Annette laughed at the thought, then went over and put her arm

48

around the older woman. "I'm just teasing."

"Is there anything between you two?"

"No." Annette sounded miffed. "He thinks only of singing. That's all he does, sing, sing, sing, night and day!"

"Yes. Philippe was upset when Monsieur Armand took Colin away from his gardening work and made a full-time pupil of him. He says it ruined a fine gardener."

"He wasn't made to be a gardener like Philippe."

"No, that's true enough. Well, get about your work. I've got to start thinking about the evening meal."

Annette left the kitchen, and as she passed down the long hallway that divided the house into two parts, she heard the pianoforte in the music room. She stopped, tiptoed over to the door, then opened it cautiously. This was where the marquis gave singing lessons to Colin, but there had been no sound of singing, only the piano. She poked her head inside and saw Colin with his back to the huge window that admitted yellow beams of light. A smile turned up the corners of Annette's lips, and her eyes sparkled. Stepping inside, she walked up silently behind him. She put her head next to his and whispered in his ear, "Oh, you play so wonderfully, Colin!"

Colin was startled. He took his hands off the keys and turned around and smiled. "Well, you do sneak up on a man, Annette."

"That's good for you," Annette said. She moved closer and leaned against him, the rich curves of her body pressing against his shoulder. He suddenly stood, and she looked up at him and asked, "What was that you were playing?"

"Oh, something the marquis wrote for the new opera."

"Is he ever going to finish that? He's been working on it for a long time."

"You know, I think it's really finished. I wouldn't be surprised if he published it."

"Will you be singing in it?"

"I doubt it. He can have anyone he wants, with his reputation."

Annette reached up and brushed his shoulder as if there were something there. But her touch lingered, and she lowered her voice and said, "Colin, do you only think of music? Don't other thoughts ever cross your mind?"

"Why, of course."

"No," Annette said, shaking her head in disapproval, "I don't think you ever think like most young men do."

"What are you talking about?"

"Well, you've never tried to kiss me or

even once touched me. I've been waiting for two years, but it's never happened."

"You know I wouldn't do a thing like that."

"Why not?"

"Well, because —" Colin broke off and looked embarrassed. Suddenly he grinned and said, "All right. I'll behave like other young men." He reached forward, pulled her into a tight embrace, and kissed her on the lips firmly. Stepping back, he said, "Now, I'm like all the rest of the fellows who chase you around."

"You're not very good at kissing. You haven't had enough experience." Humor lit Annette eyes, and she said, "Let's go out this evening. You haven't asked me out a single time."

"Where would we go?"

"We'd go have fun. You don't know what it is to have fun."

"Of course I do."

"No, you don't. You go hunting sometimes with Philippe and fishing by yourself, but aside from that, all you do is sing."

"I have to take advantage of the marquis' teaching. He's a hard master."

Annette looked disgusted. "Poof!" she said. "You're nothing but a machine. You don't even know how to kiss." She turned around and left the room, huffily slamming the door behind her.

For a long moment Colin stared at the door, then scratched his head thoughtfully. *What's wrong with her, I wonder? I guess she wants me to chase her like all the young bucks in the neighborhood do. I don't have time for that.*

Going back to the piano, Colin looked over the music. He sang softly the words to the solo until he was interrupted when the door opened, and the marquis entered. Colin stopped playing at once and stood. "Good morning, sir. A fine day."

"Yes, it is. I've been thinking I might go out for a ride. Would you like to join me?"

"Very much. We've good weather for it."

Armand looked at the music on the piano-forte. "You're playing the new solo. Do you like it?"

"I think it's one of the best things I ever heard."

"You're not very critical, Colin. You never find fault with anything I do."

"That would be wrong of me indeed, for all that you do is right."

The marquis smiled. Smiles had come rarely to him since his wife had died, but during the past year he had found a great deal of consolation in pouring himself into the young man who stood before him. "You're wrong about that, but keep on thinking it if it pleases you. Now, go ahead. Sing that as it should be sung."

Colin sat down and began to play. He had a natural gift for the piano, and the marquis had hired a master for him. It had been a pleasure for Colin to learn so that he could accompany himself. He was not an accomplished pianist, of course, but he did well enough. He lifted up his voice and poured himself into the song. When he was finished, he struck the last chord, then shook his head ruefully. "I didn't do the phrasing on that very well."

"You're never satisfied with yourself — which is what I taught you." Armand smiled. "Never be satisfied. There's always something better." He hesitated, then said, "I've got something to tell you."

"Yes, sir. What is it?"

"Actually one never finishes a work. At some point you just have to stop and say, 'At this point in my life, this is the best I can do.' Don't you agree?"

"Well, that's what I have to say to myself. I'm never happy with my singing."

"I've been waiting for two years for you to show some signs of artistic temperament or vanity, but I haven't seen any. That's a miracle." Armand shook his head, and wonder was in his eyes. "You don't seem to care for anything but learning and singing."

"That's why I came to France."

"Well, I've got a bit of news for you. We're going on a journey."

"Where to, sir?"

"We're going back to your home in America. New Orleans, to be specific."

"New Orleans! Do you mean it, sir?"

"Yes. I've decided to take this new opera to New Orleans. They are a rather rough, crude bunch, though they would never admit it, but I thought it would be interesting to try out my new work on them before we perform it here."

"Why, it will be a tremendous success. I know they've been trying to get you to come to America for a long time."

Armand smiled and laid his hand on the young man's shoulder. "So, you'll be seeing home again and old friends. You never talk about things like that."

"Actually," he said, "I don't have all that many people. I didn't have many friends."

Armand understood that Colin's life had been an unhappy one, hard and harsh in a land that was noted for such things. "Well," he said, "I've got another surprise for you. You're going to sing the second lead."

Colin stared at Armand with astonishment. "You mean it, sir? Of course you mean it." He shook himself, and his eyes glowed with excitement. "Do you think I can do it?"

"I think you could do the first lead, but it would be better to get a more established figure. This will be a good introduction to your career. We'll have to be careful, though."

"Careful about what, sir?"

"Whomever we get for the first tenor, you'll be better. And you know how these opera singers are — jealous as Caesar. Well, we'll be leaving in a month. Then, when we get there, I've made arrangements with a man called Herzhaft, Enoch Herzhaft, to get things ready."

"I know that name from when I worked in the opera house."

"Yes, he's the owner of the largest opera house in New Orleans. I've met him a few times. He had ambitions of being a singer himself, but he didn't have the voice for it. So, he's become the biggest figure in opera in America. Even though he can't sing, he has good judgment. I've told him not to worry about the second tenor — that I'll take care of that." He put his hand again on Colin's shoulder and said, "It will be a change. I've needed it for a long time now. Get yourself ready."

"I could leave today."

"Well, I can't leave quite that quickly, but the voyage will be good for us, and you can show me around New Orleans."

The Marquis Armand de Cuvier leaned on the rail of the *Diana,* his eyes fixed on the teeming harbor of New Orleans. "A crowded place," he remarked. "I hardly see where the captain can find room to dock."

Colin was excited at the first sight of his native land. He avidly took in the mixture of steamships and sailing ships that seemed in competition for spaces along the wharf. Turning to the marquis, he said, "This trip over was a little different from my voyage to France two years ago. Then I slept in the foul straw of the cattle on the cattle boat, but this time I ate at the captain's table and slept between clean sheets. I've come up in the world."

The two stood on deck until finally the *Diana* was tied up to the dock. "Come along," said the marquis. "I'm anxious to see this city of New Orleans. I hear it's like no other city in the world."

"It can be a very rough place, sir. I'm afraid you won't find much polish here."

As they walked off the dock, Armand asked, "Who are those fellows over there? They're a rough-looking bunch."

Colin followed the marquis' gesture. "Oh, those are what are called *Kaintocks.*"

"Kaintock? What does that mean?"

"Well, Kentucky is a state, and many people find their way down-river hauling freight from that place. But it doesn't matter which state they're from — they all are called Kaintocks."

"They look like wild men," the marquis murmured. "But we have our own gangs of criminals, called *apaches,* in Paris, and they're probably wilder than these fellows."

The two disembarked, and Colin saw that the luggage was located and stored in one of the many carriages that were for hire. Etienne, the marquis' valet for years, had remained at home, protesting that he was too old for such a trip. Colin had vowed that he would see to it that his master did not have to deal with the problems of travel. Then they got into the carriage, and he said, "St. Louis Hotel, driver."

"Yes sir." The driver was a small, dark-skinned man with flashing white teeth and a ferocious mustache. He touched his top hat with his whip and then touched the horses with it, calling for them to step out.

As they made their way through the city toward the hotel, Armand was fascinated by it all. "It's a very cosmopolitan place, isn't it?"

"Sir?"

"I mean there are many nationalities here. I see a great many Spanish people and even more black people."

"Well, there are Cajuns and Creoles and just about any other peoples that you'd like to meet. They come in on the big ships, and some of them stay."

"Who are the Creoles?"

"Creoles are people who are descended from both the French and Spanish," Colin said. "There are always some very prominent Creole people here. Many of them are interested in the arts, from what little I picked up. Of course, you understand, sir, I wasn't moving in high circles in those days. They would have thrown me out of their homes."

"Well, they won't throw you out this time."

"No, sir, not as long as I'm in your company."

The driver pulled up in front of a block-long building simple and dignified in design. "St. Louis Hotel, sir." He hopped out, unloaded the carriage, and Colin asked a porter to take their luggage inside. "I think you'll find the hotel impressive," Colin told the marquis. He led Armand into the lobby, past a large rotunda covered by a magnificent dome sixty-five feet in diameter. The ceiling rose at least ninety feet.

"What going on in there, Colin?"

"Well sir, I'm afraid it's a slave auction. They use the rotunda for that sometimes. It's not a pretty sight."

The marquis insisted on stopping, and for a while the two men watched as the blacks were led up to the slave block and auctioned off.

"Why, it's as if they were vegetables or animals!" the marquis exclaimed.

"It's very bad, sir. New Orleans is the slave market for the rest of the country. A very bad thing. I never liked to see it."

The marquis shook his head sadly. Colin led to him the desk, where they registered, then to their rooms upstairs. He asked, "Would you like to lie down and rest, sir?"

"No. We should get ready for the reception."

Enoch Herzhaft, a portly man, presided over the reception for the marquis. His hair and beard were blond, and his eyes were electric blue. Every sentence seemed to be a proclamation rather than a mere statement of fact.

He had greeted the marquis effusively, and when introduced to Colin, he had been fully as enthusiastic. He was a man who lived in a constant state of excitement.

"My dear marquis, you honor us with your presence, and the opera — what a triumph it will be!" Herzhaft exclaimed, waving his hands. "The entire world will hear of it."

"Well, I would be content with a little less success than that, but I am very interested in my protégé's doing well."

"He will be fantastic, I am sure. I have persuaded Dominic Elfonso to sing the leading role. You have heard him?"

"Oh yes, I have heard Señor Elfonso many times. A fine voice indeed. Not much of an actor."

"No, indeed, he is not, but never tell him so. His ego is even larger than his body." Enoch Herzhaft turned to Colin. "Have you had much experience, may I ask?"

"None whatsoever," Colin answered. He saw Herzhaft's surprise and smiled. "I hope I will not ruin the performance."

"Oh, I'm sure you will not." There was less assurance in Herzhaft's voice than before. "Come. We will eat, and then there will be speeches."

"I hope I'm not expected to make one,"

the marquis murmured.

"But of course you are! They have all come to hear you. Come now. We have the finest chefs in New Orleans, and you will taste Creole cooking."

The meal was indeed unusual. It consisted of shrimp Creole, a spicy dish that the marquis tasted for the first time. There was shrimp remoulade and *pompano en papilote.* Colin said to Armand, "This Creole cooking, is it too spicy for you?"

"I don't think I'll have any taste buds left after I get through with this, but it is good."

The meal ended with small cakes served with black chicory coffee. The marquis took one swallow, and his eyes flew open. "This is strong stuff, Colin!"

"Yes, it is. You can barely stir it with a spoon! But you'll get used to it."

Finally, when the meal was over, Herzhaft made a glowing speech proclaiming that the Marquis de Cuvier was the greatest composer the world had ever seen. He painted a picture that no man could have lived up to, and when Armand stood amid the applause, he said, "I will disclaim 90 percent of all of my friend, Mr. Herzhaft, has said. Not even Mozart and Beethoven rolled into one could live up to such a reputation." The marquis was a good speaker, though his remarks were brief. He knew how to address a crowd, and when he sat down, the applause was enthusiastic.

After more speeches, Herzhaft said, "Now I must introduce you to our guests. I know they are anxious to meet you."

Colin stood away from the pair but followed closely enough to hear the introductions. He lost track of the names, but he did see a young woman who stood out from all the rest somehow. She was of medium height; her blonde hair was as fair as anything he had ever seen. Her complexion was perfect. But the most striking thing about her was her large, well-shaped, dark-blue eyes. For some reason she seemed familiar. Colin put that thought aside. He had not moved in society such as this before going to France!

The woman glanced at him once, then looked back at the marquis, and Colin heard Herzhaft say, "And this is Monsieur Louis d'Or and his wife, Renee. This is their son, Bayard, and this is Mademoiselle Simone d'Or." He waved his hand toward the marquis, saying, "Of course, Lord Beaufort needs no introduction."

Colin watched as the marquis bowed to the family and called them each by name — but he saw that Armand's eyes were fixed on the young woman. It struck him that she bore a resemblance to Jeanne de Cuvier! The facial structure was the same, the hair was the same color; the eyes were different, but there was a general resemblance.

The marquis could spend little time with the d'Or family, as others were waiting to be introduced. When Armand turned to greet another family, Louis d'Or approached Colin and asked, "Pardon me, Monsieur, are you a relative of the marquis?"

"Oh no, sir. Merely a pupil."

"Ah," Louis d'Or said. "Enoch has told me about you. You will be singing in the master's new opera."

"Yes, sir. My name is Colin Seymour."

"But you are not French."

"No, as a matter of fact, I'm an American."

"Oh, let me introduce you to my family. We are all aficionados of the opera." He introduced Colin to his wife, his son, and his daughter, and said, "Simone will ask you a million questions. She is a great fan of the opera."

"I'm afraid you would be disappointed, Miss d'Or. I have very little background."

Simone d'Or looked at the young man curiously. She stepped forward and said, "I will interrogate him, Father."

"Be careful of her, Mr. Seymour. She's a dangerous woman."

"Pay no attention to Bayard, sir. Now, you must tell me all about yourself. Where are you from?"

"Well, mostly from Louisiana."

"Oh, you must have been in France a long time then."

"No. Only two years. Before that I lived here in New Orleans."

Simone gave Colin an odd look and tilted her head to one side. She was the most provocative woman Colin had ever seen. It was not just her outward beauty, which was great indeed, but there was a fiery spirit within her that he had never seen before.

"But I never met you. Who was your family?"

Colin hesitated. He had an inkling that the truth would not endear him to Simone d'Or, but he said rather bluntly, "I was an orphan, Miss d'Or. Mostly I was raised by a distant relation. He was a fisherman."

Something changed in the woman's eyes then, and Colin knew that she had placed him in a completely different category than before. She lifted her chin and said, "A fisherman?" in a voice of disdain.

"Yes. I left here on a cattle boat to go to France. I was determined to become a singer and to study under the marquis, and that's what I did."

Simone stared at him for a moment, then shrugged her shoulders. "That's very interesting."

At that moment a tall, lean man with black hair and dark eyes approached. "Simone," he said, "I've been looking for you."

"Oh, yes. Claude, this is Monsieur Colin Seymour. Mr. Seymour, Claude Vernay."

Vernay looked puzzled, but he said, "Happy to make your acquaintance."

"Mr. Seymour will be singing in the marquis' new opera."

Vernay smiled. He had a thin, black mustache, and his black eyes were smoldering. "Never could sing myself. Not my style."

"You'll have to forgive Mr. Vernay," Simone said, her eyes sparkling. "He's more interested in swords and pistols than he is in art."

"Now, that's not so!" Vernay protested. He was a fine-looking man and dressed at the height of fashion. "I do like to shoot, and I keep in form by fencing, but I like opera."

"Don't listen to him, and don't offend him, whatever you do, Mr. Seymour. He's deadly with either weapon."

"I'll try to be as inoffensive as possible."

Vernay laughed. "Simone always makes things seem more dramatic than they are. I'll look forward to seeing you in the opera. Are you ready, Simone?"

"Yes." She nodded slightly and said, "I will be interested in hearing you when the opera takes place. When will it be, do you know?"

"I would think at least two weeks, from what the maestro has told me."

She nodded, and Vernay said, "Enjoy your visit, Mr. Seymour."

Colin watched the two leave and then snorted, saying under his breath, "What a snob! I've never seen such a proud pair in all my life."

Later, however, he saw that Simone d'Or speaking with the marquis. Colin was startled to see the eagerness with which Armand conversed with her. Of course it was true enough that Simone d'Or behaved much better to a nobleman than she had to an ex-fisherman. The idea troubled Colin for a moment, but then he thought, *Don't be foolish. He's not interested in any woman — especially a woman like that.*

In the two weeks that followed, Colin often thought of his first opinion of the marquis' interest in Simone d'Or. He had seen nothing to trouble him at first, but then it became clear that the young woman fascinated Armand. She was no more than twenty-two, he guessed, while the marquis was in his late forties. The d'Ors were a prominent family interested in opera, and Simone went often to the rehearsals. Afterward, Armand escorted her out, and Colin could not help but notice that his master came in very late following these trips.

As the days passed, the marquis' infatuation with the young woman became obvious, not only to Colin, but to others of the company.

The lead tenor, Dominic Elfonso, was talking once with Rosa Calabria — the diva — the star soprano. She was a vivacious woman with thick chestnut hair and warm brown eyes. During a break, Colin had been standing near when he heard Calabria say, "Well, Dominic, have you noticed the old maestro?"

"What about him?"

"He's gone crazy over the d'Or woman."

Dominic Elfonso was a big man with black hair, dark eyes, and a bristling mustache. He shrugged his beefy shoulders, saying, "She's a good-looking woman. Why not?"

"He's too old for her."

"You're just jealous, Rosa."

Rosa glared at him. "Jealous? I have no feelings for him, not in that way."

"Well, if I understand correctly, the marquis lost his wife a couple of years ago. I suppose he's lonely for feminine company."

"I think he's found it then. But something is foolish about an older man falling in love with a young woman."

Later that day, after rehearsals were over, Rosa said to Colin, "Let's go out and have something to eat. I'm starving."

"All right, Miss Calabria."

"Don't be so formal. You can call me Rosa." She took his arm and pressed herself against it, then led him outside. She knew every restaurant in New Orleans and directed him to a small, intimate place. There she proceeded to eat like a stevedore and at the same time pump him with questions. The fact that he had grown up as a fisherman amused her. "I worked in a cigar factory in Madrid. That's even worse than being a fisherman."

Colin liked the singer very much. She was in her mid-thirties, he guessed, somewhat older than himself, and she had no inhibitions that he could discover. He found out more about this when she invited him to her room. She made the offer as if she had been offering him a cup of coffee, and he saw that it meant little more to her. He stood for a moment, awkwardly trying to think how to answer without hurting her feelings, when she laughed out loud.

"I can't believe it!" she cried, her eyes sparkling. "You're blushing! I didn't think there was a man in America that had a blush left in him."

"I'm sorry, Rosa. I don't mean to be —"

"It's all right, lover," she said. She patted his cheek. "I'll have at least one man that I can trust in this world. That's quite refreshing."

"I suppose I'm a fool, but that's the way I feel."

"Oh, you're saving yourself for some woman down the road!"

"That's part of it, I suppose. Rosa, I heard you and Dominic talking about Simone d'Or and my friend the marquis. Were you serious?"

"Haven't I seen enough old men make fools of themselves? Not that he's that old. He still has desires. Did he love his wife?"

"More than I've ever seen any man love a woman, and to tell the truth, Miss d'Or does resemble her."

"There you have it." Rosa shrugged.

"She's turned down enough men, but one thing worries me about his infatuation."

"What's that?"

"You met Claude Vernay?"

"Yes, I have."

"He's cock-of-the-walk in New Orleans. Loves to fight duels. He's killed at least a couple of men and wounded a great many more. You know about this code duello that the young bucks follow?"

"I don't know much about it."

"They go around looking for someone to insult them so they can call a duel and hack at each other. Stupid, if you ask me, but they spend a great deal of time talking about honor, and Vernay's the worst. He has a crowd around him — Byron Mayhew and Leon Manville are a couple of his prominent friends. All of them are wealthy, and they all lust after victims! Tell your friend the marquis to steer clear of them and to be careful."

"Thank you, Rosa. I'll talk to him."

"Well, up in my lonely bed I'll dream about you."

Colin reached out and took her hand and kissed it. "You're a good sport, Rosa."

"Yes, I suppose I am. Go along with you now before I change my mind."

■ ■ ■ ■

The opera was a smashing success. The house was packed on opening night, and the critics raved in their reviews. Colin even rated a few lines, though, of course, Rosa and Dominic got the lion's share of the praise. But Colin was satisfied with his first endeavor into the opera.

What did not please him was the fact that nothing he could say to the marquis about Simone d'Or made any difference. "For such a wise man, he is blind as a bat!" Colin said angrily to himself. He had been in the presence of the woman enough to know that she was selfish to the bone and cared very little for anyone but herself. He had tried to hint to Armand that though she resembled the marquis' dead wife physically, she was totally different in character. There was little kindness in her, and in Colin's mind it would be a disaster if he were to marry her.

But nothing he could say to the marquis seemed to have any effect.

One day late in summer, the marquis, his eyes sparkling, said to Colin, "I have good news."

"About the opera?"

"No, not about that. That's a success, and

you're doing very well. No, this is a personal thing."

An alarm went off in Colin's mind, and he held his breath.

Armand said, "I have decided to ask for Miss d'Or's hand in marriage."

Colin tried desperately to think of an answer, but he could only say, "Well, that — that is quite a surprise." Actually it was not. He had seen it approaching but could no more stop it than he could have stopped an avalanche on its inexorable path.

"She's such a handsome woman — and so like my Jeanne."

Colin wanted to cry out, but he knew that there was no hope that Armand would listen to him. He heard the glowing hope in Armand's voice as he spoke of Simone, and finally he said, "I want only your happiness, sir."

Armand replied, "And I will find it with Simone. She is what I have been looking for since I lost my dear wife!"

CHAPTER FOUR

"Simone, you must know by this time how deeply I care for you. I want to marry you, and I would be honored if you agreed to be my wife."

Simone could not believe what she was hearing. The marquis had been attracted to her ever since they had first met — that had been easy enough to ascertain. Simone, of course, was accustomed to the admiration of men, and that Armand had shown her such attention flattered her. Her parents had been even more impressed, and her father had said, "It would make a fine marriage, Simone. He's a famous man, wealthy, and you could not do better."

Simone d'Or had formed a habit of doing those things that a woman can do to attract men. It had been a game with her and one at which she had learned to excel. Her natural beauty had been augmented with a spirit that was quick and active, and the game of courtship was to her very much like a game of chess or tennis. Men pursued women, women tried to evade them — or at least gave the appearance of it. If the man was persistent enough, and attractive enough, the woman perhaps allowed herself to be captured. Simone had never found a man she loved enough to marry, and she certainly was not in love with the marquis. Still, he was quite a catch, and the society in which she moved, the Creole world of New Orleans, was watching the progress of the courtship avidly.

Simone, however, was taken quite aback when Armand had come on one of his many visits to her home and almost immediately proposed to her.

Only rarely had Simone d'Or been at a total loss for words. She was quick-witted, and as a rule, quite able to handle any situation. But the sight of the marquis standing before her and the impact of his words caught her unaware. She had, of course, thought that *someday* he might come to that point, but obviously he was more enamored of her than she had supposed. She hesitated so long that Armand said, "You do not speak. Is my case hopeless?"

"Oh, no, Armand, certainly not!" Simone said quickly. "It's just that — well, you've

74

taken me off guard. I wasn't expecting you to say such a thing."

Armand took her hand, lifted it to his lips, and kissed it. "I know," he said, "that you are highly sought after and that you have refused many suitors. I come without much hope, for I am aware of the difference in our ages. You do not need to marry money, for your family is wealthy. I am aware also of the many dashing young men who are pursuing you even now. Still, I could do nothing else. The affection I feel for you is too strong for me to ignore. I beg you, Simone, do not refuse me."

As Armand spoke, Simone was able to gather her thoughts and said, "Armand, I have a great admiration for you. You are famous the world over, and there are so many women who would be happy to become your wife."

"But I am not interested in those other women. Only in you." Armand shook his head and said, "I can say only this for my own cause. I was married once, as you know, and my wife was the light of my life. We lived together in perfect peace. You remind me so much of her, Simone. She was such a good woman, and I thought I would never find another to put beside her. But in you I have found such a one."

A slight warning went off in Simone's spirit; she was wise to the ways of men and women. She knew that she could never be what Armand's first wife had been. From all reports, coming mostly from him, she had been an excellent woman but totally unlike Simone herself. He had spoken so often of her gentleness, and Simone was not blind to the fact that she had an impetuous spirit that she had not yet learned to control.

"I am honored by your proposal, Armand, but I must have time to think."

"That is all I ask." Armand's eyes brightened. "I was so afraid that you would refuse me outright. It would be a better match for me than for you, but my dear, you must believe that I am willing to do whatever will make you happy."

"That's very sweet of you, Armand. Just give me some time."

"Why, of course. In the meantime, I trust I will learn more about you and your family, and perhaps you will learn more about me."

"Oh, I know a great deal about you, Armand," Simone said, relieved that the crisis was over, at least for the moment. "But women always know more about men than men do about them."

Armand laughed. "I think that is probably

76

true. I must go now. Will I see you at the opera tonight?"

"Oh yes. I wouldn't miss it."

"What do you think of my protégé?"

"He sings very well. I think he has great potential."

"I'm very proud of him. If I had had a son, I would have wanted one exactly like Colin. Well, I must go." He took her hand, kissed it, and took his leave.

As soon as he left, Simone took a deep breath and stared at the door. "Well, it's too bad he's not twenty years younger. He would have been irresistible then. But even now it would be quite an honor to be the wife of a famous man such as the Marquis de Cuvier."

"But you can't even think of such a thing, Simone!"

Claude Vernay had been fearful of exactly what had come to pass. When he arrived to escort Simone to the opera, she told him almost at once about the marquis' proposal. Vernay stared at her and exclaimed, "Why, he is an old man!"

"He's not old, Claude."

"Of course he's old! He must be fifty."

"He's not. He's only forty-eight."

"Even if it weren't for the age difference,

he's not the sort of man who can make you happy."

Simone laughed and teased Claude. "Are you an expert in what sort of man would make me happy?"

"I should be," Vernay grinned. "I've studied you enough. I know what you are, Simone." He reached over and took her hand, and she made no attempt to prevent him. He stroked it and thought for a moment, studying her intently. He was impressed, as always, by the ripe, self-possessed curves of her mouth. She had the richest lips a woman could possess, and now her smile illuminated her face. Her skin was fair and smooth and rose-colored, and her hair was the same color as a very clear honey, a rich yellow that gleamed whenever the light caught it. He was also aware of the shape of her body within her dress, and not for the first time thought she was the most beautiful woman he had ever seen — and he had seen a great many.

"You're a woman of fire, and the marquis' fires have burned low. You need excitement and a man who will challenge you."

"Can you recommend one, Claude?"

Vernay knew that she was laughing at him, but it didn't trouble him. The thought that she might marry the marquis did. She was an impulsive woman, he knew, and he said, "If you gave it time, you wouldn't marry him, but you are always jumping into something, Simone. Marriage is something you can't jump out of easily."

"Still, the wife of the marquis would have a lot. You would have to call me Lady Beaufort."

Claude pulled her to him and kissed her. She did not struggle, and when he released her, he said, "You'll not marry that old man!"

"Don't be too sure. I would be part of the nobility in France as well as in this country. I'm sure he has a castle, too, and everywhere I went, people would look at me."

"That would please you for a while, but not for long. You'll never marry him."

Simone gave Vernay a curious glance. "You seem very sure of that."

"I am sure. You know I want to marry you myself. The time's not right yet, but no other man can have you."

"You're very possessive, and I don't want to be a possession."

"Yes, you do. You want to belong to a man, and you want the man to belong to you."

The astute quality of Claude Vernay's mind impressed Simone. He was the most dashing of the Creole gentry, and he stirred her physically in a way that no other man had. Still, he demanded a great deal more than she was willing to give. Quickly she said, "Let's not talk about marriage. Let's talk about the opera."

"Very well. But remember what I said."

During the intermission, Claude Vernay encountered his friend Byron Mayhew. Mayhew was a small young man, no more than five foot six, with fair hair and gray eyes. His family was prominent, and Mayhew himself was a much more steady individual than his friend Vernay. The two of them made a strange pair, but both were passionately devoted to fencing, and both had engaged in duels. Mayhew was not as enamored of the practice as was Vernay, but still the two were close.

"I've heard rumors that Simone might marry Lord Beaufort, Claude."

Claude shot a glance at his friend. "That will never happen, Byron."

"I don't see why not. The old man is panting after her in full chase, and she must be flattered to have a world celebrity after her."

"It doesn't matter. I've already talked to her about it and warned her."

Byron laughed. "You know Simone better than that. The surest way I can think of to make her do something is to tell her she can't."

An angry light burned in Claude Vernay's eyes. He was a man of unstable emotions, at times perfectly amiable, but at the slightest provocation his temper could explode. "I'll call him out if she agrees to marry him."

Byron stared at his friend. "Why, you can't do that!"

"Why can't I? There's always some way to provoke a man into an insult."

"Now, wait a minute, Claude," Byron said with alarm. "It's one thing to have a duel and pink some unmannerly puppy in the shoulder, but this is no puppy. This is a marquis, and you can't treat him as you would an ordinary man."

Vernay did not answer, but the fixed expression on his face told Byron that he was wasting his time. Still, Byron repeated, "Mind what I say. You can't challenge this man to a duel."

"You're right, I can't. But if he challenges me, I can certainly accept."

At the same time these two were talking, Rosa and Colin stood waiting for the opera to begin. The two had become close friends despite their differences. Rosa admired the steadfastness and the honesty in Colin that she herself lacked, while Colin admired the peppery qualities of the diva. He did not admire her morals, but he knew that she was a faithful friend when there was no amour involved. Rosa asked, "Did you see the marquis sitting beside Simone d'Or?"

"I saw it," Colin said grimly. "I didn't like it."

"Why should it bother you?"

"She's not the kind of woman to make my master happy."

"She's beautiful and rich and young."

"She's also selfish and arrogant and filled up with pride."

Rosa shook her head. "I suppose she is, but that doesn't seem to bother the marquis."

"He's trying to regain something that was lost forever."

"And what is that?"

"He loved his first wife more than I ever saw a man love a woman. Simone looks like her, in a way; she's more beautiful but has the same features and hair. But she's different. Jeanne de Cuvier was a gentle, sweet woman always ready to show a kindness. I see none of this in Miss d'Or."

Rosa was silent for a moment, studying her young friend's face. "I've seen something that you haven't."

"What's that, Rosa?"

"For a long time Claude Vernay has been pursing Simone. Do you know him?"

"I met him briefly."

"He's a volatile man, always looking for a fight. He's had more duels than you can count, and he's killed men. He won't see another man take Simone d'Or. He'll kill him first."

"Why, that's impossible!"

"No, it's not. These youngbloods know how to provoke fights. They get someone to insult and challenge them, then they take them out to the oaks and kill them."

"I can't believe this. He wouldn't dare!"

"He was my lover for a short time. I know him. He's as deadly as a snake. If you have any influence with the marquis, be certain that he never has anything to do with this man."

"Miss Simone, you have a visitor."

Simone looked up from her dressing table. Her maid, Lucy, had gone to answer the door. "Who is it?"

"It's the young man from the opera. The student of the marquis — Mr. Seymour."

"All right. I'll see him in the drawing room." Simone rose from the dressing table, left her bedroom, and went downstairs. She found Colin waiting, and he said at once,

"I'm sorry to come without an invitation, Miss d'Or, but I felt I had to see you."

Simone studied the young man coldly. Since she had found out about his humble origins, she had been unable to show anything other than cool civility. "Would you care to sit down?"

"This will take only a moment, but I had to speak with you privately."

Simone saw that Colin Seymour was nervous. She also noticed that his dress was not the current style of the young men of New Orleans. He was wearing a pair of fawn-colored trousers, a white shirt, and a rust-colored jacket. He seemed to care little for dress, but she had to admit that there was a rugged handsomeness about the man. His auburn hair caught the sun as it came through the window with just a trace of gold, and he had the bluest, most direct eyes of any man she had ever seen. "What is it, Mr. Seymour?"

"I know this will seem strange, but I wanted to talk to you about the marquis."

"The marquis? What about him?"

"I think you need to understand him better. You see, he was very much in love with his first wife."

"He has already told me that, and I must say I cannot see your concern."

"He has been a friend to me more than any other man. I can't stand by and watch him make a mistake."

Simone stared at Seymour, her eyes fixed on his face. "What mistake is that, sir?"

"He tells me he wants to marry you, and I think — I *know* that would be a sad mistake."

Anger touched Simone then, as it often did when she was crossed. "It's very impertinent of you to interfere in my personal affairs!"

"Please don't be angry with me, Miss d'Or. The marquis would be ruined if —"

"If he married me?"

"Well, yes. You see, his first wife was a very gentle woman with a sweetness of spirit. You resemble her a great deal physically, but —"

"But I am not sweet and gentle."

Colin met her gaze evenly. "No, Miss d'Or, you are not sweet, and you are not gentle. You are a woman who has to have a great deal of attention and would not be happy at all leading the life a marchioness leads."

"I think you may leave, sir!"

"But I haven't —"

"You have finished. Now, get out of the house!"

Colin walked toward the door. He turned

85

long enough to say, "If you marry him, you will make two people very unhappy. You are not suited."

"Leave the house, sir, or do I have to call the servants to help you out?"

"No, I can find my way."

As soon as she heard the door slam, Simone began muttering and pacing. She walked over to the window and saw the tall young man leave. "He's a boor, an uneducated boor of a fisherman! Who does he think he is, to tell me what to do?"

Claude Vernay was a brooding sort of individual, one who worried over a thought constantly until he could take some sort of action. When he had first heard of the possibility of Simone's marrying the marquis, he had shrugged it off, but finally he saw that she was becoming more and more attached to the idea, and they had quarreled over the matter more than once, the most serious being on a muggy July evening. In reality, Simone had grown tired of Claude's interference and had been influenced by Seymour's visit. She had disliked the young man intensely before he had come to warn her off from the marriage, and now, without realizing it, she was more receptive to the idea of the marriage because of his visit.

She had told Claude Vernay that she probably would marry Armand, and he had grown terribly angry.

He slept little that night and started to drink early the next morning. At two o'clock he stepped into a salon where he saw the Marquis de Cuvier sitting with Enoch Herzhaft, the owner of the opera house. A recklessness came over Vernay, and he walked over and greeted the two men. Herzhaft knew him well and invited him to join them. He sat down and listened as the two men talked of music. Finally the liquor that he had consumed already that morning made him say, "So, Marquis, you are courting my friend Miss d'Or?"

Surprised, Armand stared at the man across from him. He hardly knew him. "I have been seeing Miss d'Or, yes."

"I think it would be an unfortunate match."

Armand had a temper of his own, and the man's words insulted him. "It's hardly a matter for discussion in public."

"I suppose it isn't," Vernay said. "But I've often seen such things turn out badly. A young girl marrying an older man — it never works out."

"Claude," Enoch said hastily, "I don't think —"

"I hardly think it is any of your affair, sir," the marquis said. "And I would appreciate it if you would leave the table."

"I'm not good enough to sit with you?"

"You are a boor."

Claude continued taunting the marquis: "If you weren't an older man, I would demand satisfaction from you."

Enoch Herzhaft was alarmed. He knew Vernay's reputation. "Claude," he said, "you're drunk."

"No, I'm not drunk, but I know when a foreigner comes over with his European ways and tries to take advantage of a young woman."

The marquis stood and said, "I will not listen to this!"

Vernay stood also. "You're after her money, and everyone knows you're making a fool of yourself."

The marquis was not accustomed to such talk. He had received respect most of his adult life, and the insult inflamed him. His arm seemed to fly out on its own accord, and he slapped Vernay on the cheek. He said coldly, "There will be no more mention of Miss d'Or in this public place."

Vernay stared at the marquis. "You have struck me, sir. You can't take refuge behind your name and your age."

"I take refuge behind nothing. I challenge you, sir."

"I've never refused a challenge. My man will call on you."

Vernay turned away, a slight smile on his face. As soon as he left, Enoch Herzhaft jumped to his feet and said, "My lord, you must not fight this man! He is deadly with either a pistol or a sword."

"My honor demands it."

"Don't be foolish! These young men make a game out of it."

"It's a matter of honor."

Herzhaft threw his hands up. "Honor! I'm sick of that word! All that word means to these youngbloods is an excuse to destroy a man of lesser ability."

"My mind is set. I will ask you to act for me."

New Orleans had very few secrets, and the story of the proposed duel between the two men aroused everyone's interest. Whispers were exchanged, bets were made, and Simone, of course, heard of it almost at once. Unfortunately she heard of it from Colin, who again visited her home. He burst into her house, saying, "I beg your pardon, but I must speak to you."

"I told the servant that I wouldn't see you."

"You *must* see me. The marquis has challenged Vernay to a duel."

"I know about that."

"Please, Miss d'Or, you must see now what a dangerous thing this is. You must talk to the marquis."

Simone shrugged her shoulders. "I cannot interfere in such things."

"You must!" Colin said loudly. He walked over and took her by the shoulders. "You brought this on, and now it's up to you to break it off. Vernay is your friend, and the marquis is a man you profess to have some affection for. You must cause them to be reconciled."

Simone struggled to free herself, but his grip was like iron. "Let me go!" she said. When he did, she glared at him. "I wouldn't marry a man who would accept an insult. Now get out of my house!"

Colin stared at her. "You're worse than I thought," he said quietly. "You'd see a good man butchered because of your pride. I despise you." Quickly he turned and left the house.

Immediately Simone sent for Vernay, who came within the hour. She said at once, "Claude, you must not fight the marquis."

Claude said only, "He struck me. You know the answer to that."

"But he's an older man, and a powerful one."

"That's no excuse. He should have kept his temper. Don't worry. I won't kill him. I'll just teach him a lesson."

"This is madness, sir! You must not do it!"

"This is no time for you to talk like that, Colin."

The dawn was beginning to break, and the two men stood on a field in the vicinity of a large oak tree. News of the duel had spread, and many had gathered there. They stood silently, watching the drama unfold before them. Enoch Herzhaft was speaking with Byron Mayhew, who was acting for Vernay. Vernay himself stood off to one side, saying nothing. Beside him stood a tall man with dark brown hair and hazel eyes. Colin learned later this was another cohort of Vernay's, a man named Leon Manville.

Colin shivered in the coolness of the morning and could not contain himself. "This man has a lifetime of practice. Have you ever even fired a gun?"

"Of course I have," the marquis replied. "I've never had a duel, but I have practiced often enough."

"What if you kill him? Could you live with that?"

"I will not kill him, I assure you. I'm a better shot than that."

"But he may kill you."

"I do not think so. He usually shoots only to bring blood."

"He has killed," Colin said. But he had no time to argue further, for a short man in a black suit had moved forward and said, "My lord, if you're ready."

Colin watched the marquis march steadfastly to where the tall man stood. Herzhaft moved to stand beside him. His teeth were chattering. Neither of the men would budge. "God grant it may not be fatal," he said quietly.

Colin was silent as he watched as the two men heard the instructions from the duel master and then turn their backs to each another. He watched them as they stepped off ten paces, then turned, and the marquis fired first. He missed, and a coldness clamped around Colin's heart. Vernay laughed. He leveled his pistol and fired. At the same instant the marquis had turned so that his back was toward the man. The shot caught him in the back and drove him forward, then he collapsed.

"Armand!" Colin cried out, using the marquis' first name for the first time. He ran to his master and saw the blood spreading on the white shirt. The shot had caught the marquis just above the lower back.

Vernay walked over and asked, "Why did he turn? I intended only to pink him."

He was shouldered aside by a burly man in a snuff-colored coat. He knelt down and said, "I do not think it is fatal. Can you hear me, Monsieur?"

"I — can't move my legs."

A chill ran through Colin, and he said, "It will be all right, won't it, Doctor?"

The doctor turned and said evenly, "I trust so, but no one is sure of these things. I must have the bullet out. Some of you help me get him inside."

As they moved the wounded man inside, Colin turned to Vernay. Rage filled him, and he ran at the man and with all of his might struck out. His blow caught Vernay squarely on the chin and knocked him down. At once Mayhew and others of Vernay's friends seized Colin.

"Don't make a fool of yourself, sir," Mayhew said.

"If my master dies, I'll kill him!"

"Don't be a fool," Mayhew whispered. "Go see to your master."

The men released Colin, and he ran to catch up with the doctor. He had never felt such an icy anger in his life. There had been something inhumanely cruel about what had taken place, and he followed the wounded man with a feeling of helplessness.

"I can't believe it!" Simone exclaimed. "How could he have done such a thing?"

Leon Manville had gone to Simone with the news of the duel, and although he had tried to be gentle, he could see that the young woman was shaken. "I know it's a terrible shock, Miss d'Or, but it's not all bad."

"How can there be anything good in such a thing?"

"The gentleman will not die," Manville said quickly. "I understand that the wound was serious, but not fatal."

"Well, thank God for that!" Simone said. "Did you see it, Leon?"

"Yes, and I wish I hadn't. It was not at all a thing that Vernay should be proud of." Manville had heard that Simone d'Or had some sort of an attachment to the marquis and was as curious as to its nature as the rest of the city. "I trust that you will not let this influence your plans with the marquis."

Simone hated gossip, and glaring at Leon, she said, "Don't concern yourself with such things. Now, thank you for coming, but I must ask you to leave me."

Manville made a hasty retreat, and Simone walked nervously around the house, troubled by the news. She was grieved at the incident, but in her heart she knew that she did not love Armand. *I wish him well, and a speedy recovery,* she thought, *but I would never have married him.*

CHAPTER FIVE

Dr. Marcus Grigsby proved to be a good friend to Colin and Armand during the recovery period after the duel. The bullet had lodged itself in Armand's back so close to the spine that Grigsby had been unwilling to take a chance on removing it. "If I make the slightest mistake, he will be completely paralyzed," Grigsby warned Colin. "As it is, his legs are paralyzed, but at least he'll have the use of his upper body. It's just not worth the chance."

Three months had passed since Grigsby had made his pronouncement, and October had come. Grisgby arrived at the dock to see the pair off. He stood beside Armand, looking at him with a worried expression, but quickly he smoothed it away and said heartily, "Well, my lord, you are going home again. I know that will be good for you."

Armand looked up. His features were still, and his eyes showed little sign of life. He had been quiet and listless ever since learning that he would be confined to a wheelchair for the rest of his life. "I want to thank you, Doctor," he said quietly, "for all of your attention."

"I wish I could do more. Really I do."

"You've done all anybody could do, and I will miss you when I am at home."

A steam whistle uttered a mighty blast, and Colin said, "It's time to go on board."

"Yes. Good-bye, Doctor. Thank you again."

Colin nodded to a steward, who stepped behind Armand's chair. "I'll be on board right away, sir." Armand nodded briefly, and the steward pushed him up the gangplank. As soon as he was out of hearing distance, Colin put his hand out. "Thank you, Dr. Grigsby."

Grigsby shook the young man's hand. "It's one of those cases when I wish I'd become a blacksmith or a stockbroker — anything except a doctor! I hate to give bad news, especially to good men like your master."

"Any final instructions?"

"I think the problem is twofold. The first is the physical one, of course. That's obvious. His spine is damaged, and sometimes that causes other damage. We doctors still don't understand all that goes on inside the body. Just see that he gets all of the exercise he can. Get him to use dumbbells to make his upper body as strong as possible. Keep him outdoors a great deal." Dr. Grigsby hesitated.

"What is it, Doctor? You're leaving something out."

"Well, aside from the physical problem, there's the emotional one. He's had a great chunk of his life removed. Some people can't handle that, Colin. Keep him as busy as you can." The doctor was a burly man with a blunt face and sharp, gray eyes. "You've told me how much he's helped you, and now it's time for you to return the favor."

"I'll give him my life, Dr. Grigsby. You can depend on that."

"One thing you might do is get him interested in your career."

Colin shook his head. "He's doesn't seem to have much interest in music anymore."

"You must see that he does. Make him compose. Make him help you. Somehow show him you want to go on and become a topflight tenor in the opera."

"That seems selfish."

"Not in the least. Furthest thing from it," Grigsby protested. He raised one fist in a pugilistic gesture and said, "You're going to have to fight for his life, Colin. Making you into a star isn't selfish. He wants it anyway. He thinks so much of you. Now, fill up his life as best you can."

"I'll do that, and I'll ask you to pray for us, Doctor."

Grigsby nodded, and his face softened. "I'll do that, my boy. You may be sure of it."

"Good-bye, Dr. Grigsby." Colin turned and climbed the gangplank. The steward was waiting beside Armand's chair, but Colin said, "I'll take care of it, Ernest."

"Thank you, sir," the steward said, pocketing the coin that Colin gave him.

Turning to look at the teeming crowds on the wharf, Colin was silent for a moment, and then he remembered Dr. Grigsby's admonition. "Let's find our rooms. I want you to help me with that new piece from *La Traviata*. I can't get it."

"I really don't feel like it much, Colin."

"None of that. I'm going to become a great star, and I can't do it without your help."

Armand looked up and smiled faintly. "You have ambition. I never noticed that before."

"It's going to take everything both of us have. I got a late start, but on the way home

99

there's not much scenery to look at, so I'll entertain the passengers with my singing. They will probably want to throw me overboard."

"I doubt that," Armand said. He took a last look at New Orleans, and something crossed his face, an emotion that Colin caught at once. "All right, Colin. There's nothing left to see here."

Colin grasped the wheelchair and pushed it down along the walkway. His mind raced to make plans. *I've got to keep him active and busy. He mustn't have time to brood.* He lifted his voice and began to sing "Amore Ti Vieta," startling all of the passengers within hearing distance.

The booming sound of his powerful tenor voice filled the air, and one well-dressed and attractive woman turned to watch him with admiration. She leaned over and whispered to the woman with her, "What a handsome man and a beautiful voice! I wonder who he is."

"Well, you can find out. We've got a long voyage."

Unaware of this, Colin sang lustily, and when they reached the stateroom door, he saw that the marquis was smiling broadly. "You ought to charge them, Colin."

"Maybe I can talk the captain into letting

100

me give a concert. We can take up a collection afterward." He saw that his actions had taken Armand's mind off of his problem for the moment. In the cabin, he wheeled the chair around and said, "Now, let's get to work. How does the phrasing go in that duet in the second act?"

Philippe Gerard stepped up silently behind his wife in the kitchen, put his arms around her, and lifted her off the floor. She was a large woman, but he handled her as easily as if she were a child.

"Stop that, Philippe!"

Philippe kissed the back of her neck and whispered, "I'm overcome with passion for you, my little dove. Come away with me."

Josephine Gerard had been a spinster for many years. She had given up all ideas of love, but when Philippe Gerard had proposed to her and she had accepted, she discovered that he had the ability to make her feel like a young girl. "Put me down, you fool!" When he placed her on the floor and turned her around, he winked.

Josephine flushed but smiled. "Now you get out of my kitchen."

The sound of Colin's voice drifted down to them. "He sings all the time. How long have they been home — six months? And

101

Colin sings every day," Philippe noted.

"Yes, and he keeps the master busy too. I think it's a good thing. You remember how sad he was when he came home."

"Yes, what a tragic thing." His dark eyes flashed. "I'd like to go to New Orleans and find that man who put the bullet in the marquis. I'd take him off at the neck!"

"And I would bless you if you did it."

"When he first came home, he was so depressed, and Colin told me that we would have to keep him occupied all the time. That's why I make him go look at the garden and help me make plans."

"You've done wonderfully well, my husband." Josephine patted his cheek and said, "The whole staff has made it the business of life to cheer up the master."

"Colin said he was composing again. That's good."

"Yes, it is. Now, you get out of here. I'm taking their tea up."

Philippe left the kitchen, and Josephine took the tray and walked down the hall. The marquis' bedroom had originally been upstairs, but Colin had had a large room remodeled. He knocked out a wall so that the room itself was fifteen feet wide and twenty-five feet long. Colin decorated it tastefully and put new windows in so that sunlight flooded it. It was a cheerful room with thick carpet and a fine pianoforte positioned where the player could catch the sunlight on the music. Colin was sitting at the piano, and the marquis was seated where he could watch his face. As Josephine entered, he was saying, "No, no, no! You sound like a sick puppy!"

"I do not!" Colin protested. "I sang that last part exactly right."

"You will argue with your teacher!"

Colin laughed. "You are right. I did sound awful." He turned and said, "Oh, Josephine. Tea! Is there cake as well?"

Colin walked over and watched as Josephine poured the tea, then he pulled a chair up close to the tea table beside the marquis. "Thank you, Josephine."

"I did make a few cakes. They're not very good."

Colin picked up a cake and bit a piece off. "It's terrible. Leave them all. They're so bad I'll have to eat them to keep someone else from suffering."

Josephine's eyes sparkled and she grinned. "You always think of others, Monsieur."

"Unselfish — that's me."

As Josephine left the room and the two men drank the tea and ate the cakes, they talked about the music. Colin had soaked

103

up an immense amount of knowledge from the marquis during the past six months. He had studied Italian and German, and day after day he had sung until his throat, at times, grew raw, but Armand had thrown himself with passion into making him into the finest tenor in Europe — or in the world, for that matter.

"I need to speak to you about something, Colin."

Colin groaned and put his hands on his head. "Every time you say that, it means you've found something I am doing wrong."

"That's not at all true, but in this case it is. You are doing something wrong."

Colin straightened up. "Well, what is it?" he said wearily. "I don't think I'll ever become the singer you want me to be."

"It's not your singing," Armand said. "It's something else."

"What is it, sir? Tell me."

"I've noticed that you have a bitterness concerning the man who put this bullet in my back."

"Why, I've never mentioned him!"

"I know you haven't directly, but it shows, and besides, you talked to Philippe about it, and Philippe told Etienne. Both of them, of course, agree with you, but I want to tell you that hatred and bitterness are more dangerous than a pistol or a sword."

Colin could not meet the marquis' eyes; he had spoken the exact truth. For months now, he had not gone to bed a single night without thinking of Claude Vernay. He had begun to indulge in violent thoughts about how he would make the man suffer and daydreamed scenarios in which he put Vernay into terrible tortures.

"I can't help it, Armand. I just can't."

"If I've forgiven the man, surely you should. I think the Bible says somewhere that it's wrong to take up the offenses of another. I'll have to look it up. Don't remember the exact place, but it's true enough."

Colin was silent. The marquis had done so much for him, and the idea of Claude Vernay's taking from him a precious part of his life was hateful. Finally he lifted his head and said, "I'll do my best to put the thing out of my mind."

Armand reached out and grasped Colin's arm. His grip was strong, for Colin had insisted on his doing all the physical exercises he could. "I have something else to tell you."

"What have I done now?"

"Nothing, really. You will like this, I hope." He hesitated and then said, "I have decided to adopt you as my son. Legally, I mean. If you agree."

Colin stared at him. "Why, sir, I've never asked for such a thing."

"I know you haven't, but I want to do it. I have no other kin, and I want you to have all that is mine when I die."

"Don't speak of that."

"It comes to all of us, Colin. One day you will be the marquis. It would give me pleasure to think of it. You'll have sons, and the name will go on. Besides . . ." His voice grew quiet. "I have thought of you as a son for some time, and I know Jeanne would have been very happy at such a thing."

Colin's eyes were dim with tears. He cleared his throat and said, "It is an honor that I do not deserve."

"We will speak no more of it. The papers are being drawn up. They will be ready later in the week. Until then we will continue our work."

CHAPTER SIX

"I wish you would talk to the master, Mr. Colin. He's really not well enough to go to your opening."

Colin had entered the front door and started down the hallway into the marquis' bedroom when Josephine stopped him and made her plea. He halted and turned to face her, his brow furrowed with worry. "I've tried my best to get him not to go, but you know how stubborn he can be."

"I'm worried about him, sir. What did the doctor say?"

"He told him flatly that he would be risking his life to go to Paris, but he won't listen. He says he's worked too hard for this to miss it."

Indeed, Armand had worked very hard for nearly two years since his return from New Orleans. It had been a good thing for him to stay busy, and he had done well for eighteen months. But then something had happened to his heart. Colin had entered his room to find him gasping and holding onto his chest in pain, his left arm numb and useless. The doctors pronounced him the victim of a stroke. Some of the effects had passed away, but the marquis had lost part of the use of his left hand. His speech and memory were affected.

Nevertheless, Armand had asked Arnaud Heuse, the owner of the Paris Opera House, to put on a production of *The Marriage of Figaro,* by Mozart, starring Colin. It had not been hard to convince Heuse, for Colin had progressed tremendously, his talent becoming obvious to everyone who heard him. He had sung second tenor in several operas under Heuse, and Armand had set March 2, 1837, as the beginning of Colin's new life as a starring operatic tenor.

Colin bit his lip and shook his head. "I'm worried. I wish he'd stay home, but he won't."

"Be as careful with him as you can, but then I know you will. You care so much for him."

"We all do, Josephine. It'll be a slow, careful trip. Where's Philippe? I want him to help me get the marquis into the carriage."

Armand de Cuvier sat in his box. Philippe,

dressed in a decent black suit, had been pressed into service to get him up the stairs. The big man had simply picked up the wheelchair containing Armand and bore the burden as lightly as if it were nothing. He sat behind the marquis, who was speaking with Arnaud Heuse, the owner of the opera house. Philippe watched carefully as Colin sang the song that closed the opera. He had difficulty associating the man on the stage, so tall, strong, and handsome and full of life, his voice filling the tremendous opera house, with the skinny ragamuffin who had come up to the door in rags five years earlier. He was filled with pride, and once he leaned forward and said, "Our protégé is doing fine, my lord."

"Yes, he is, Philippe," Armand whispered back.

"Still, you spoiled a fine gardener."

Armand could not but help smile. He was thin now and spoke little, for it embarrassed him that he sometimes stuttered and could not find the proper words.

He relished the opera, drinking it all in. As the curtain fell and the cast members began to take their bows, Heuse leaned forward and said, "You have written many fine works, Maestro, but your finest work is down there on that stage."

"Thank — thank you for those kind words, Arnaud. I believe you are right."

The marquis enjoyed the sound of the crowd calling out Colin's name, the young man who had come to fill his life. He was pleased to see that his adopted son still had humility. He had undertaken to drill into Colin that pride was a deadly sin. Many times he had said, "God gave you the voice. It's none of your doing. You simply must use it for His glory." The marquis knew that Colin had been struggling with his faith since Jeanne had died.

Finally the curtain closed for the final time, and Philippe asked, "Shall I take you backstage?"

"I would like that."

Arnaud said, "It's so crowded. It will be hard for you."

"This is his opening night. I must be there."

At once Philippe wheeled the marquis to the stairs. He picked the chair up again and made his way down the stairs, calling out, "Make way there for the maestro!" in a booming voice. The crowd parted as the waters had parted for Moses, and Philippe continued to call out until Armand asked, "Could you please not be so loud, Philippe? You're making —" He could not get the rest of the sentence out, and Arnaud Heuse said, "Here. I'll get the door."

They went in without knocking and found that Colin's dressing room was already full. They all stepped back, however, as Philippe wheeled the marquis in. Colin went to him at once and took the thin hand that Armand held out.

"It was magnificent," Armand whispered.

"All your doing, sir! All yours!"

The crowd listened, and one beautiful young woman, famous and rich and very prominent in the Paris social life, stepped forward and said, "I must congratulate you, sir, on your pupil." The diamonds on her neck, arms, and hands glittered, but only slightly less than her eyes, which were fixed on Colin. "I must insist that you come to my home for refreshments."

"Ordinarily it would be a pleasure," Colin said quickly, "but I must get the marquis home. It's been a trying time."

"Then you must come, sir, next Tuesday. I'll be waiting for you." She swept away, and as she did, Heuse leaned over and said, "Stay away from that woman. She's a carnivore. She eats opera stars for breakfast."

Colin laughed. "Thanks for the advice," he said, planning to follow Arnaud's recommendation. He turned back and said,

"Come now. We've got to get you to the hotel and then back home tomorrow."

"I will never forget this night."

"And I will never forget the years, sir, that you have given to me."

Colin's debut marked the beginning of a professional triumph. All of Paris was speaking about the young American tenor. No one could understand how anyone not European could sing so well! Colin found it amusing, more than anything else, and he spent a great deal of time avoiding the women who flocked to him.

But opening night had marked a decline in the health of the marquis. In the days that followed, he grew weaker, and by the time the month was out and Colin's engagement was over, he was confined to his bed and growing weaker daily.

"I must tell you, Monsieur, that your benefactor is failing."

Colin had caught the doctor leaving the house, and he said, "But you must be able to do something."

Dr. Marteau answered sadly, "We doctors have no control over the final illness. It may come when a man is ninety or when a child is one, but when the good God decides that it is a man's appointed time, there's nothing we can do."

"How long will he live?"

"At the rate he's going, no more than a month. Possibly much less. I'm sorry. Stay very close to him, for you will lose him soon."

The end came two months later, on a Monday evening at sunset. Colin was sitting beside Armand, looking out as the light faded in the west. The dying sun threw a crimson ray that tinged the clouds, and Colin watched as the sun seemed perceptibly to sink behind the hills to the west.

"Colin."

Colin turned, and seeing something in the marquis' face, he took the frail hand and said, "Yes, what is it, Father?"

"I — must ask you . . ." He had trouble continuing, and Colin leaned forward to catch the words. Gathering strength, the marquis said, "Many times I have asked you — to trust in Jesus Christ." The silence seemed to fill the room, but the words echoed in Colin's ears. He had once believed, but he had lost his faith after Jeanne died. He saw that life was leaving this man who had done so much for him, so he said quickly, "Yes, you have, my father, and I will put my faith in Jesus."

"Will you do that right now, my son?"

Colin bowed his head. He felt the presence of God at that moment, and in a faltering, stumbling voice, he cried, "Oh, God, I have been a sinner all my life, and I am so sorry!" He began to weep, and for some time he could not utter a word. Finally he said meekly, "I ask you to save my soul, Father, in the name of Jesus! I believe He died for me! Forgive me, please, and make me Your child!"

Armand cried out with joy, "My son — my son! How happy you have made me! Now, give Him your life, my dear boy. Serve God with all your heart!"

The marquis lay quietly for five minutes, and then suddenly he stiffened, and his eyes opened. Colin saw that his life was fading. Armand smiled and put his hand up to touch Colin's cheek. "Good-bye, my beloved son."

The arm grew limp, and Armand lay very still. For fifteen minutes he lingered, and then he simply stopped breathing. Colin stood over the bed, holding the frail hand in his own. Tears filled his eyes. He leaned over, kissed the thin cheek, and whispered, "Good-bye, best of men."

"I don't understand what you're doing,"

Philippe said. "You are now the marquis, Lord Beaufort. Why are you leaving France for that awful country of yours?"

Colin was packing one of his trunks. He was taking most of his clothes with him. Three months had passed since the death of the marquis. The legal work had been done, many papers had been signed, and now Colin Seymour was the Marquis Lord Beaufort. He himself preferred the simple American name, but everyone on the staff and the lawyers insisted on calling him Lord Beaufort. "Why must you go to America? The last time you went, it was nothing but a tragedy," Philippe protested.

Colin dropped the shirt into the trunk and turned to face Philippe. He smiled. "I promised Armand that I would follow Christ, but first, before I begin that life —" He hesitated and then said, "I have business."

Suddenly Philippe, who, though uneducated, was a clever man, watched Colin carefully. His eyes narrowed, and he said, "It has something to do with the man who shot the master, doesn't it?"

Colin shook his head. "I refuse to talk about it. Let us just say that I have a chore to do before I can really begin living."

Philippe gripped the young man's shoulder. "You are now Lord Beaufort, but I think of you as the young man who came years ago. I never thought you would become anything, but now you are a man. And I say to you: avenge Armand de Cuvier!"

"That is exactly what I plan to do, Philippe. Then I will come back here."

"It will be lonely until you return." Philippe suddenly reached out, put his massive arms around the younger man and squeezed him, then turned and left the room abruptly. Colin stared after him, and his lips tightened. "Yes, just one more chore to do, and then I can think about life itself."

■ ■ ■ ■

PART TWO:
1838
SIMONE

■ ■ ■ ■

Chapter Seven

The d'Or family usually gathered in the parlor after dinner if they were not going out. The parlor was one of the most comfortable rooms in the house. The large room was decorated very warmly with dark-green paint on the walls and brown rugs scattered on the highly polished wooden floor. The furniture — a large sofa, two side chairs, and three easy chairs — was upholstered in green damask and had hand-carved arms and legs of dark mahogany. The walls were decorated with colorful landscape paintings framed in gold and dark wood, and the fireplace was made of white marble with flecks of gold running through it. A small table, flanked by two of the easy chairs, had a brass and wooden chess set on it, and a desk took its place beside one of the two large windows along one wall.

Ordinarily Simone played either the harp or the pianoforte, both instruments she had mastered, but on this particular night she was engrossed in a new novel and had begged off. Her mother was working on one of her interminable bits of sewing, while her father read the newspaper thoroughly. He was not a man who loved literature but studied the paper as if it were Holy Scripture.

Noticing his daughter's intense concentration, Louis asked, "What are you reading now, Simone?"

Looking up, Simone smiled. "A new novel by the Englishman Charles Dickens. It's called *Oliver Twist.*"

"What's it about, my dear?" Renee asked. She was not a reader herself but was proud that her daughter was.

"It's about a young boy, an orphan, who has a terrible life. He goes to London and is made into a thief by an awful Jew named Fagin. Before that, he had spent a terrible time in a poorhouse. It's very moving."

Louis d'Or shook his head with disbelief. "I don't see why you want to read such sordid books. Surely there must be more pleasant novels."

"I suppose there are, Papa, but Dickens has the ability to make things so real."

"Those novels! They're all nothing but lies. Just stuff made up out of some man's head. If you want reality, listen to this." He began to read from the paper.

More than fourteen thousand members of the Cherokee Nation from tribal lands in Georgia, Alabama, and Tennessee have been pulled up from their homes and transported eight hundred miles to the Indian Territory west of the Red River. General Winfield Scott oversaw the move in which it was estimated four thousand people, mostly infants, children and old people, died — most of them of whooping cough, pneumonia and tuberculosis.

He lowered the paper and said, "There's real tragedy for you. Not something made up out of a book."

Simone looked at her father in disbelief. "Why did they move the Indians out of their homes?"

"Because they stand in the way of progress, my dear. It's the old story. The weak must give way to the strong."

"Well, I think it's terrible," Renee said indignantly, putting down her sewing. "After all, the Indians were here before we were."

Louis laughed. He was a jovial man who could find humor in most situations. "If we followed that line of thinking, the Indians would be sitting on this very spot, naked and killing each other off with tribal wars. You wouldn't have this beautiful home if somebody hadn't moved them out."

"Well, I don't like to hear about such things as that. Please don't read any more, Louis," Renee said and went back to her sewing.

"None of us likes to hear about terrible things, but they exist. As a matter of fact, I think a real tragedy is shaping up for this country."

"What do you mean, Papa?" Simone asked. She knew her father kept up with current events, and she herself was interested.

"This slavery thing, daughter. It's going to blow up like a bomb one day."

"I suppose you're right. I read the other day in the paper that the abolitionists in the North have organized some sort of method of stealing slaves and taking them to northern cities and Canada."

"That's right," Louis said, "and it's going to cause trouble. It's called the Underground Railroad."

"What in the world is that — a train?"

"No, not a real train, my dear. It's just a manner of speaking. The abolitionists steal slaves from those of us who own them in the South and spirit them away. They take them to where slavery is illegal."

"Not everyone in the North is sympathetic to that, Papa. A mob in Philadelphia burned down a hall there where people were having antislavery meetings."

"People in the North don't understand our problems. How in the world would we raise rice or cotton without slaves to do it? It takes a lot of people. We couldn't afford to pay hired hands."

The three sat talking about political problems, primarily about slavery, until Louis drew out his watch and opened the case. "Why, it's getting late," he said. "Where in the world is Bayard?"

"He went out with some friends," Renee said.

Louis snapped the case shut, rubbed the back of the golden surface with his thumb, and shook his head. "I don't know what's going to become of that boy if he doesn't settle down."

"Well, he's young, dear."

"He's twenty-five years old!" Louis snapped. He tugged at his whiskers and stared moodily at the picture on the wall across the room from him for a moment before answering. "I don't like this notion of his of being an artist anyway."

"But Papa, he's so talented," Simone said. "Monsieur Dupree at the art institute said he could be a great painter." Simone had softened in recent years after watching the struggles of her older brother.

"He'd be better off painting houses or doing something practical."

"But suppose there were no painters," she said, quick to defend her brother. "Look at how these pictures brighten up our room."

"That's all very well, but Bayard doesn't work at it. I don't think he's serious. It's not too late for him to find a real profession. He could become a lawyer."

"Bayard would hate that," Simone countered. "He's a young man of imagination, and staying in a stuffy old office all day and studying dull documents would kill his spirit."

"Well, he's headed the wrong way."

"Don't be so hard on him, dear. He'll find his way," Renee said. "After all, he's —"

A sudden loud knocking at the door brought Renee d'Or's words to a halt. She said, "Who in the world can that be at this time of the night? It can't be Bayard. He wouldn't knock."

"The servants must have gone to bed. I'll see," Simone said. She got up and walked quickly from the room, then turned down the wide hallway and passed through the foyer. She opened the door and saw her brother, Bayard, and Claude Vernay. She caught a quick breath, for Vernay was practically supporting Bayard, who was obviously inebriated.

"I brought the wandering prodigal home, Simone," Claude said. He shook his head and said, "I'm afraid he's a bit the worse for drink."

"Come in, Claude." Simone drew the door back and moved to help support Bayard, who was slumping in Claude's grip. He opened his eyes and stared at her. "Who's this? Oh, Simone, it's you."

"You're drunk!" Simone said with disgust.

"Not drunk. Just had enough."

"Will you help me get him to his room, Claude?"

"Certainly."

The two steered Bayard down the hall, but when they got to the parlor door, Louis and Renee stepped out. Louis glared at his son and shook his head with disgust. "He's drunk again."

"No, not drunk, Father," Bayard grinned foolishly.

Louis said, "Claude, I've spoken to you about this before. You're ruining Bayard."

"Not me, sir," Claude protested. "I was

home in bed. Leon Manville came and got me up. Bayard was in trouble, he said, so I got dressed, and the two of us went down. We pulled him out of a rough place. He was trying to fight everybody, but I had nothing to do with it."

"Well, I apologize, Claude. Here, let me take him upstairs. Come on, Bayard."

"I'll go with you," Renee said. The two held onto Bayard, who began singing a drinking song at the top of his lungs. His words were slurred as they led him down the hall.

"Come into the parlor, Claude, and tell me what happened," Simone said after they had settled Bayard in his bed. Simone led him into the parlor and turned to face him. "I'm sorry you had to be dragged into all this."

"It's all right. I was glad I was there. It could have been rather nasty."

Simone could not think of anything proper to say. She knew that Claude had been a bad influence in many ways on Bayard, although he professed to care for her brother. He was the sort of man who had influence — of a certain type — over others. She sat down in one of the easy chairs, saying, "Here, come and tell me all about it."

Claude sat in another of the easy chairs and told her the details. "I know you think I'm a bad influence on Bayard, but honestly, I'm going to try to help him slow down on the drinking."

"I hope you can. He's throwing his life away," Simone said. "I wish he'd stop drinking and start working more on his painting."

"I'll talk to him about that. I have already, but he's young."

"That's no excuse."

"No, I suppose it isn't. I'm no priest to preach at a fellow, but I'll do the best I can with Bayard."

"I'd appreciate that, Claude."

"I haven't been able to see much of you lately. Have you been avoiding me?"

"Of course not."

Claude studied her. He had pursued the woman for years, for the last year in the most fervent way he knew how. He reached over, took her hand, and said, "Have you thought about us, Simone?"

Simone let her hand remain in Claude's. He was a strong man, virile, and he had a streak of romanticism in him. He was easily bored, she knew that, and had enough money that he did not need to work. He had a taste for the arts, and she had thought about his proposal long and hard. She could not explain to herself why she did not accept him — only a short while ago, she would have, but she had seen a rash and fiery temper in him. It seemed he was ungovernable, and of course, she knew his record of dueling. It was something that she was coming to find less and less appealing. At first such things had been romantic to her, but a good friend, Charles Daschelle, with a bright future, a young bride, and a young son, had died in a duel. It was a foolish, useless duel over a hand of cards.

"I just don't think I'm ready for marriage, Claude."

"Why, you're twenty-four years old. Many of your schoolmates have already married."

"That's true, but I'm just not ready." She stood up and said, "I'm really upset tonight, Claude. I can't talk about this."

"Well, come for a ride with me tomorrow."

"All right, Claude."

He reached out to embrace her, but she put her hand on his chest. "Not now. I'm just too worried about Bayard."

"All right. I'll be by tomorrow about one o'clock."

"That will be fine. And thank you for bringing Bayard home."

After showing Claude out, she went upstairs to find her mother coming out of Bayard's room. "How is he, mother?"

"He's drunk. How else can I put it?" It was unusual for Renee d'Or to be bitter. She was a sweet woman, agreeable almost to a fault, but now she was depressed. "Our only son, and he's a drunkard."

Simone put her arm around her mother. Squeezing her, she said, "You mustn't worry about it. It will come out all right."

"I don't see how. I don't see anything but trouble ahead for him."

"Go to bed, mother, and try to rest."

She watched as her mother walked down the hall and then looked at Bayard's door. She herself had become doubtful about her brother's life. They had been very close as youngsters, but Bayard had pulled away after getting caught up with the young bucks of New Orleans. Now Simone shook her head and went to her room, falling into bed soon after.

Sleep would not come, and she recalled Claude's words, "Many of your schoolmates have already married." The words evoked memories of when she and her three friends had been called the Four Musketeers during their schooldays at the convent. Simone had a vivid memory, and she relived the last time the four of them had been together . . .

The party was noisy, but none of the guests was more lively than Assumpta Damita de Salvedo y Madariaga! She floated around the room, followed by young men, but she refused them all. She drew her three friends Chantel Fontaine, Leonie Dousett, and Simone to her, saying, "Come, let's hide ourselves and gossip!" Her dark eyes flashed, and she ran through the large room, leading the others outside. When they were alone, she said, "I'm going to tell your fortunes."

"Why, fortune-telling is wicked!" Leonie Dousett was the least impressive of the three girls. She did not have the dark beauty of Damita, the blonde attractiveness of Simone, or the prettiness of Chantel — indeed, many considered her flatly unattractive. But there was a steadiness in her gray eyes, and her modest air set her off well in most company.

"Then we'll be wicked," Damita said, grinning. "Give me your hand, Leonie." Ignoring the girl's protests, she took her hand and studied it. "Ah, you will have a sea voyage — and you will meet a very handsome and daring and rich man! He will fall madly in love with you. He is of noble blood! You will be Lady Leonie!"

Leonie pulled her hand away, laughing. "That is your fortune, not mine, Damita."

"Here, tell my fortune," Chantel said, extending her hand. She was a quiet girl who had grown even more reserved after the death of her father. She had an unfortunate history, losing her father, mother, and for a time, her only sister. But tragedy had not defeated her, and she smiled as Damita began to make wild predictions of her future. They all involved rich young men who were ready to die for her.

"I wish one of them were here now," Chantel laughed. "I don't need half a dozen — one would be plenty."

"Now you, Simone," Damita said, taking her hand. "Ah, I see a troubled future! You will have grief and loss."

Simone laughed and said, "No, tell me good things, as you've done to the others."

Damita grew serious. "You probably will have trouble, Simone — but then, we all will. Life is like that."

Simone started as the memory came sharp and clear. She had kept up with the other girls after a fashion and knew that they were well — but none of the three had found a rich husband. She could not help thinking of how close the four of them had been, and now they were almost like strangers! A pang ran though her, sharp and keen, at the thought that something precious had been lost. She whispered, "I'll have to get in touch with them." But she knew that she probably would not. Life was like that — you touched a life and felt its power, and then it drifted away and became only a memory.

Rising early the next morning, Simone had breakfast with her father, and then accompanied him to his office — at least as far as the shops. She kissed him and stepped out of the carriage, saying, "I'll need some money, Papa."

"You always do," Louis said. He sighed with resignation and handed her some bills from his pocket. "Simone, I'm upset about Bayard."

"So am I, but we'll both talk to him."

"We've talked and talked, but nothing's come of it. Come by and have lunch with me."

"I'll try, Papa."

Simone made her way along the streets for an hour, shopping for a few small items. She stopped by the jewelry store to try on a ring that she especially wanted, an opal that would go with a new dress she had just bought. She was tempted strongly but did not have enough money to buy it at the moment. She said as much to the clerk.

"Certainly, Mademoiselle d'Or," the clerk

said, smiling. "When you purchase the ring, it will look very beautiful on your hand."

Leaving the store, Simone decided that she would go visit one of her old classmates after all — but not one of the Four Musketeers. This was another friend from the convent named Marie. She made her way down to Royal Street and climbed the stairs to the second floor, where Marie had rented an apartment.

She knocked on the door. When it opened, she smiled and said, "Hello, Marie. I've come to visit."

"Simone, I'm so glad to see you! Come in at once."

Marie Devois was a large woman of twenty-seven, three years older than Simone. She was strongly built with the big chest of a singer. Her coloring was spectacular: red hair, flashing green eyes, and a beautiful peachy complexion. She wore too much makeup for Simone's taste, but she had found Marie to be a good friend. Marie had been at the convent only one year and had been an older girl, but the two had become close during that time. Marie could not tolerate the discipline of the convent and left with the professed intention of becoming a singer at the opera. She had traveled quite a bit and led an independent life for a woman.

"I'll make some tea, and we can have some beignets."

"Well, I had breakfast, but that sounds good."

Marie fixed the tea and the two went out on the balcony, where they watched the crowd through the black grillwork. Several times men looked up and saw the two women; they called out greetings, lifting their hats.

"How's your career going, Marie?"

"Oh, all right, I suppose. I'm a stand-in for Louise Perlotta." She took a bite of the beignet, which left a dust of powdered sugar on her upper lip. She licked it off and turned to Simone. "I want you to help me pray for something."

"Pray for what?"

"That she'll break her leg!"

Simone laughed and shook her head. "I couldn't pray for that." She barely believed in prayer, but she still couldn't ask for such a silly thing.

"Of course you can! She's got plenty of money, and I don't have any at all. If she broke her leg, I could become a star."

"Think of an easier request."

"All right. There's a new opera going to be put on. It's called *Juliet.* It's written by a

Frenchman named Cuvier."

"Yes, I've heard of it," Simone said. Marie had obviously not heard of her doings with the marquis, and she did not want to discuss them. "Tell me about it."

"They say it's beautifully done. The last work that Lord Beaufort wrote. That's the older Lord Beaufort. His son now has the title. But it's going to be a smashing opera."

"You always say that, Marie."

"Well, this time it's true. The lead's going to be sung by Lord Beaufort himself. He's the sensation of the French opera, Simone, a nobleman, and I hear he's frighteningly handsome."

"I think his name is Colin Seymour."

Marie stared at her. "I thought he was Lord Beaufort."

"Well, Colin Seymour is his American name. Lord Beaufort is his title. And he wasn't really the son of Lord Beaufort except by adoption."

"Well, I want you to pray that I'll get a role in that new opera! Everyone says it's going to be the best thing that ever hit New Orleans."

The two women chatted for a while, and then Simone rose to leave. "I hope you get the role, Marie. I may even actually pray about it!"

"If he's as good-looking as they say, and as rich, I'm going to try for more than just a little singing part." Marie winked and said, "I may get the fellow himself."

"You mean fall in love with him?"

Marie laughed. "That would help, but it's not entirely necessary. When a man's got a title, looks, and money, love can wait in the closet!"

It was Monday, three days after Simone's conversation with Marie Devois, that Simone found Bayard out in the garden. His easel was set up, and he was painting a picture of a spectacularly colorful bank of roses.

Standing beside him, Simone looked at what he had done and said, "That's very good, Bayard."

"I suppose it's all right." He turned and looked at Simone. "Are you still angry at me for coming home drunk?"

"It hurt Papa and Mama."

"I know. I wish they wouldn't feel so bad about my bad behavior."

"How can they help it, Bayard?"

"It's quite a burden being an only son." He turned back, made several more passes with his brush, then asked abruptly, "Are you going to marry Claude?"

"Oh, I don't know."

"He's very determined."

"I'm not sure we're suited for each other."

"That's not what he says."

Simone did not want to speak of it and began to ask more questions about his painting. He answered them absentmindedly. Finally he said, "Do you ever think about Lord Beaufort?"

"I haven't forgotten him, of course."

"The more I think about the duel, the more I hate it. Lord Beaufort was a nice chap, and he wound up a cripple. Do you feel any guilt about it?"

"Why should I feel guilt?" Simone answered sharply. "It was none of my doing."

"Of course it was, Simone. The fight was over you."

"I didn't ask them to fight over me."

"You didn't do much to stop it, either. Well, it's all in the past now, and I've done worse things. But do you remember Beaufort's protégé?"

"Yes, his name was Seymour."

"That's right. Well, he's back in New Orleans."

"Yes, I've heard. He's going to do an opera that his adopted father wrote."

"How did you know that?"

"Marie told me. She wants a part in the opera."

"Well, I'm worried. Claude has said something about Seymour. You know Seymour punched him at the duel. Claude doesn't forget things like that. He may call Seymour to account for it."

"You must try to talk him out of it, Bayard," Simone said quickly.

"I have tried, but he's not very reasonable about things like this."

"I wish you'd find a different set of friends. Claude and his group aren't good for you."

"Why, I thought you were half in love with him."

Ignoring his comment, Simone said, "They're not the kind of people an artist needs. All they think about is drinking and wenching and going to balls. If you're going to be a great artist, you're going to have to work at it."

"No sermons, Sister."

"Well, I think they're bad for you." She suddenly took his arm, and he turned around to face her in surprise. "You're the only son in our family, Bayard. Our hopes are in you."

Bayard's eyes softened, but he shook his head. "I'm just a prodigal, born to be so." He dipped his brush in paint and returned to his work.

As Simone left, she thought of what he had said about Colin Seymour. *I wish he had never come back,* she thought. *I'll have to talk to Claude. He mustn't fight the man.*

CHAPTER EIGHT

"Bayard, I want to speak to you about this young woman you're taking to the ball."

Bayard, who was just putting the final touches on his tie, gave his father an odd look. Arching one eyebrow, he said, "You mean Miss Eileen Funderberg? Why would you want to discuss her?"

Bayard was standing in front of a full-length mirror, examining his costume, which consisted of a black-and-green silk waistcoat, a white shirt, black tie, a single-breasted long-skirted frock coat made of green velvet, and a pair of black trousers. He was a fine-looking man and had the art of making anything he put on look fashionable. Even his oldest clothes showed style and good taste.

Louis d'Or studied his son glumly. He had gone to Bayard's room specifically to speak with him on a rather touchy subject, but now he seemed to have difficulty finding the words. He paced up and down the room for a moment, pulling at his beard, which was beginning to show signs of gray. Finally he blurted out, "You've got to be careful how you treat this young woman, Bayard."

"I'm always careful with young women."

"No, you're not."

Bayard turned, slightly shocked. "Why, what do you mean, Father?"

"I mean you do what you please with young women. And to be blunt about it, with Claude Vernay's crowd, you've been running with the wrong kind of young women. Do you think I don't hear the stories of things that you and your friends have done?"

"I've guarded myself against bringing any disgrace on you, sir."

"Well, you've got to be cautious tonight." Taking a deep breath, Louis said, "Eileen Funderberg's father, Oscar, is an important man in this town. He's also a man filled up with family pride."

"I thought you liked family pride."

"I do, and I wish I saw more determination in you to have it."

"I'm sorry I disappoint you, Father."

"No, you're not sorry, Bayard. Don't pretend you are." Sadness came into Louis d'Or's voice, and his shoulders slumped. "I don't know what to think of you. You're smart, fine-looking, and you could be anything you want to, but all you do is play with paint and run around after women at these Creole balls and worse. I'm ashamed of you, Bayard."

Bayard flushed. "I know you are. To tell the truth, I'm ashamed of myself."

"Then why don't you change, son? Why do you keep pursuing this disastrous life-style?"

"I don't know. I wish I did."

Louis threw his hands out in a gesture of despair. "Your mother and I want the very best for you, and your sister, too, of course. I've been against your becoming a painter because it seems a frivolous occupation to me, but if that's what you want to do, then by heavens, be a good one! You're nothing now but a dabbler. You need to find something and throw yourself into it with all of your heart."

Bayard d'Or listened as his father continued to speak passionately. He had grown pale and could find no argument to confront his father's words. He was, indeed, rather weary of the endless round of parties, balls, hunts, and other social functions that had filled his life since he was seventeen years old. For a time he had been excited about becoming an artist. He knew he had talent, but he did not have drive. His professor of art had grown angry at him. "You are throwing your life away," he had shouted, "and your talent also! I'm fed up with you!"

The professor's words seemed to echo in Bayard's memory, and he stood silently as his father continued to speak. Finally, when he saw an answer was expected, he shrugged his trim shoulders and said, "I wish I were a different sort of man, but I'm just what I am."

"But people can change, son."

"Maybe some people. I don't seem to be one of them."

Louis stood silently, his lips drawn tightly together. Of all the disappointments in his life, Bayard's failure to grow up and become a man of purpose, a man who counted, was the keenest. He said wearily, "Well, we've argued about this for years now, but I want to tell you that you must not play with Miss Funderberg's affections."

"I have no intention of doing so."

"You never have an intention of doing so, as you put it, but her father is a good friend of mine. He's also very protective of his daughter. There have been enough young bucks trying to marry her for her money, and he's suspicious. If you have any sense at all, you won't trifle with her."

"I think I can promise that, Father." Bayard pulled at his tie and said, "She's a nice girl, but not at all the sort of woman that interests me."

"Then why did you ask her to the ball?"

"Mother talked me into it. I wish she hadn't."

Louis stared at his son, then turned and walked out. As he reached the door, Bayard said, "Father, I'm sorry I'm not the kind of son that you had hoped for."

"I haven't given up, Bayard. You need something to bring you out of this mood of helplessness. You are our hope. You'll bear my name, and I hope you will bear it proudly. That's my prayer."

The door closed, and Bayard sat down. He leaned forward, put his forehead against his open palms, and sat slumped over, the picture of misery. Finally he lifted his head and whispered, "I just wish you had a better son, but you don't." He got up then, and thoughts of the ball were almost painful. He liked Eileen Funderberg well enough, but he knew that she was not the kind of woman who could make him happy, nor indeed the kind he could make happy. He moved toward the door, wishing that the evening were over.

■ ■ ■ ■

The ball was held at the rotunda of the St. Louis Hotel — the same place sometimes used during the daylight hours to sell slaves. The mayor had spared no expense to make a spectacular scene.

The room was large and very ornate. The walls were white, the floors marble, and chandeliers of delicately cut crystal hung in a line down the middle of the room. These were lit with hundreds of candles. Tables stretched along one long wall of the room and were covered with fine, white linen. The finest china and crystal dishes held delicate foods of all sorts. Damask-covered chairs of gold, green, and blue lined three of the four walls of the room, and along the back wall was the orchestra, sitting four deep in a half circle.

As Simone entered the ballroom holding Claude's arm, she whispered to him, "The mayor is going all out."

"Yes, he is. I expect all this money could have been spent better on something else — but I can't think of what that might be."

Music filled the room, and Simone and Claude glided around the floor. They knew almost everyone, and soon Bayard entered with Eileen Funderberg on his arm. She was a small girl with cinnamon-colored hair and light green eyes. When the dance concluded, Simone and Claude walked over to greet them.

"Eileen, you look beautiful," Simone said and kissed her cheek.

"Thank you, Simone. Of course, you outshine everyone here."

The two talked for a moment, and then the orchestra — which Simone noticed was the same one that played for Enoch Herzhaft's opera house — provided the music. They were excellent musicians, and Simone enjoyed herself.

Thirty minutes after Simone and Claude arrived, the mayor, George Ahern, stepped up on the podium. As soon as the music stopped, he said, "My dear friends, I have already welcomed you to the dance celebrating my daughter's betrothal, but I have a very special treat for you."

"He's probably going to take up a collection to pay for this party," Claude whispered.

Simone shushed him but smiled. "I think he's got enough money to take care of that himself."

"I am happy to announce that we have a very special guest with us tonight. Some of you are aware that the Marquis Colin Seymour, Lord Beaufort by his title, has come to our fair city to put on an opera by his late, lamented father. Lord Beaufort, as some of you who follow the opera know, has become the sensation of France with his performances there in Paris. I have prevailed upon the marquis to favor us with a song. Lord Beaufort, we await with expectation your offering."

Simone was shocked. She stared at Colin Seymour, who stepped up on the podium and stood smiling over the crowd. *I would never have known him!* she thought. Then the orchestra began to play, and he sang an aria in Italian from *Julius Caesar* by Handel. Simone could not believe the tone and the quality of Seymour's voice as he sang. There was a sweetness to it that she had never heard in the voice of any man, but at the same time a robust power that she knew he held back; he could have rattled the chandeliers if he had chosen.

And his appearance! He had gained weight and wore a plain gray suit with a frilled white shirt and no ornament except a simple ring on his right hand. More than that, he had matured beyond belief. When she had seen him before, he had been almost a callow youth, but now there was strength in every aspect of his body and maturity in his face. He was clean-shaven, and his skin was a slight bronze. The freshness of his complexion made his cornflower-blue eyes even more noticeable, and she saw that time and something else had tempered him and made him into a man of purpose and determination.

Colin sang the love song, which was humorous at times, and his eyes reflected the quick wit that lay behind the words, but when he reached the part of the solo that called for the profession of love, there was something real and startling about him. She knew that most singers were poor actors indeed, standing woodenly on the stage, not moving except from one side of the stage to the other. But Seymour moved his arms and once lifted his hands when he held a note that spoke of his feelings for his beloved.

When the song ended, the crowd burst into a spontaneous ovation. People called, "Bravo!" just as they did at the opera, and Simone saw that Colin Seymour took the applause with dignity, smiling and bowing slightly and finally stepping off the podium.

"Well, he's back."

Simone turned to look at Claude. "Yes, he is. He looks so different."

"I agree. He's moved up in the world.

Come, let's dance."

Simone caught the curtness of Claude's voice and noted the hard look that came into his eyes. She started to say something about what Bayard had warned her of, but she decided it was not the place. She moved around the floor, and then when the music ended, they applauded. Simone turned with Claude to leave the floor, but Mayor Ahern met her instead.

"Ah, Miss d'Or, how lovely you look tonight."

"Thank you, Mayor. How kind of you to say so."

"I say only the truth. But Miss d'Or, you must allow me to introduce our guest to you. I promised him a dance with the most beautiful woman at the ball, and of course, you can't refuse." He turned and said, "Lord Beaufort, may I present to you Miss Simone d'Or. Miss d'Or, the marquis."

Simone could not move. Very rarely in her life had she found herself completely speechless. She was aware of Claude's standing on her right, and that he had gone stiff, but her eyes were fixed on Colin Seymour. She hadn't expected to have to converse with the man she'd only fought with previously. A tiny smile tugged at the corners of his lips, and as he stepped forward and bowed slightly, he said, "It's been a long time, Miss d'Or."

"Yes, it has."

Mayor Ahern was surprised. "Oh, you've met before!"

"Yes. It seems like a long time ago," Colin said. His eyes went to Claude Vernay, and their gazes locked. Something passed between them, and then Colin said, "Our dance, I believe, Miss d'Or." He stepped forward, and without thinking, Simone accepted his arm. He led her back onto the dance floor. When she turned toward him, he was considering her in a strange way. The music started, and he put his arm behind her waist. She lifted her hand, and he took it, and they began to move around the floor. He was an excellent dancer, but Simone was silent. She could think of absolutely nothing to say. He was, unexpectedly, as fine a dancer as she was herself.

"You're looking very well, Miss d'Or."

"Thank you, sir."

Simone had thought much about the terrible thing that had happened to Armand de Cuvier. She had heard little about his life, really only once. A friend had visited the Beaufort estate and she had overheard him telling someone else, "It's a real tragedy. Armand de Cuvier died still stuck in that wheelchair. He was such a lively, cheerful man before, and his life seemed to have been stolen from him."

The words came floating back to her, and she tried desperately to think of some way to express what she felt. She remembered the scene when the man who now held her in his arms had begged her to stop the duel, and she had coldly refused. She had changed, she knew, for if such a thing happened today, she would react much differently.

"You're doing well professionally, sir."

"Yes. I've been very fortunate."

"You're not married."

"No, I'm not."

"I'm surprised."

"Well, music leaves little time for such things. You're not married either."

"No, I am not."

Simone was conscious of Colin's masculinity. He was holding her loosely enough, but still, from time to time, they brushed against each other, and she knew that if they had had no past history, she would think of him as one of the most attractive men that she had ever met.

The dance ended, and they both applauded. Then he extended his arm, and taking it, she allowed him to lead her off of the floor. "I wish you well with your opera."

"Thank you very much, Miss d'Or."

When they reached the open area off the dance floor, Claude Vernay was waiting. His eyes were hard and adamant, and he spared no look for Simone.

"Thank you for sharing your partner, Mr. Vernay."

Vernay listened to his words, seeming to hunt for something deeper than their surface meaning. "I see you are back, Mr. Seymour."

"Yes, the bad penny shows up again."

"I think, sir, we have some unfinished business."

Colin paused for one moment, and the two men stared at each other. "I'm always at your service, sir."

"Please, Claude, I would like some refreshment." Simone took his arm and gently tugged. Reluctantly he wheeled, and as he walked toward the refreshment table, he said, "I can't stand that fellow!"

"Claude, we've got to talk about this."

"About what?"

"About the marquis. I know how you are about things like this."

"He struck me, and I haven't forgotten."

Simone stopped, and he turned to meet her gaze. She was looking up at him with an intensity that he had seldom seen in her eyes. Her back was straight, and she said clearly and distinctly, "Claude, I will not be fought over again. I am not a bone that two dogs will battle for."

"Why, Simone —"

"I mean what I say, Claude. If you pursue that stupid quarrel any longer, I will never speak to you again. Do you understand me?"

"But my honor is involved."

"No, your pride is involved. I'm not going to argue. You have my word that if you fight this man, I will never speak another word with you as long as I live."

Claude Vernay watched Simone turn and walk purposefully away. He knew very well that beneath the beautiful exterior, Simone d'Or had a will of iron. He had laughed at it before but always felt that he could get around her. Now as he followed her off the dance floor, he knew that she meant exactly what she said. *I've got to get at that fellow, but it won't be easy.* His mind was working as he took the glass of wine an attendant handed him, and when he turned back to Simone, he said nothing. His eyes were on the Marquis Lord Beaufort as he danced with a woman, his head high and his smile bright.

Chapter Nine

"Well, my dear Colin, that was a fine ball the mayor gave last night."

"Very impressive."

"I saw you dancing with Miss d'Or." Herzhaft hesitated and studied Colin's face. Seeing no expression there, he said, "I take it you two have made up your differences?"

Colin did not answer. The two were sitting in Herzhaft's office to discuss launching the new production of *Juliet.* In all truthfulness, it had taken some effort for Colin to show no response when Herzhaft had mentioned Simone d'Or. He had been shocked to realize how deep his feelings toward the woman ran. Ever since the duel, he had struggled with his emotions and usually lost the battle. Toward Claude Vernay he felt no ambiguity. He despised the man and had come to America with the idea of revenge. All of the long months and arduous labor that he put into making himself into an expert swordsman — not to mention the hours spent with a pistol in practice — he had found himself picturing Vernay as his opponent.

His feelings toward Simone d'Or were more ambivalent. He had remembered her as a haughty woman filled with pride and had known that she had despised him as one beneath her station. What he had forgotten, however, was the beauty of the woman. She had grown, if anything, more attractive during the years he had been gone, and as he had danced with her, he felt himself drawn to her in a way that made him despise himself. He had been glad when the dance was over, and he could concentrate on Vernay.

There in Herzhaft's office, though, he knew better than to bring Herzhaft into his personal life. "We have little enough in common, I think. And the duel was a long time ago."

"I'm glad you can put it behind you. It was a tragic thing."

"Indeed it was."

"Well, I can't tell you how excited I am about doing this opera. Imagine, the introduction to the world of *Juliet* by Armand de Cuvier! It's such a privilege, and I can't thank you enough for choosing me as your producer."

Colin could not help but smile slightly as he thought, *I chose you only because you were in New Orleans, and I was determined to come back and get my revenge on Claude Vernay.* Aloud he said, "You are a good producer, Enoch, and I trust we are going to have an outstanding opera."

"I have had singers from everywhere begging for a part. The auditions will be today, as I told you."

"That's good. I think we need to get the major parts assigned as quickly as possible."

"We won't have any trouble with the chorus. I have a good stable here, better than when you were here the last time. Do you have any preferences about who will sing the role of Juliet?"

"None whatsoever."

"Well, you'll have your pick of some very fine voices." He pulled out a watch as big as a turnip from his waistcoat and looked at it. "It's time. I think they'll be waiting. Nobody will be late today, I think."

Colin was growing tired. He had already selected the singer who would play Mercutio after listening to several candidates, and then he had heard three women who had come to audition for the part of the nurse

— a very key figure in Shakespeare's drama. "Are there any more?"

"One more. Next," Enoch called loudly.

Colin watched the woman as she crossed the stage. He straightened up. "Why, it's Rosa!"

"Yes, Rosa has gone downhill a little bit. She can no longer sing leading roles."

Colin listened, and as Rosa Calabria sang, sadness gripped him. She had grown very heavy, which didn't matter as far as the nurse part was concerned, but he remembered her as a beauty, and she had lost that. "What happened to her, Enoch?"

"Hard living. She fell in love with a baritone. He treated her abominably, and she took to drink. I didn't want her to audition, but she insisted."

"She's still got the voice," Colin whispered. When the song was over, he got up, vaulted over the front seats, and walked around to the stairs leading to the stage. "Rosa, it's good to see you."

Rosa halted, and he saw tears come into her eyes. "Hello, Colin," she whispered.

Colin stepped forward and took her hand. "I'm so glad to see you again. I've thought about you often."

"I've thought about you too."

"You were such a help to me. I've never

forgotten."

"That — that seems like such a long time ago."

Colin smiled and said, "I'll be seeing you."

Hope flared in Rosa's eyes. It was obvious that she was not used to good news, and she whispered brokenly, "Thank you, Colin," and slipped off the stage.

Two hours later, Colin had listened to three sopranos trying out for Juliet's role, all of them adequate. The trouble was that one of them was nearing forty and looked it, and Juliet was closer to thirteen or fourteen. Another was much younger but was also short and chunkily built with none of the slender, lissome quality that he pictured in the romantic heroine. The third was a possibility, but in all truth Colin was not thrilled with her vocal range.

"Do you like any of them?" Herzhaft whispered. He was sitting in the second row of seats with Colin, and his face was anxious. "They're all qualified."

"Yes, I suppose they are."

Herzhaft said, "I don't want to pressure you, but Margaret Fleming is the sister of the governor. It would give us some prestige to have her sing the part of Juliet." Fleming was the third of the singers who looked the part of Juliet, more or less, but whose voice was rather weak, in Colin's opinion. "I'll think about it."

Colin looked around and asked, "Are there any more auditions for the lead role?" No one answered, and he nodded, saying, "Thank you all for coming. We will be letting you know our decision by tomorrow. If any —" At that moment a voice cried out, "Just a minute, sir!" He turned to see a young woman charging down the aisle of the theater.

"Yes, Miss, what is it?"

"Please, I'm sorry to be late. I was detained."

Colin waited until she had stepped up on the stage. She was an impressive-looking woman with exotic coloring. Her hair was bright red, and she had green eyes deeply set and beautifully shaped. Her lips were full and mobile, and she had a perfect body for an opera singer: tall, barrel-chested, and well padded. "What is your name?"

"I am Marie Devois."

"Well, Miss Devois, you're not very prompt."

"I am sorry, Lord Beaufort."

"Mr. Seymour will do. You want to try out for the leading role?"

"Yes, sir."

"Very well. Let's hear what you can do."

He went back to sit with Enoch and asked, "What do you know about this girl?"

"She's a good singer. Great voice and a good actress too. She just hasn't had a break yet. But I really think that the governor's sister would be the best choice."

"You're a politician, Enoch. I'm not." Colin listened as the woman sang an aria from Rossini's opera *La Cenerentolea.* It was not a well-known opera but it had always been a favorite of Colin's. He leaned forward halfway through, his attention fully fixed on the woman. The role of Juliet was highly important, and he knew that this one had the capability.

When she finished, he stood up and said, "Thank you very much, Miss Devois. Now, once again, you will all hear one way or another tomorrow. Thank you all for coming."

Enoch asked, "Do you want to talk about the candidates?"

"No, I've heard them. I must make the decision myself."

"Very well. Can you do it by tomorrow morning?"

"Yes, I think so. We need to begin rehearsals day after tomorrow."

Enoch left, and for a while Colin wandered around the theater. He moved around the stage from one place to another, trying to get some feel for it, and he was almost ready to go when he heard his name called. "Mr. Seymour?"

Colin turned to see Marie Devois, who was standing in the aisle close to the orchestra pit. "Please, may I speak with you?"

"I don't think that would be fair, Miss Devois."

Marie ignored his words. She climbed the steps to the stage and stood directly in front of him. "I don't always play fair."

Colin could not help but smile. "Is that right? Then I must be very careful with you."

"Opera stars never do. In the last opera I was in, the two female singers hated each other. Right in the middle of the performance one of them leaned over and whispered to the other, 'Your right false eyebrow is falling off.' Immediately the other woman pulled off her left eyebrow to make them match — only the right one hadn't fallen off, and the audience laughed uproariously."

Colin laughed. "I suppose all is fair in love, war, and opera."

"I don't want to ask for special consideration —" Marie stopped and laughed. She had a delicious, deep laugh. "I, of course, do want special consideration. We all do."

"I liked your singing very much."

"I know the pressure will be on you to pick Margaret Fleming."

Colin blinked in surprise. "I hadn't known it was that obvious."

"Well, it's always been that way with Margaret. She gets roles because of who she is, not because of how well she can sing."

"That's a rather bad thing to say about a woman behind her back."

Marie gave Colin a direct look. "I'd say the same thing to her face, sir."

"I believe you would. Well then, tell me why I should choose you rather than any of the other ladies."

"Because none of them will work at this like I will. I may not be as attractive as some of the others, but I'm sturdy. I can sing for eight hours at a stretch, and I will. I'm big enough to take the hard work that opera demands. Nobody knows any better than you how hard it is."

"Indeed you are right, Miss Devois. People often don't understand how arduous opera is."

"Please give me a chance. That's all I can say."

The woman strangely moved him. Colin knew something about being on the bottom of the heap. He had been there, and he admired her pluck and her determination.

Perhaps it wasn't fair to ask for a special treatment, but as he looked into her green eyes, he saw a fierce, driving desire, and he liked that. He felt also something of the passion that was in the woman, and not just from music. He was not a womanizer, but there was a powerful aura about Marie Devois that he could not miss. She was a woman made for love in every sense of the word, and it troubled him that she managed to stir him simply by looking into his eyes. Quickly he said, "Well, you'll have to wait just like all the others, Miss Devois."

"Yes, sir. I just wanted to let you know that I will do anything to get this role, and I will give it everything that's in me."

"I believe you."

Marie was pacing the floor when the knock sounded. Quickly she turned and ran to the door and flung it open. Disappointment swept across her face. "Oh, it's you, Simone."

"Well, nice to see you, too, Marie," Simone said, surprised at her friend's ungracious welcome. "Can I come in?"

"Yes."

Simone closed the door behind her. Marie's shoulders were drooping, and anxiety showed in her face. "What's wrong,

Marie?"

"I don't think I got the role I wanted in the new opera."

"Oh, I'm so sorry!"

Marie shrugged her shoulders, and bitterness pulled her lips thin. "I didn't much expect to. You know that the governor's sister was trying out for the role of Juliet."

"Yes, I heard about that."

"I'm sure she got it."

"But you can sing so much better than she."

"That doesn't seem to matter." Marie sat down, and Simone went over and sat beside her. She took Marie's hand and said, "I'm so sorry. I wish I could help."

"Well, it's just part of this business. There's more heartache in it than there is in selling dresses in a shop."

Simone set out to try to cheer Marie up, but she had little success. Finally a knock at the door sounded, and Marie said, "That's probably the note telling me that I haven't been accepted. I didn't think I'd even get that."

She got up and walked to the door, and when she opened it, she stood stock-still.

"Hello, Miss Devois."

"Mr. Seymour!" Simone jumped up and saw Colin Seymour standing in the doorway.

His eyes swept past Marie's and met hers. "Oh, you have company."

"Oh, it's just a friend of mine. Come in, please." She stepped aside, and Colin entered. "This is Miss d'Or," Marie said quickly.

"Yes, we've met."

Simone nodded.

"I'm a little late. I sent your note by messenger, but I put the wrong address on it. I wasn't aware that you hadn't received it until thirty minutes ago." He handed her the note and said, "You can open it, but what it says is that you will be in the opera."

"You mean in the chorus?"

"Don't be so negative, Miss Devois," Colin smiled. "You are my Juliet."

Marie let out a glad cry. She grabbed Colin's hand and kissed it enthusiastically. "Oh, sir, how I thank you! How I thank you!"

Simone saw that Colin was embarrassed, but he laughed and said, "You won't be kissing my hand next week. You'll probably be calling me vile names."

"Never!"

"You say that now, but I intend to make this opera the finest in the country — even if I have to kill all of us to do it."

"Nothing will be too demanding. Oh,

Simone, did you hear?"

"Yes. I'm so happy for you, Marie."

Colin said, "Rehearsal begins in the morning. Have a good breakfast. You'll need it." He gave a slight bow to Simone and said, "Good to see you again, Miss d'Or."

"I think you're making a wise choice, Mr. Seymour. Marie has a wonderful voice, and I know she'll be a great success."

"That's why I chose her." He turned and said, "Tomorrow at nine, Marie."

"I'll be there."

Marie closed the door and flew to Simone. She picked up the smaller woman off the floor and practically crushed her. "Isn't he wonderful?"

"Don't break my ribs, Marie," Simone said, laughing. But then she kissed Marie and said, "Congratulations. But as he said, you may hate him before it's over."

"Have you lost your mind? How can I hate a man who's giving me this chance? Besides," she said, and a smile spread across her face, "he's rich and has a title and is good-looking and can sing like an angel. Do you think I'm going to disappoint a man like that? There will be some romantic love scenes in this opera, and I'm going to do what any diva would do."

"What's that?" Simone asked.

Marie's eyes danced. "I'm going to be sure that not all the romantic love scenes take place on stage."

Simone laughed, but she knew that Marie Devois was a passionate woman. "I don't think he's that kind of man," she said.

"They are all that kind of a man when the right woman finds them."

CHAPTER TEN

"Bring another bottle — and be sure it's not any of your rotgut. I want the best you have." Claude Vernay, who was stooped over the table, lifted his head and glared at the waiter. "And bring some clean glasses. Don't you ever wash dishes in this place?"

Byron Mayhew leaned back in his chair and studied Claude carefully. He had joined Vernay at the Blue Rose, one of the less-attractive saloons in New Orleans, earlier in the evening. The two of them had played cards, and Vernay had drunk steadily from a full bottle that was now empty.

"You're hitting that bottle pretty heavy, Claude."

"So what? What are you, a preacher of some kind?"

Mayhew shrugged and glanced out at the dance floor, where Bayard d'Or was dancing with one of the hostesses of the Blue Rose. She was an overblown woman of some indeterminate age. Her face was painted, and her laughter was shrill. She was pressing herself as close to Bayard as she could, and her skimpy, low-cut dress left little to the imagination.

The cheap woman fit well in the Blue Rose, Mayhew thought. The room was hazy with smoke, and the smell of raw liquor, cheap perfume, and cigar smoke made an unpleasant mixture that seemed to choke him. The piano against the wall made a cacophonous racket, and the dancers seemed to have no connection whatsoever with the music. Most of them staggered around the floor, clinging to each other. The sounds of quarrels and cursing and the high-pitched laughter of the women was enough to deafen anyone.

"Let's get out of here, Claude. This place is no good."

"It's good enough for you."

"You're quarrelsome tonight."

"Why not? Do I have to be smiling all the time to make you happy?"

Mayhew did not answer. When Vernay was in one of these moods, there was no reasoning with him. He wondered why he wasted his time with Claude Vernay. They had been friends for years, but it seemed to Byron that the man was getting coarser. When he was younger, he had had flashing good looks and charm, but something seemed to have gone wrong in Vernay's life. *He's really going downhill fast, and I suspect it has something to do with his failure with Simone d'Or.* Mayhew's thoughts were interrupted as Leon Manville approached the table, dragging a tall woman with rouged cheeks and bad teeth. She had eyes harder than agates, and her smile was cold. "Come on, let's have a drink, Roseanne."

"Fine with me." The woman fell into a seat, and as the waiter brought the bottle, Manville picked it up and stared at it. He was a tall man with dark brown hair and light hazel eyes. There was a coarseness in his face, and he had allowed himself to get out of condition so that his belly hung over his belt. "Everybody have a drink. Come on, Claude. You look like a funeral."

Vernay glared at him and said, "Shut up, Leon, and keep your remarks to yourself."

"What's the matter with you? A fellow can't say anything to you." He poured the drinks for himself and the woman, they drank up, and then he dragged her out on the floor again.

"I'm about ready to get out of here, Claude. This place is depressing."

"What's your hurry? It's only ten o'clock."

Looking out on the floor, Byron kept his eyes fixed for a moment on Bayard, whose partner was practically pushing him around the floor. "Bayard's drunk. He can barely stand up."

"He can't hold his liquor."

"You're not going to please Simone by getting her brother drunk."

Claude tilted his glass up, drank the liquor, and then refilled it. "I can't stop him from drinking. He's a full-grown man."

"But you could stay away from him. You told me how Simone felt about it. What's the matter with you, Claude? You used to be brighter than that. You want to marry the woman, don't you?"

"I will, too."

"Not if you keep getting her brother drunk. Simone is a proud woman. The whole family is ashamed of Bayard, and you've become the villain in their eyes."

Vernay shook his head and put both arms on the table. He stared at his hands, clasped them into fists, and looked up. His eyes were cloudy with drink, and he said harshly, "I can't forget Seymour."

"You'd better forget him, Claude."

"He struck me and knocked me flat. You saw it."

"He was younger then, and he was upset

about his teacher. They were more than teacher and pupil, I think. The fact that the marquis made Seymour his heir proves that."

"He thinks he's something special with his singing and his title, but I haven't forgotten. I'll never forget."

"There's nothing you can do about it."

"I can slice him to ribbons or put a bullet in his brain."

"A duel? Don't be a fool," Byron said shortly. "He's an important man. You got in trouble enough by shooting the old marquis."

That was true enough, and it left a bitter picture in Vernay's memory. After the duel, Vernay had lost his popularity. Shooting the older man in the back had not sat well even with the dueling element of New Orleans. Vernay protested that the man had whirled at the instant he shot, but few listened to him. He had also had a visit from the sheriff of the parish, who warned that he could bring charges against him. Somehow Vernay had escaped that, but the memory of it was still raw in his mind.

"Maybe I can't fight a duel with him, but someone else could." Vernay's eyes lit up then, and he studied, as steadily as he could, the young man in front of him. Mayhew was a smaller man, slightly over five foot six. He had fair hair and steady gray eyes, and he was studying the law under an uncle. For some time Vernay and Mayhew had not been as close as in days gone by, and Vernay was aware of it. Still, he had to try. He leaned forward, his eyes taking in the younger man. "You could do it, Byron."

"I could do what?"

"You could fight Seymour."

Byron shook his head. "You've had a great deal too much to drink. In the first place, I could get killed, which would interfere with some things I've got planned. In the second place, I don't have anything against the man. He hasn't done anything to me. And in the third place, he's a prominent man. Get that in your head, Claude. Anyone who kills him or even hurts him would be up for some pretty stiff charges. You almost went to jail for shooting the old man."

"You're making too much of it. He's not that important."

Byron shook his head. "I'm going. You're not making any sense."

"You're not much of a friend, are you, Byron?"

"Not enough to kill another man for you. Take my advice, Claude: forget about this."

Byron Mayhew got up and left. Leon

Manville stumbled back and threw himself down in the chair that Mayhew had vacated. "Where's Byron going?"

"Home, I guess. Who cares?" Vernay studied the other man, noting the brutality of the features. Leon Manville had come from a fairly good family, but when his family died, he had taken over the business and run it into the ground. He endured bankruptcy, and now he lived on a small annuity plus what he could pick up gambling.

Vernay studied Manville and made up his mind quickly. "You've been having a hard time. Short of money, aren't you, Leon?"

Cursing, Manville poured another glass of whiskey, downed it, and slammed the glass on the table. "Yes, I'm short of money! I haven't had the breaks."

"You really haven't. Things have been tough. Well, I've got a little job that needs doing that I'll pay five hundred dollars for."

Manville leaned forward. "Five hundred dollars? What's the job?"

"You know the trouble I had with the marquis."

"I heard about it. Shot the old buzzard in the back, didn't you?"

"Wasn't my fault. He turned just as I fired. But anyway, he's dead now. He adopted a man named Seymour, and he's the one you probably heard about that struck me after the duel."

Manville laughed roughly. "I heard he put you right on your back."

"He did, and I haven't forgotten it. I can't fight him because I've been warned off by the sheriff. But you could, Leon."

Manville leaned forward. "You want me to put a bullet in him?"

"Yes, and I wouldn't care if you put it right between his eyes."

Manville was quiet for a moment, then he grinned. "I'll do it for a thousand. Not a penny less."

"We'll talk about it."

"Is he a good shot? Has he ever been called out?"

"I doubt it. Remember, Leon, this is strictly between us, and if it happens, you'll have to make him challenge you. I know how you could do it: insult him in public. If he's any kind of a man, he won't stand for it."

Manville rolled the glass around in his thick fingers while staring at his friend. "You carry a grudge pretty good."

"It's what I do best."

Manville looked over at the dance floor and remarked, "Bayard's really drunk. Maybe we'd better take him home."

"Let the fool take care of himself."

"That's fine with me. About this job — are you in a hurry?"

"No. It's got to look right. I'll teach him that nobody can hit me and get by with it."

"All right, d'Or, get up."

Bayard had been lying on a cot that stank abominably. The light through the window of the jail struck him in the face, and he sat up slowly, holding his head. "What is it?" he groaned.

"You're gettin' out of here. Get your coat and your hat."

Bayard slowly put on his coat, jammed his hat down on his head, and stumbled out of the cell. He followed the jailer down a long corridor flanked by cells on both sides and passed through two doors, finally stepping into the main office of the city jail of New Orleans. He stopped abruptly, for his father was standing beside a long counter. Behind the counter an officer was filling out a paper. He said, "Sign right here, Mr. d'Or."

Dreading what was to come, Bayard shuffled over to stand beside his father, who said nothing but signed the paper and handed over the cash that the officer demanded. Then Louis d'Or turned without a word and left the office. As Bayard followed him, one of the officers laughed loudly, saying, "I'll see you soon, Bayard. You like our accommodations. I reckon you'll come back."

The sunlight was bright in Bayard's face. He waited for his father to speak, but the older man didn't say a word. Bayard braced himself for the lecture as the two walked down the boarded street. When they reached the carriage, Bayard started to get in, but his father stopped him.

"We've got to have an understanding."

"All right, Father. Let's have the sermon."

"No sermon. Not this time." Louis d'Or was flinty as a rock, and his eyes were hard and glittering. Something in them sobered up Bayard. He straightened his back and said, "I don't want to hear any admonitions, Father."

"You're not going to hear any, but you're going to hear an ultimatum. I've put up with you as long as I intend to. You have embarrassed your father and especially your mother. Both of us are ashamed to call you our son." Louis d'Or had spoken this firmly before, but the disgrace that Bayard was bringing upon him made his face dark and drawn. His words were sharp, and they struck Bayard almost like bullets.

"I should have taken steps long before

this. I was too lenient when you were younger, but I thought you had more stuff in you than to become a drunk and even worse. You've caroused with the worst kind of lowlife women in New Orleans. You come home stinking drunk, and your mother has to see you. Well, Bayard, I'm telling you right now: I'll have your word this moment that you will not drink anymore."

"I'm old enough to make those decisions myself, Father."

"Decisions for what? Decisions to stay a drunk? Is that what you want out of your life?"

Bayard felt the sting of his father's words down to the very center of his spirit. It was not that he did not know what sort of life he was living, for he did. He had purposed many times to leave his lifestyle and change it for something better. Actually, he loved and revered his parents, but something in him kept him from embracing the life they desired for him. The memories of past scenes like this one flashed before him. Always before his father had relented, and as Bayard faced him, he expected the same thing now.

"I can't promise you I won't drink anymore. I'm not a boy, Father."

"No, you're not a boy. You're a miserable

excuse for a man."

"I won't hear that kind of talk!"

"You'll hear it from me right now. You don't understand, Bayard. I'm telling you, unless I have your word right now that you'll change your life and stop this useless drunkenness and chasing after women, I'll not have you in my home."

"That suits me fine."

As soon as the words were out of his mouth, Bayard regretted them. He said, "All I can promise is I'll try to do better."

"I've heard that before, Bayard. It won't work this time. Give me your word right now. No more drinking at all, and no more of the company you've been keeping."

"I can't give that word to you. I'm a grown man."

"All right. I'll have your things sent to you. I don't want you coming back to my house."

"You're throwing me out?"

"You're throwing yourself out, Bayard! I was so proud when you were born, and when you were growing up, I saw a goodness in you — a lot of your mother. But when you grew into manhood, you began to take the wrong paths. I wasn't stern enough with you then. Maybe it's too late, but I'm starting now. Send word where you want your things sent. And don't come to me for money, for you won't get any." Louis climbed into the carriage, shut the door, and then leaned out of the window. "Your mother and I will pray for you, but until you change your ways, you are no longer my son. Go on, Robert."

The carriage driver spoke to the horses, and they started out at a brisk trot.

As soon as Louis got home, he went to his wife. She was in the parlor, sewing, and when she looked up and saw his face, she asked, "What's wrong?"

Louis sat down beside her on the sofa and took her hand. "I got Bayard out of jail."

"Well, that's good. Where is he?"

"He's not coming home. Not until he changes his ways, Renee."

"What do you mean, 'not coming home'?" Renee dropped her sewing and turned to face him. "What happened?"

"I gave him an ultimatum. We can't go on as we have been, and I told him so. In a way it's my fault, I suppose. I did a poor job of raising him."

"You were always a good father."

"No, I wasn't. I was too indulgent. Both of us were, I think."

Renee began to cry. She pulled out a handkerchief and buried her face in it, sobbing softly. Louis put his arm around her

180

and said, "I know this is hard on you, but we're going to have to let him find out for himself what life is really like."

At that moment Simone entered the room and was startled by her mother's weeping. "What's wrong?" She sat in the chair across from them as her father explained what had happened. Her face grew still, and she said, "I'm not sure that's the right thing to do, Father."

"There's nothing else left to do."

"But if we cut ourselves off from him completely, we won't have any influence on him."

"Influence! What kind of influence do we have now?" Louis said in an agonized voice. He got up and began to pace the floor. "I know you two are opposed to this, but he's going to ruin himself completely if something isn't done."

Both Simone and Renee knew that when Louis d'Or was in a mood like this, there was no arguing with him. He had made up his mind. Still, Renee said, "He'll starve on his own."

"Let him go hungry. He'll come back one day when he finds out what it's like out there in the real world."

"I'm afraid, Papa. I'm afraid for Bayard."

Louis d'Or's face twisted, and both

women saw with shock that there were tears in his eyes. "I'm afraid, too, my dear, but we have to do something, or we'll lose him forever."

Simone glanced out the carriage window. "Robert, are you sure this is the right address?"

"Yes, Miss Simone," he said from the driver's seat. "This is the street. According to the numbers it ought to be in the next block."

Simone looked at the broken-down section of New Orleans. She had found out from Byron Mayhew where Bayard was living, and after a week she could stand it no longer. She had to see him!

"I think that must be the place right there, Miss."

Robert helped Simone step out of the carriage. "No place for you, Miss," he warned. "I wouldn't want to be here after dark."

"That's why I came at noon."

"I'd better go with you inside."

"No, you wait here with the carriage."

"Yes, ma'am, but if you ain't out soon, I'll be in to look for you."

"Thank you, Robert."

Simone looked up at the two-story building with a faded sign reading *Royal Hotel.*

As she entered, she smelled decay and other rank odors as well. Going over to the desk, she found herself facing a tall woman, bigger than most men, and broader. "I'm looking for Mr. Bayard d'Or."

The woman grinned, revealing large, yellow teeth. "Up on the second floor. Room 203."

"Could — could someone go up and get him for me?"

"This ain't the St. Louis Hotel. You'll have to go up yourself. You'll be all right. If anybody bothers you, just holler. I don't put up with anything here."

"Thank you." Simone walked over and climbed the stairs that were fastened loosely to the side of the wall. The treads gave under her feet, and the carpet was worn down, revealing the bare wood. She followed the dark corridor to the room and knocked on the door.

"Who is it?"

"It's me, Bayard — Simone."

After a long time, the door opened. Bayard stood unshaven in a pair of filthy trousers and a once-white shirt without a collar. "Welcome to my humble abode."

Ignoring his sarcastic tone, Simone stepped inside. It was a single room with a window that had been broken and was covered with some sort of paper. She could hear the street sounds.

"Have a chair. It's the only one," Bayard said. He sat down on the bed that was unmade with unwashed covers. "How are you?"

Simone was disgusted and shocked at Bayard's appearance. His cheeks were sunken in, and he looked as if he had been ill for a month. He had been away from home only a week, and yet he had gone downhill in every way: his hair needed trimming, his fingernails were grimy, his clothes were gray and smelly. He had always been a fanatic about cleanliness, and he had descended to this.

"Bayard, I want you to come home."

"I can't. Didn't Father tell you his terms?"

"Are they so very bad? Would it be worse than this?"

"Yes, it would. This is bad enough, but I've got some prospects. I'll be out of here soon."

"Mother is grieving herself away."

Bayard looked down at his hands. "I'm sorry about that," he said. "But I can't just give in to Father."

Simone begged and pleaded for fifteen minutes but got nowhere. He was angry, she saw, and hurt. Finally Bayard stood, saying, "There's no point in arguing, Simone. Thank you for coming, but I'll be all right."

"At least let me give you some money."

"I don't want your money."

Simone was fumbling in her reticule, but she saw the anger in his face and knew that it would be useless to protest. She went to him, pulled his head down, and kissed him on the cheek. "We all love you, Bayard. Please, don't do anything desperate."

Bayard cleared his throat and said, "Thank you for coming, Simone. I'll be all right. Don't tell Mother how bad this looks. Lie a little bit."

"Yes, I'll do that. Please — think about what you're doing." She turned and left the room, descended the stairs, and returned to the carriage. Robert opened the door. "Did you find him, Miss?"

"He was there."

She got in the carriage, and Robert asked, "Be he comin' home — Mr. Bayard?"

"I don't think so. Now, take me back home, Robert."

CHAPTER ELEVEN

Simone had worried herself almost sick over Bayard, and on Thursday morning she got up and spent the day trying to put the whole thing out of her mind. This proved to be impossible, and finally, late in the afternoon, she went to her mother and said, "Marie's invited me to come to one of the opera rehearsals. I think I'll go."

"Don't be out too late, dear."

"No, I won't, Mother."

Leaving the house, Simone had Robert take her to the theater. When she got out, she said, "Why don't you go get yourself something to eat?" Reaching into her reticule, she pulled out a bill and handed it to him. "Have a nice supper on me."

"Thank you, Miss."

Simone turned and entered the theater. There was no one at the door, and as she stepped inside, she was surprised that the theater was completely empty except for those on the stage. The stage was lit up, but the rest of the theater was dark. She had been in the opera house only during actual performances, and there was something gloomy about the rehearsal setting. She walked down to the front, aware that the orchestra was there, but only Marie and Colin were on the stage. He was speaking to her in a low voice, and Simone took her seat, wondering where the rest of the cast was. She must have made some sort of noise, because Marie looked out and saw her. "Oh, Simone, you came!"

"Yes. I thought I might like to see a rehearsal."

"Not a very good day for that, Miss d'Or. The rest of the cast is finished. Marie and I are working on a number that's rather difficult."

"Would you rather I leave?"

"No, but I don't think it will be very entertaining." Colin Seymour seemed distracted, and he turned to the orchestra leader and said, "Let's try it again, Steven."

"Yes, my lord."

As the music rose and filled the theater, Marie and Colin disappeared into the wings, and then after a few moments Marie came out slowly. She was not wearing the costume that would be worn in the opera but a simple, cream-colored dress that set off her red hair. She began to sing, and Simone understood just enough Italian to know that Juliet was singing of yearning for her lover to return.

As Marie's song ended, Colin stepped out from the opposite side of the stage. He stopped and looked at her and then began to sing a beautiful song. His voice was clear and very muted, soft, and gentle. As he continued to sing, the volume rose, and Marie turned to look at him with surprise. The two of them came together and blended their voices in a duet. When it was over and the orchestra was still playing, he kissed her in a lingering fashion.

Simone saw that Marie was making the best of the kiss. She was clinging to him, pressing herself against him. When the music died, Colin stepped back and shook his head. "It's still not right, Marie. We'll have to do it again."

"But we've done it five times."

"We'll do it five more if we have to."

"I need to take a break, Colin."

"All right. Take fifteen minutes. This song is the key of the first part of the opera. It must be done right, or we're lost."

Marie sighed. "I'll be back, and we'll try it again."

Marie left the stage, and Simone saw Colin look at her. He leaned over and said, "Why don't you take a break, too, Steven, you and all the orchestra?"

The orchestra members began to chatter, and Colin walked down the steps and stood in front of Simone. "It's not much like the real thing."

"No, it's not. I guess I never thought about how much work went into an opera. All I've ever seen is the finished product."

"Sometimes I think that's the hardest part, the getting ready. Shakespeare said, 'Readiness is all.' "

Colin stretched himself, arched his back, and shook his head. "I'm just about groggy with rehearsal, and by now everybody in the cast hates me. The orchestra, too."

"Oh, I'm sure that's not true."

Colin smiled, which made him look much younger. "Well, I guess the trick is to keep those who don't hate me away from those who do. That way maybe we can all last without someone killing me."

"How is Marie doing?"

"Very well indeed. She has a fine voice."

"I like the part you just performed. Tell me," she said, "I've never been into drama, but I've wondered. That — that kiss between you and Marie. Does it mean anything?"

189

"It's part of the opera."

Simone was puzzled and did not know how to ask the question. "It seems such an — well, intimate thing to do."

"I think professionals get over that."

"You mean you can hold a beautiful woman in your arms and kiss her and feel nothing?"

Colin laughed and sat down on the chair in front of her. Turning around, he said, "I'd be a liar if I said that. I suppose the professional thing is to put it aside, no matter what you feel."

"It must be very difficult."

"Just part of the work."

The two sat for a while, Colin speaking of the difficulties of producing an opera, when he suddenly stood and peered into the gloomy part of the theater, up toward the front doors. "What is it? Can I help you?"

Simone turned around to see a roughly dressed man enter. He was a hulking figure and wore his hat pulled down low over his face. "I'm lookin' for a woman named d'Or." He pronounced it *Door*.

"I am Miss d'Or," Simone said. She stood. The man was obviously from the lower rung of society, and she could not imagine why he would want to see her.

"I've got a message for you, Miss, from

your brother."

"From Bayard?"

"Yes. He's in trouble."

Simone's hand went to her throat. "What's the matter? Is he hurt?"

"Not yet, he ain't." The man grinned, but it was not cheerful. "But he's liable to be if somebody doesn't come to where he is."

"Where is he?"

"He's in a place over on Rampart Street. It's called Sally's Parlor. You know it?"

"I don't think so."

"Well, it's just down the street from Jackson Square, like I say, on Rampart Street. You keep goin', and you'll see Sally's Parlor — and don't bring no police, neither!"

"What's wrong with my brother?"

"Like I say, he needs help. I reckon you'd better get there pretty quick." The man turned and left, and Simone watched him, speechless. She picked up her reticule and said to Colin, "Excuse me."

"Wait a minute," Colin said as she reached the end of the line of seats. "You can't go down in that part of town by yourself."

"I have to."

"No, you don't. Stay right there. I'll go dismiss the cast, and I'll take you."

Simone wanted to refuse, but he gave her no chance. He walked over to the leader of the orchestra, who was smoking a cigar and laughing with one of the musicians. He spoke with him, and then he turned and got his coat, picked up a cane, and put on his hat. "Come along, Miss d'Or."

"I really shouldn't let you do this, but I don't have time to go get my father."

"It sounds urgent. It might be wise to send word to the police."

"But he said not to do that."

"All right. As you wish. Let's go."

"Oh, my driver will be coming back sometime soon. He'll have no way of knowing I'm not here."

"I'll leave word with one of the stagehands to tell him not to wait." Colin delivered the instructions, then the two left the theater, and Colin hailed a carriage. He opened the door, put her in, and said to the driver, "Rampart Street. You know a place named Sally's Parlor?"

The driver grinned and said, "I knows it. It ain't your kind of place, sir, if you don't mind my sayin' so."

"It is today. Take us there."

Colin got in and sat down next to Simone. He saw that her face was pale and said, "Try not to worry. Things aren't usually as bad as they seem."

"We've had — difficulties with Bayard."

"Well, maybe this will be a simple matter."

"I hate to ask you to bother yourself with my troubles."

Colin shrugged. Actually he was half-amused at his own actions. He would not have imagined himself going to any trouble for this woman who had shown him nothing but an arrogant spirit. That had been some time ago, though, and as he glanced at her, he saw the fear that kept her drawn up tight with her fists clenched. He knew that, at least for now, he had gotten past some of his animosity toward her.

Neither of them spoke until the driver pulled up in front of a shabby three-story building. "There's Sally's Parlor," he said as Colin got out and helped Simone step down to the pavement. He took the money that Colin gave him and asked, "Should I wait, sir?"

"I think you'd better." He handed him another coin and said, "There'll be another of those if it takes longer. I'll pay whatever your time is worth."

"Thank you, sir."

Taking Simone's arm, Colin led her to the front door. "It's a pretty coarse place. Why don't you wait in the carriage while I go find out what the problem is?"

"No, I have to go with you."

"Very well."

They entered and found what they had expected, a bar with disreputable characters drinking and shouting and loose-looking women dancing. A burly man in a striped shirt approached the couple. His hair was slicked back with grease, and he wore a black tie. "What can I do for you, sir?"

"We got word that a man named Bayard d'Or was in some difficulty."

The burly man grinned. "Back there — first door on the right. It's a private party, so knock before you go in."

"Thank you."

Colin and Simone walked down the short hallway, found the door, and Colin knocked on it. It opened almost at once. "What do you want?" the individual demanded.

"My name's Seymour. This is Miss d'Or. We're looking for her brother, Bayard."

"Well, come in, mate. My name's Tyrone."

Tyrone was a wolfish-looking man of some six feet, lean, with a patch over his left eye. He was dressed in the attire of a typical gambler but was obviously one of the rougher sort. As they stepped inside, Simone saw that there were three other men in the room in addition to Bayard, who had risen to his feet. "You shouldn't have come here,

Simone."

"Now, don't be like that," Tyrone said and grinned. There was a feral quality about the man, and Simone felt repulsed at the very sight of him. His single eye gleamed as he looked at her, and his face twisted in a leering expression. "We've got a little problem here, Miss d'Or. Your brother here has been gambling with me for some time. I'm ashamed to mention it to you, but he ain't actin' like no gentleman."

Bayard was half-drunk, at least. His clothes were wrinkled. His shirt was stained, and his hair hung down in his eyes. "Get out of here, Simone. This is none of your business."

"But Bayard, you sent for me!"

"No, I didn't."

Simone looked puzzled and asked, "How much does he owe?" It was hard for her to speak, but she faced the man as squarely as possible.

"Nine hundred dollars."

"Simone, they just sent for you to get your money. The game was crooked. I won't pay it," Bayard said defiantly.

"That's always what a cheater says," Tyrone grinned. "Ain't that right, fellas?" The three other men in the room looked as dangerous as Tyrone. It was clear to Simone and Colin that they comprised some sort of setup that fleeced unsuspecting victims.

"He ain't leavin' here until we get it, and we're gonna rough him up if we don't get our money right away."

"My father will pay it," Simone said quickly.

"No, he won't! Don't you ask him, Simone!"

"Be quiet, Bayard." Simone said, "My father is Louis d'Or. He's a prominent man in the city. I promise you he'll pay the nine hundred dollars."

"Well, Missy, ordinarily I would take a lady's word, but your brother here has put this off long enough. I got to have more than a word. I've got to have cash."

"Please let him go!"

"Sure. I'll let him go," Tyrone said. He moved closer, and Simone could smell tobacco and alcohol on his breath. "And you stay here with me. He can bring the money back from Papa." He reached out and took Simone by the arm, but Colin stepped forward and struck a sharp blow on his bicep.

"Take your hands off the lady," he said pleasantly.

"And who might you be?"

"Just a friend. I'll give you some good

advice, Tyrone. Let Mr. d'Or make you out an IOU. The lady says that her father will pay it. I suggest you take her word for it." Colin felt the tension in the room and wished Simone were outside. "Come, Bayard. Make out the IOU."

Bayard stared at him and could not think clearly. "I've already made out an IOU," he said thickly.

"Then we'll leave. I'll promise you as a gentleman, you'll get your money."

Tyrone laughed. " 'As a gentleman.' Well, that makes it all right, because gentlemen never lie, do they?"

Simone could not think clearly. She had never been exposed to real danger, and danger lay in the room thick as a blanket. She shot a quick glance at Colin and saw that his face was calm, but he did not take his eyes off Tyrone. "Please," she said, "I promise you you'll get your money."

"I'll get it all right, but I'll take a chunk out of your brother there while we're waiting."

"He's leaving with us, Tyrone. Come along, Bayard."

Simone gasped when Tyrone pulled a knife. He did it so quickly that she barely caught the action. It was a long-bladed knife, and he held it out in front of him, pointed at Colin. His voice was deadly as he said, "Get yourself out of here, Mister, before I cut you wide open."

Colin suddenly pulled at the top of his cane, and it separated from the rest. Simone saw that he held a gleaming sword almost three feet long. She had seen sword canes before on display but had not dreamed that Colin would have one.

Tyrone leaped forward, stabbing with the knife, but Colin's sword moved and caught the man in the arm. The steel cut him, and Tyrone cried out and dropped the knife to the floor.

Things happened very quickly then. Tyrone yelled, "Get him!" and all three men leaped to their feet. One pulled a pistol from his belt, but Colin dropped the cane from his left hand and pulled a small pistol from his belt. He shot quickly, and the man grabbed his own shoulder, the pistol clattering to the floor.

Colin said in a grating voice, "There are more bullets in here. Which of you would like to have one between the eyes?"

Two of the men were bleeding badly, Tyrone holding his arm, pain etched on his face. The other man slumped back in his chair, hollering, "Get me a doctor! I've been shot!"

"You'll be all right. You other two, pull your pistols out with your finger and thumb. If you do it wrong, you'll never know it. You'll be dead."

Simone watched as the two men pulled out their pistols and put them on the table. Then Colin stooped to pick up the one that had been dropped. He reached inside Tyrone's coat, pulled out another gun, and said, "Take these pistols, Miss d'Or." He waited until Simone had picked them up and said, "Take your brother outside."

Bayard's eyes were wide with shock. The explosion of violence had sobered him up, and he followed Simone without question. When the two were outside the room, Colin said to Tyrone, "You got off easy. I could have put that sword in your throat." He stooped down, picked up the hollow part of the cane and put the sword back in, all the time keeping his eye on the four. "I expect you'll get your money. If I hear of you troubling Miss d'Or anymore, I'll have to come back and finish what I've started."

"I won't forget this," Tyrone gasped, holding his bleeding hand.

"I hope not," Colin said coolly. "I'll leave your weapons at the bar." He stepped outside and shut the door. After depositing the weapons with the barkeeper, the three stepped quickly outside. Colin helped Simone back into the cab. He turned to Bayard and said, "You'd better go home with your sister."

"No, I won't do that." He turned to Simone and said, "Tell Father not to pay. That was a crooked game." He turned and walked off unsteadily.

"Shall I go get him?" Colin asked.

"No, it would be useless."

Colin got in the cab and gave the d'Or family address to the driver. He saw that Simone was trembling and said, "I'm sorry you had to see all that. It wasn't very pleasant."

Tears ran down her cheeks. Her shoulders began to shake, and she put her face down in her hands. "Bayard — Bayard!" she cried. "What's going to become of you?"

When they reached her house, Colin stepped out and helped her down. She turned to him, and he saw that her eyes were desperate.

Strangely enough, at that moment Simone had the clearest memory of the time he had come to her, begging her to get the duel between Armand and Claude called off. She remembered how cold she had been when she had refused. Shame flooded through her, and she said, "You have no reason to think well of me or to help me, but believe this, sir: I thank you from the bottom of my heart. Accept the thanks of my family and myself."

Colin was struck by the vulnerability that he saw in her face. He was relatively sure that she was not a woman who cried a great deal. Perhaps she had had nothing to cry about, but this had brought her face-to-face with one of the ugly realities of life. He felt a sudden gust of compassion, and when she put her hand out, he took it and held it for a moment, then leaned forward and kissed it. "I think you've changed for the better, Miss Simone."

Simone's hand seemed to burn where his lips had touched it, and when he released it, she dropped her eyes, unable to meet his. "I hope so," she said.

Colin asked, "Did you ever hear of the ancient science of alchemy?"

"I — don't believe so."

"It was the search of scientists in the Middle Ages to turn base metals such as lead into gold."

"Is such a thing possible?"

"Not with cold metals, I believe — but there is an alchemy of sorts. It occurs when a heart that is cold and hard is turned into one that is warm and gentle and tender."

His grip tightened and he whispered, "I think I've seen something very close to this kind of alchemy in you, Simone."

Simone lifted her head and saw a depth in his eyes she had never noticed before. His words were like balm to her wounded spirit, and she whispered, "That was a lovely thing to say."

She felt like weeping and murmured "Good night," then turned and went into the house. As soon as she was inside, she leaned back against the door and closed her eyes. She knew that Colin Seymour had saved her, and Bayard, from a great deal. She did not dare to think what. As she heard the carriage drive off, she thought how strange it was that this man she had once so disdained had put himself in danger for her. "I don't understand him," she whispered. Then she straightened up and went to find her father, dreading what she had to tell him.

■ ■ ■ ■

PART THREE:
1838
BAYARD

■ ■ ■ ■

CHAPTER TWELVE

A banging noise awoke Bayard from a deep sleep. With a groan, he rolled over and peered around for a moment, not recognizing his surroundings. Then a voice said, "Get up! Do you hear me? Get up!"

Groaning, Bayard sat up in the bed, then paused as a sharp pain struck him in the temples, almost forcing him to lie down again. The banging and the voice continued insistently, and finally he called out, "All right! All right, I'm coming!"

Getting up, he stifled a cry as the pain hit him again. The taste of stale liquor in his mouth and the pain in his head made him feel as bad as he ever had in his life. He was still dressed, and he vaguely remembered falling into bed after drinking a quart of whiskey. Staggering to the door, he shot the bolt and opened it.

"Well, I thought maybe you was dead." The speaker was a tall, slatternly-looking woman. Snuff ran out the edges of her mouth. "I want my money, you hear me? And I wants it now!"

"I'll get it to you today."

"That ain't good enough. You said that yesterday and the day afore. You pay up, or you get out."

Bayard felt the room reel. He shut his eyes for a moment. He said, "I'll have it today."

"If you don't, I'll throw your stuff out in the street. You pay me or out you go!"

Bayard slammed the door, and the noise seemed to echo inside the confines of his skull. He leaned against the door with both hands and waited for the room to stop spinning. Then he straightened up. He had eaten practically nothing, and the hangover was fierce. It was as if someone were driving steel spikes into both sides of his skull.

Finally he walked over to the wash basin, lifted the pitcher, and drank the tepid water thirstily. He poured the remainder into the basin, leaned over, and sloshed his face. The water helped clear his mind, and as he dried with the filthy towel, he knew he had to do something. With a vague idea of trying to sell his easel and his paints, he pulled on his dingy white hat and left the boardinghouse. As he slammed the front door, he heard the landlady calling after him, "Mind you, money or you're out!"

He looked in his pockets and found that he had nothing. He remembered losing the last five dollars he had in a penny-ante poker game at some bar. Hunger gnawed him. He had been drunk for over a week and had eaten only when the mood struck him. He wandered into two shops and offered his equipment, but in both places the proprietors took one look at the rickety easel and box of paints, mostly dried, and laughed at him.

When noon arrived, he finally came to a conclusion: "I can't go home again. I've got one canvas left. I'll paint a picture. Someone will buy it for a few dollars."

Weak and nauseated, he started walking out of town eastward, toward the bayou. He had walked for over an hour and was growing weaker when a wagon passed by, driven by a black man. Bayard waved his hand and asked, "How about a ride?"

The black man drew up and stared at him. "You wants to ride with me, suh?"

"I'm going out to the bayou."

"Yes, suh, I go close. Get in."

"Thank you."

Throwing his equipment into the bed of the wagon, Bayard climbed up into the seat. He was feeling worse by the moment.

"Been lots of rain lately. The swamp pretty high."

"Yes, it has been wet."

"You not huntin' no 'gators, is you?"

"No, I'm a painter. I'm going to paint a picture of some of the wildflowers by the swamp."

"Plenty of them."

That was the extent of the conversation. An hour later, Bayard got down out of the wagon with his equipment and nodded. "Thanks for the ride."

"You welcome, suh. You be careful. Bad 'gators in that swamp could eat you whole."

"I'll watch out."

Bayard began walking toward the swamp. Fifteen minutes later, he was out of sight of all humans, and the smell of humus was thick in his nostrils. He watched as mallards rose in squadrons above a group of willows, trailing in long, black lines across the sun that was yellow as an egg yolk. He continued to walk, and the big cypress trees began to grow thicker. He could hear the bass flopping, breaking water, and more than once he saw the solitary V-shaped ripple of a nutria swimming through the dark waters. Bayard splashed through the muddy pools that began to gather, keeping his eye out for the beautiful, wild orchids. He passed through large areas green with lily pads clustering along the bayou's banks. They were bursting with flowers, and he muttered, "I can come back and paint the lilies if I don't find any orchids."

On and on he walked, until the trees hid the sun overhead, and the air grew cooler. Once he stirred a flight of egrets, and a blue heron lifted its long legs carefully, its long beak darting down on a fish. Bayard's breath grew shorter, and finally he reached the very center of the bayou. The air was moist and cool, and it smelled of fish and mud. There was also the smell of something dead that lay heavy in his nostrils. Finally, stepping over roots and struggling with his easel, Bayard came to a spot where he caught the colorful gleam of the wild orchid.

"Now," he muttered, "I've found you." The water was around his ankles, but he sought a dry spot, spread the easel, put the single canvas on it, and opened the case of paints. He felt disgusted at how sparse his supply was, but grimly he began to work.

For two hours he tried to transfer reality to canvas, and as sometimes happened, he grew so consumed with the act of painting that he forgot his hunger and the headache that continued to nag at him. He reached a point where the paint seemed to flow onto the canvas, and he wished that he had more of the brilliant colors. Still, he did the best he could.

Twice he stopped to rest, and once, with his back against a tree, he dozed off. He slept for over an hour and came awake with a start. "Got to finish this blasted painting! Don't want to get caught in the dark in this bayou."

He stayed with the work until finally he had done the best he could. He admired the painting for a moment, and he thought, *If I worked at this, I would be really good.* Remorse filled him as he thought how he had squandered his talent, but hunger growled like a live thing in his belly. He folded up the canvas, closed the paint box, and put it under his left arm. He carried the easel with his left hand, and the painting he held with the painted side away from him. He started back and paid little attention to where he was going. He thought of how pitiful a sight he had become. Shame rushed through him as he realized what he had thrown away.

He suddenly realized that he was wading in water up to his knees. Looking around, he saw nothing familiar. "I came this way," he muttered. "I *must* have." He surged forward, but the water grew deeper. "It can't be." Bayard turned and traced his way back, and for the next fifteen minutes he followed a track that he thought he had taken into the bayou, but then, too, the water grew deeper. "This is wrong," he said. He tried to ascertain his direction, but the sun was low in the west, and the shadows were deep in the bayou. He heard the sound of a bull 'gator grunting somewhere and grew afraid. He found another path and started stumbling, hurrying to get out. He nearly fell once, and finally the path he had chosen faded out completely into vegetation that seemed to close around him.

His fear deepened, and Bayard started to run blindly. A root tripped him, and with a cry he fell across a rotten log coated with green moss, his painting flying into the water. He put his arms out to brace himself, but his chest crashed onto the log, and suddenly a pain struck him in the left bicep. Bayard jerked madly and glimpsed a bit of white. He didn't recognize it at first, thinking it was a flower, and then he saw it was the inside of the mouth of the biggest cottonmouth he had ever seen! It was as big around as his own arm, and with a cry of panic he threw himself over backwards. He scrambled to his feet and saw the huge snake glide away from him.

But his arm! He tore the button off his sleeve, pulled it up, and saw the deadly twin punctures.

Fear can drive a man into frenetic activity, or it can stun and paralyze him so that he cannot move. Bayard d'Or stared at the twin punctures and remembered the stories he had heard of the deadly cottonmouth. "I've got to try to find help," he gasped. He started walking, stumbling through the water, but he had not gone far before he began to feel the effects of the poison. It burned like fire, and five minutes later he felt so ill that he tried to vomit. He leaned forward on his hands and knees, retching. The ground was dry beneath him, and finally the heaving stopped. He knelt, willing himself to get up, but all around him the swamp was growing darker. He was lost, his body was full of deadly poison, and a terrible dizziness was overtaking him. He cried out, "Help! Somebody please help me!"

The echo of his own voice came back to him, and he realized the futility of the attempt. He called out again, this time not for human help. "Oh, God, I'm dying! Help me, God! Don't let me die in this swamp!"

Again the echoes of his voice came back to him. He felt the presence of live things around him moving in the dark waters. Night was coming on, and he bent over and touched his head to the ground, covering it with his hands and crying out again, "Oh, God, don't let me die! Please don't let me die!"

CHAPTER THIRTEEN

The darkness that surrounded Bayard seemed to be almost palpable — soft, thick, and warm as a blanket. But at other times he felt a coldness like the frozen northlands where snow enveloped everything. These two extremes covered him, and he cried out at times, for one seemed as painful as the other.

The voices he heard seemed to come from far away. He strained and tried to make them out but failed. They were the voices of strangers, and he felt frightened that there was nothing familiar in his world of blinding whiteness and stygian darkness. One of the voices came more often than the other, and in time he came to look for it and to try to make sense out of the words. He was not able to do this, but the voice had a soothing tone, and that comforted him.

The sense of touch was within this world, wherever it was. Besides the burning heat or bitter chill, he felt hands touching him, and he came to look forward to it. They were strong hands, he knew, but they were gentle at the same time. There was the feel of sheets, some sort of cloth, a breeze that touched him lightly, but there was no sense of the passage of time. He might have been in the terrible place for as long as it took to build the pyramids — or it might have been only a day or less.

Finally the heat and the cold seemed to modify, and he groaned with pleasure as the pain left him. The words began to have meaning, but there was still something about them that he could barely understand. He longed to know who spoke and who touched him.

Finally reason and order and sense came, almost as if someone threw a switch. One moment he was deep in the warm darkness, knowing that the hands were touching him and the voice was speaking, and the next instant he realized that he was lying flat on his back, a sheet was covering him, and something wet was touching his face and the upper part of his body. He opened his eyes then, and directly over him was a face — one he had never seen before. His thoughts swarmed and confusion stirred him, and then he felt fear.

Where have I been? Who is this? Bayard blinked and stared at a young woman with jet-black hair and eyes that seemed black at first, but as he studied them, he noted that they were a dark blue. Her face was oval, she had broad, full lips, and her expression was friendly but focused. His eyes dropped, and he saw that she had a cloth in her hand and was sponging his chest. He watched as she put the cloth into a basin, wrung it out with one quick motion, then began to wash him again.

"Where is this place?"

His words came from his throat hoarsely and creaked almost like a hinge that had frozen in place. They startled the young woman, whose eyes widened. He noticed she had the thickest eyelashes he had ever seen, and that they curved upward gracefully. She answered him, saying, "Ah, you are awake!"

At first he could not understand her, and then he realized that she had spoken in French. *"Oui,"* he said. His French was very limited, so he muttered in English, "Who are you?"

The young woman's eyes were deep pools, it seemed, and she studied him a moment before she said, "My name is Fleur Avenall. You are in our house, yes."

Bayard closed his eyes for a moment, trying to put together what was happening, and then it all came rushing back. He remembered falling in the bayou and the enormous snake and the pain in his arm. Alarm filled him, and he looked down and saw that a bandage was on his arm. "A snake — a snake bit me."

"Yes," the young woman said, nodding. "You almost died, I think. Me, I think you will not live for a time." Her English was broken, but Bayard understood her. He struggled to get up, and she bent over and put her arms under his and pulled him to a sitting position. She set the pillow upright and pushed his head against it. "You have been ver' sick," she said. "*Ma mere* and I think you will die maybe."

Bayard could hardly speak, but he managed to gasp, "Water! A drink of water!"

"*Oui, certainement,*" the girl named Fleur said. She picked up a pitcher on a table by the bedside and then a glass. She poured the water and handed it to him. His left arm was sore, and he flinched and took the glass in his right hand. Thirstily he drank the water, and he had never had a drink so good.

Fleur took the glass and asked, "What you are called?"

"Bayard d'Or."

She considered that, then nodded. "Can you eat something?"

"How long have I been here?"

"Me, I fin' you last Tuesday. Tomorrow will be a week."

Alarms went off in Bayard's head. "My family! I've got to get word to my family!"

"I would have send, but I not know who your people were. You must eat."

Bayard watched as the young woman put the glass down, then turned and walked over to the fireplace. A series of hooks suspended blackened pots over the fire. It was warm in the cabin, and as she began to stir something in one of the smaller pots, Bayard looked at his surroundings. The room he lay in was part of a log cabin. His bed was against the wall, and he reached out and touched the smooth, rounded logs. The furniture was sparse, consisting of one small table and two chairs, both obviously homemade. A large bearskin was on the rough, plank floor, and the walls were covered with shelves on which were placed various objects: seashells, a tiny skull of a small animal, a vase with blue flowers in it.

Two windows admitted pale sunshine. The smell of cooking meat was in the air, stirring Bayard's hunger. A door to the left led to what was evidently another room, and on the far side another door led outside.

He lay quietly, and Fleur came back with a bowl and a large spoon. He tried to lift his left arm to take it, but it was so sore that he winced.

"Here, Monsieur," she said, "Me, I will feed you."

She dipped the large spoon into the bowl, and he saw that the food was smoking. She blew it and tasted it herself, then said, "It's ver' hot, but it's good."

Bayard opened his mouth, feeling like a child, and swallowed a spoonful. The first bite aroused a raving hunger, and he ate until she had emptied the bowl.

"Not good to eat too much at once," Fleur said. "You have little bits not far apart." She blinked and said, "Oh, I forget to pray over the food. Maybe you want to pray now?"

This struck Bayard as odd. At his home sometimes grace was said, but only rarely. "I am thankful for it," he said.

"The good God, He takes care of you. If He had not, you would be buried in a grave."

The food had somehow produced sleepiness. Bayard felt his eyelids drooping, and he asked, "Where is this place?"

"It is our house where I live — me and

ma mere." She saw that he was going to sleep and helped him lie flat with his head on the pillow. She touched his chest and said, "You sleep now. It will be good."

The smell of cooked meat awoke Bayard, and as he came out of the sleep, he knew the fever was gone. He struggled up and saw the young woman named Fleur across the room, stirring something in a pan. "That smells good," he said.

Fleur turned and smiled. Her hair was long, tied with a thong, and hanging down her back almost to her belt. She was wearing a pair of man's faded trousers and a man's shirt, and moccasins without any stockings. Her petite frame looked odd in a man's clothing. She straightened up and said, "You are hungry, no?"

"I am hungry, *yes.*"

"This will be ver' good for you. You want to try to sit at the table?"

"I'll try." He threw the sheet back and saw that he was wearing only his undergarments. "Where are my pants?" he said.

"You do not need them, no. You will go back to bed and sleep some more after you eat. Come." Fleur went over and pulled him to his feet, then draped his arm over her shoulders. The room seemed to reel, and he clung to her as she guided him across the floor. Slumping down in one of the two chairs, he shook his head. "I'm weak as a kitten!"

"You be strong ver' soon," Fleur said. She plucked a plate off of a shelf and pulled some of the meat out of the frying pan with a fork. She brought it back to him and furnished him with silverware. She said, "You eat. I get you some milk." She stepped outside. He noticed that she moved quietly and gracefully, almost like a young deer. When she came back, she had a jug in her hand. Retrieving a cup, she poured and said, "The milk, she is fresh."

Bayard found that he had some use of his left hand, and putting the fork in it, he steadied the meat while he carved out a bite-sized chunk. He put it in his mouth and chewed. It was tough and had a rather fishy flavor. "This is good," he said. "What is it?"

" 'Gator."

Bayard had been about to insert another forkful of meat but halted. " 'Gator?" he said. "You mean *alligator?*"

"Yes. I soak her in saltwater. Is good?"

Bayard grinned. "Very good," he said.

She got up and spooned something out of a pot on the fireplace and brought a bowl

221

back to him. "Gumbo," she said. "Ver' good."

Bayard ate hungrily and drank the milk, and then he asked, "Where is your family?"

"Only *ma mere.*" She gestured toward the door. "That is her place."

"Your father?"

"He is with God."

Her way of speaking of God seemed very familiar. "I'm sorry to hear it," he said.

"He was very sick — ready to go." A tiny line suddenly appeared in the girl's smooth brow. "*Ma mere,* she very sick also. She will go be with God soon."

"What's wrong with her?"

"I do not know, except she's sick."

Bayard studied the young woman. Her strange garb lent her a foreign look. Her hair was black as the blackest thing in nature, and he guessed her age was somewhere between sixteen and nineteen. She had a long, composed mouth, and her skin was olive with a smoothness and a slight rose tint that did not come out of a jar. The light that came in through the window was kind to Fleur, showing the full, soft lines of her body, the womanliness in breast and shoulder. She was still not quite out of that part of youth that marks girlhood, but she was a woman. He saw the hint of her will and her pride in the corners of her eyes and lips, and as she spoke, she made little gestures with her shoulders and expressive turns with her hands. "I need to get word to my people, Miss Avenall."

Fleur laughed. "No one call me that. I am Fleur. I cannot leave *ma mere,* but someone will go."

"One of the neighbors?"

"I will ask Lonnie Despain to go."

"Who is he?"

"He lives five miles from here, but he come by twice a week to pick up the meat to sell."

"What meat is that?"

"I catch 'gators, and I trap. Lonnie takes the meat into the city to sell it."

"What sort of meat is it?"

"I catch many fish," she smiled. "I am a good fisherman. Also there are wild pigs in the bayou, and I shoot them. Also some people eat the coon, so I shoot him too. Squirrels and rabbits. Everything I sell. People like almost any kind of meat."

It seemed strange to Bayard. "Do you have other family besides your mother?"

"No. She is all I have."

"Has a doctor been here?"

"When *ma mere* first got sick, Lonnie, he fetch a doctor out, but he said that she cannot live. I think he's right. When I pray, the good God, He tells me that I must say good-bye to her soon."

"I'm sorry, Fleur," Bayard said, and indeed he did feel pity for the girl. He wondered what she would be like if she had been born into different circumstances, but there was no way of knowing. He glanced at the door and asked, "Does your mother ever get up?"

"*Oui,* some days she feel ver' good. I think she get up today later, and I fix her something good to eat." For a moment the girl's face changed, and he saw her vulnerability. "I feel ver' bad that she suffers so much. I wish I could suffer for her, me. But none of us can suffer for another."

"I suppose that's true."

"You have family?"

"Yes. My father and mother, of course, and I have one sister."

"It is ver' good to have people. I know they will be afraid for you. Lonnie will be here later on in the day. He always come on Tuesday. I do not think you are fit to move, but if you will write, Lonnie will take it to your people."

"I'll do that now if you have paper."

After some searching Fleur found a scrap of paper. She also found a stub of a pencil, and Bayard wrote as clearly as he could, but he found himself growing weary. When he ended the note, he handed it to Fleur, and she looked into his face. "You are tired. You sleep now."

"Wake me when Lonnie comes."

"Yes, I will do that. Can you get to the bed by yourself?"

"I think so." Bayard got up and found that he was indeed somewhat steadier, but he was ready for the bed, and he lay back in it with a sigh. He wanted to say something to Fleur to thank her, but sleep came quickly, and he fell asleep thinking of the strangeness of the young woman.

Bayard heard voices, and when he opened his eyes, he saw an older woman sitting in one of the chairs beside the table. Fleur was putting food in front of her. He struggled upright and said, "Miss Fleur, could I have my trousers?"

Fleur said, "Oh, you are awake." She found his trousers and said, "I wash them for you." She handed them to him, then turned back to her mother. Bayard felt better when he had put his pants on, and he stood up and bowed, saying, "Good afternoon, ma'am."

"This is *ma mere.* Her name is Gabrielle.

This man is Bayard d'Or."

Gabrielle Avenall's hair was black, her eyes were the same dark blue as her daughter's, but she was wasted away and had none of Fleur's strength. The disease that was killing her was obvious in the sunken cheeks and bony arms. Still, there was strength in her face and traces of an earlier beauty. *She must have looked exactly like Fleur when she was young,* Bayard thought. "I do not know how to thank you and your daughter for taking care of me. I was very lucky."

Gabrielle studied him with her dark eyes, her gaze intense. "Not luck. It was God who give her to you."

"I think you're probably right, Mrs. Avenall."

"Come and sit down. You can eat again."

Bayard walked over and sat down and noticed the thinness of Gabrielle Avenall's hands. He was aware that she was watching him. For some reason, this made him nervous, and he said, "I would have died out there if it hadn't been for your daughter." He looked at Fleur and asked, "How did you get me here to the house? You couldn't have carried me."

"No, I have a mare. I was riding, and I hear you cry out. When I find you, you could not speak, and the poison was already in your blood. Lonnie was riding with me, to help me drag 'gators back to the house. He brought you back to our cabin, and my mother and I treated your sickness. I think God must have been in it."

Bayard blinked with surprise. "I think that must be close to the truth."

Gabrielle said, "You cannot be the same man again. When a man comes close to death, he can't go back to being what he was. Do you ever pray, Mr. d'Or?"

"Well, I haven't been much for prayer, but I did pray out there in that swamp." Memory came flooding back, and he shook his head in wonder. "I cried out to God with every bit of strength I had just after that snake got me. I cried out until I felt life passing out of me."

"Then you must live the life of a man of God."

A silence fell over the three, and Bayard stared at the sick woman. Her eyes were fixed on him intently, and he found that he could not meet them. He nodded. "I think you are right."

"Yes, I am right. He has given you your life, and you are responsible for using it to serve Him."

Bayard lifted his eyes and found something in the expression of the woman that

227

he could not explain. He shifted his gaze and found some of the same in Fleur's face. The two women were regarding him strangely, and he heard himself saying, "I think you may be right. When God gives a man his life, he must not throw it away."

"I hear Lonnie coming," Fleur said. She had put her mother back to bed and was sitting with Bayard. Bayard had said little, but she had talked considerably. Her world was small — trapping animals, fishing, taking care of her mother, and serving Jesus. Bayard had never met anyone with such a simple faith! To her, Jesus was not a man who had lived two thousand years ago, neither was He someone who lived far off in the sky. No, for Fleur Avenall, Jesus was as real as Bayard himself. She spoke of Him as naturally as if He were a next-door neighbor. It was a fascinating thing to Bayard d'Or. And since his near-death experience, he was aware that something was stirring within his heart.

He told her, "When I believed I was going to die, Fleur, I thought of two things. One, the awful mess I've made of my own life. That was a hard thing to bear."

"You have been a bad man?"

Bayard grimaced. "Very bad, Fleur. I'm

not the kind of man you would admire."

"Tell me some bad things that you have done, you."

Bayard suddenly laughed. "You are an unusual young woman! Well, I have hurt my parents deeply. I've wasted the talent that God has given me, and I've been a drunkard and a womanizer. As a matter of fact, I'm a terrible man."

Fleur watched him. "That is sad," she said, "but God loves sinners, and we are all sinners. You remember in the Bible the man said, 'I thank you, God, I'm not like other men, that I'm good.' And the other man said, 'God be merciful to me a sinner.' "

"I'm like that second fellow."

"We are all like him, I think, Bayard." She used his name easily and added, "But God loves us all — sinners though we are."

The sound of a man's voice called from outside, and Fleur said, "There is Lonnie." She went to the door and invited him in. A small man, wiry with a dark complexion, stepped into the room. He was wearing a floppy black hat that he did not remove, and his eyes were gray and inquisitive. He stared at Bayard.

"This is Bayard d'Or, Lonnie. The one who was bitten by a snake and nearly die."

"Them snakes, they are bad. You are better, I hope?"

"Very well, Lonnie, but I need to get word to my people. I've been here nearly a week. Could you take a message to New Orleans for me?"

"*Certainement!* You tell me where."

Bayard discovered quickly that Lonnie could not read, but he was a quick, intelligent man. He listened as Bayard gave instructions and then said, "I take this to your family."

"I don't have any money to pay you, but my family will pay you. I put that in the note."

Lonnie nodded and then turned to Fleur. "You have the meat?"

"Yes. Quite a lot this time." She left the room with Lonnie, and he heard the two of them chatter as she gave him the meat. When she came back in, she said, "He is a good man, but he does not know the Lord Jesus. My mother and I pray for him every day."

Bayard admired the young woman who had done so much for him. "I owe you a lot, Fleur."

"I'm glad the good Lord had me passing by. If I had been a little later, I would not have heard your cry." She studied him and said, "God is good to you, Bayard."

■ ■ ■ ■

Evening had come. Bayard had eaten well on gumbo and fried venison steaks. He sat at the table, listening to Gabrielle and Fleur talking. They were very curious about the outside world, and he entertained them with stories. They had been interested also in his family, and he spoke of them a great deal.

Finally Fleur insisted that her mother go to bed. As she helped her to the room, Bayard went outside. He heard the two women speaking and knew that they were praying. It touched him. When Fleur stepped outside, he said, "I'm sorry about your mother. Perhaps you'd let me take her to one of the hospitals in New Orleans."

"You are kind, but she is past all help now."

"You can't know that, Fleur."

"Yes. God has told us both that she must be with Jesus soon."

The answer elicited no argument, and Bayard sat silently on the steps. She sat down beside him. He looked up in the heavens and said, "The stars are beautiful tonight."

"Yes. The Lord, He knows all their names. Every one of them."

"Do you really think so?"

"Oh, yes. In Psalm 147 He tells us that. It says, 'He telleth the number of the stars; He calleth them all by their names.' " She smiled at him. "He is a great God to know all the names of the stars, but He made them, so it is not too strange."

They fell silent for a few minutes. Then Fleur asked, "You are married and have children?"

"No, I'm not married."

"Why not?"

Fleur had a way of asking intimate questions with no embarrassment at all. It amused Bayard. "Well, I don't know why I'm not married."

"You will be one day."

"I suppose so."

"What do you do to make money?"

Bayard was embarrassed. "To tell the truth, not much of anything."

"How do you live?"

"My father has money."

"He is rich?"

"Well, he's comfortably well-off."

Bayard half expected her to follow this line, but he hoped she would not. In order to prevent it, he began to ask her questions about herself. "Why are you not married?" he asked.

"I will be one day, but God has not sent

me a man yet."

"How old are you, Fleur?"

"Eighteen. How old are you, Bayard?"

"I'm twenty-five. My sister is a year younger than I."

"What is she like?"

"She's very beautiful. She has blonde hair and the bluest eyes you've ever seen. Fleur," he said, changing the subject, "what do you do for fun out here?"

"For fun? Oh, sometimes I go to the dances, me. There's music there. It is a long way, though, and because of *ma mere,* I have not gone lately."

"Don't you get lonely out here, Fleur, all by yourself with just your mother?"

"No."

"You don't? I would think you might."

"No, I have Jesus."

The calmness of her reply and the enormity of it stunned Bayard d'Or. He could not think of anything to say. Fleur turned to him and touched his arm. She asked, "How do you live? Do you have Jesus as your friend?"

"No, I don't."

"How do you live without Him? I can never understand. I have know Him since I was nine years old, me."

Bayard had never given a great deal of

thought to religion. He had gone through the formality of it when he was younger, but even that he had given up in recent years. He was not a hypocrite and knew that his lifestyle was not pleasing to God. He saw that Fleur was waiting for an answer, and finally he looked up at the stars, at the magnificence of the display in the heavens, and thought of the God who had made them all. There had never been any doubt in his mind about the existence of God. He had merely refused to give too much thought to it. Finally he turned to her and said, "I envy you, Fleur."

"You envy me? Why's that? You have a family. You have everything that most men want."

"But I don't have God. When I called out to Him after that snake bit me, I knew that."

She smiled. "Maybe God, He send the snake to get your attention. Now," she said, and her eyes were warm, "that God has saved you, you will love Him."

Bayard dropped his head. "I hope so, Fleur. I never have. I think it's time."

Chapter Fourteen

As soon as Simone entered the house, Agnes, the housemaid, met her and said, "There's a man who's been waiting to see the master."

"To see my father? Is he here?"

"No, he and Madam left to go to visit the Dubres. They won't be back until late tonight, they said."

Simone pulled off her hat and put her parasol in the teak holder. "Why did you ask him to wait?"

"I didn't, but he insisted, Miss Simone. He's a very rough sort of man. I can't think what he would want with any of you."

Simone bit her lip for a moment and said, "Well, I'll see him."

"He's waiting out back. I didn't want to let him into the house. He's not that kind of person."

Simone moved down the long hallway and then through the kitchen. When she stepped outside, she saw a man leaning against the live oak tree. He was wiry, wore the coarsest sort of clothes, and did not look like a tradesman.

"I'm Miss d'Or. I understand you want to see my father?"

"I got a note for him."

"A note from whom?"

"A young man. I think his name is Bayard."

"My brother!" Hope shot through Simone. "He's been missing for a week."

Indeed, the whole family had been almost in despair. Ever since the altercation with Louis, Bayard had simply dropped out of sight. When Louis had gone by the rooming house, the owner said brusquely, "He left one day and didn't come back. He couldn't pay, anyway." Since that time they had waited anxiously, and more than once Louis had said to Renee, "I was too hard on him. I shouldn't have driven him out of the house."

Simone said quickly, "The note's for my father?"

"That is what he say."

"He's not here, but I need to see the letter."

The man fished in his shirt pocket, came out with a brown piece of paper, and handed it to her. Simone opened the letter and read it quickly:

Father, I have run into trouble. I was in the swamp doing a painting, and I was bitten by a huge cottonmouth. I nearly died and was unconscious for several days. I don't know how to tell you to get to this place. The people taking care of me have been very kind. Their name is Avenall. The man who bears this note is named Lonnie Despain. If you would pay him, I think he will bring you to me. I'm sorry for all that happened.

Simone looked up at the man and said, "This says my brother has been hurt."

"Yes. He was bit by a moccasin." Lonnie shrugged his trim shoulders. "He nearly die, Fleur tell me."

"Who is Fleur?"

"Fleur Avenall. She stay with her mother ver' deep in the bayou."

"But I need to get to him."

"You can't ride into the swamp. I can take you in my pirogue."

"Can you bring him out, the two of us?"

"Oh, *certainement*. Is easy."

"I'll pay you for your trouble. Let me go tell the servants where I'm going. Can you leave now?"

"Now is good. I have finished my business here in town."

Simone went inside and told Agnes the news with some agitation. "I've got to go. I think I'll be back before my parents get here. If I'm not, give them this note, and tell them I've gone to get Bayard." She did not wait for an answer but picked up her reticule and looked inside it. She saw that she had sufficient money. She put on her hat and stepped quickly down the hall and out the front door. "Robert," she called, "hitch up the horses."

"Yes, ma'am, you going to town?"

"No, a man has come saying my brother has been ill. We're going to get him."

"Yes, Miss, that's good news!" Robert disappeared around the corner, and Simone returned to speak again with Lonnie Despain.

"I'm having the team hitched to my carriage. How long will it take to get there?"

"It ain't too far, Miss. You follow me as far as my place. Then we get into my little boat, and I take you to where Fleur and her mother live. They are fine people."

Simone waited impatiently, and when Robert drove the carriage out, she got in without waiting for him to step down and help her. "Follow this man, Robert."

"Yes, ma'am, I'll just do that."

As soon as the team stopped, Simone opened the door and stepped out. Looking around, she saw that Despain had dismounted and was putting his horse into a small corral that was fenced with wooden rails. He stripped off the saddle and slapped the gelding on the rump, then came back, locking the gate behind him. "This is my place," he said. He gestured toward an enormous body of water and said, "The swamp. We cannot go farther in the carriage."

Indeed, Despain's house was right on the edge of the tremendous bayou. Few roads led into it, and the only means of transportation was the little wooden boat sitting on the bank. "We go now if you ready, Miss."

"Yes, I'm ready." Simone turned and said, "Robert, you wait here, no matter how long it takes. I'll be back with Bayard as soon as possible."

"Yes, ma'am. I'll wait right here."

Simone went down to the bank and watched as Despain pushed the small craft down the shore. "You get in the front, Miss, up there."

"Are you sure it's safe?"

"It ain't never done kill me yet."

This was not much comfort to Simone. She got in carefully and felt the boat move beneath her feet. Dropping to her hands and knees, she crawled to the end and then sat down flat on the bottom. It was a very shallow boat and looked entirely unstable.

She felt the boat move forward and then give a lurch. She grasped the gunnel, but Despain assured her, "It's real safe. You sit still now. Me, I push."

Turning around, she saw that the man had picked up a long pole. He shoved it against the bottom, and the pirogue shot forward. She resisted the impulse to cry out.

Evidently Lonnie Despain was an expert boatman, for he sent the small craft skimming across the water. The swamp seemed to go on forever, and they passed canals, sand spits, willow islands, and huge cypress trees. The mosquitoes came then in swarms, and Simone slapped her face and her neck.

"The mosquitoes are bad, yes."

"How much farther is it?"

"Not too far. Yet quite a ways too."

At this enigmatic response, Simone grew quiet. The sun was high over the cypress. They passed sweet-smelling hyacinths, and the air grew moist and cool underneath the shade of the giant trees. Once they passed a whole island covered with buttercups and bluebonnets. She saw enormous black and yellow grasshoppers flying, and when they landed in the water, sometimes fish came up and took them. Finally Lonnie said, "There is Fleur's house — right over there."

They had come out of a large body of water into a narrow inlet. The land appeared then, and fifty yards from the water a cabin sat beneath some cypress trees. Smoke rose up from the chimney, and Simone waited until Despain drove the boat up onto the land. She stepped out, and the black mud covered her shoes, but she reached down, pulled them off, and waded to shore.

"The rain, she make the ground wet," Despain remarked as he came out of the boat, agile as a monkey, and pulled it up onto dry land. "See? There's Miss Fleur. She hear us coming."

Carrying her shoes in one hand and her reticule in the other, Simone went toward the cabin, her eyes fixed on the young woman. When she was closer, the young woman said, "Hello."

"Hello. I'm Simone d'Or. My brother is here, isn't he?"

"*Oui,* he is here. He was sleeping, but I think he want to wake up for you."

Simone studied the girl, noting the rough,

masculine attire, but only for a moment. As soon as the girl opened the cabin door, Simone stepped inside and saw the bed against the wall and Bayard swinging his feet over the edge.

"Bayard!" she said. She ran toward him, and he stood up and met her. She put her arms around him, noticing the bandage on his left forearm.

"Thank God you're all right! We've been so worried!"

"I couldn't get word to you any sooner. I was unconscious."

"Are you all right?"

"Arm is a little bit stiff, but basically I'm all right." He turned Simone to face the young woman. "This is Fleur Avenall. She found me out in the swamp just after the snake bit me, and she and Lonnie brought me back to this cabin. I would have died if it hadn't been for Fleur."

Simone said fervently, "I am so grateful to you, and my family will be also."

Fleur seemed disturbed by the expression of gratitude. "If you give me your shoes, I'll clean them off."

"Oh, that's not necessary. I'd just get them muddy getting back in the boat."

"My mother, she is not feeling well today, or she would get up to meet you."

242

"Mrs. Avenall is not in good health, Simone."

Even as he spoke, the door opened and Gabrielle Avenall stepped out. She looked almost ghostly, but as Fleur introduced her, she said, "You are welcome. Sit down and have some café au lait."

Simone took one seat and Gabrielle took the other. Bayard dragged up a box, set it on end, and sat down. He told Simone how he had gone to the bayou to paint and had gotten lost. "When I saw that snake slithering off and knew he had gotten me in the arm, I pretty well gave up."

Simone was shaking, she was so happy to see her brother. She put her hand on his wrist and said, "We've all been worried sick. We thought of everything in the world that could've happened to you."

Fleur brought the café au lait in cups that did not match. It was thick and strong, and the rich odor filled the small cabin. Fleur put her hand on her mother's thin shoulder and said, "Your brother does not know God, but he is meeting Him, I think, now."

Startled, Simone gave her a quick look. "Why — that's good," she said, not knowing what else to say.

"God saved him," Gabrielle remarked. "So now he belongs to God."

Simone looked at Bayard, who reddened. "I — I think she's right, Simone. When I was dying out there, I could feel the poison of that snake killing me. I called on God. The first time I had done anything like that." He turned then and smiled at Fleur. "And then He sent this young woman to save me. She saved my life."

Simone impulsively got up and went to Fleur. She took the young woman's hand and suddenly kissed it, tears in her eyes. "How can my family ever thank you, Fleur?"

"We must all thank the good God and give glory to Him. He is the one who saves."

Bayard saw the strange look on his sister's face and laughed aloud. "You'll have to get used to it, Simone. Mrs. Avenall and her daughter are very close to God." He sobered then and chewed his lower lip thoughtfully. "I think I am too. I don't believe I can ever be the same again."

"That's so good to hear, Bayard."

"I've made resolutions in the past, but it took that snake to wake me up."

Fleur laughed. "There was one snake that got Eve and Adam into trouble, but now God, He uses another snake to bring one of His own back to Him. I think that's very funny."

Bayard d'Or smiled at the girl thoughtfully. She was like no one he had ever seen or experienced, but he knew that she was right, and something good was going to come out of that terrible experience.

Simone sat quietly listening as Gabrielle spoke of her life with God. This woman who was obviously dying showed no fear at all, which Simone found intimidating. Finally Gabrielle said, "I must lie down again."

At once Bayard stood and offered her his hand. The sick woman put her hand in his. Lifting it to his lips, Bayard kissed it and said, "I pray that God will give you peace."

"He's already done that, Monsieur d'Or, and now I think He has given you the peace as well."

Fleur took her mother into the bedroom. While the two were waiting for her to return, Simone said, "I've never met people like these."

"Neither have I. I didn't know there were such people."

As soon as Fleur came out, Simone asked, "Would you think us terribly rude if we left? I need to get Bayard back to town. My parents will be home soon."

Fleur nodded. "*Oui,* madamoiselle. You must go tell them."

Simone stood before the young woman and said, "Please, let us do something for you. There must be something you need."

Fleur seemed surprised. "Why, no. We have all we need, Miss d'Or."

Simone did not know how to answer. She was accustomed to being the one who gave things to people. There had been very few things she could not have simply by asking for them, but this young woman — poorly dressed, living in a small cabin with no luxuries — was complete and self-assured. It disturbed Simone, and she shook her head. "I can but thank you now, but we'll find some way to show our gratitude."

She turned and walked to the door and stopped. She turned to see that Bayard had gone to stand before Fleur. "How do people say good-bye, Fleur?"

"Why, they shake hands," Fleur said, smiling, "and they say 'Good-bye.'"

"Is that all?" Bayard smiled and put his hand out, and when she extended hers, he took it and held it. "Good-bye, then."

"Good-bye, Monsieur d'Or."

He said, "Is that all there is to it? It doesn't seem like enough."

Suddenly Fleur seemed shy. She was unaccustomed to such interactions. "You're holding my hand, Bayard."

"Am I? Well, I'd like to do more than that." He covered her hand with his left one and said, "I will be seeing you again, now that I know the way."

"No, you will not come back here."

"You're mistaken. I'll be coming to check on you and on your mother. But for now, good-bye."

They left the cabin, and Fleur followed them outside. Despain was sitting on a chopping block, whittling. He closed his knife, got up, and asked, "Are you ready?"

"We're ready. Will that boat hold all three of us?"

"What you think, I make a bad boat, me? You get in front, and Monsieur, you get in the middle, and I'll pole us out of here."

The three got in the boat, and although it moved more slowly and was sunk almost to the level of the gunnel, it moved easily through the dark waters. Bayard looked back, and as he did it he said quietly, "I owe her my life, Simone."

"Yes, you do. And they say you owe God your life."

"I think they are right."

They made a slow passage with the heavy load, but finally they landed at Despain's small cabin. When they were all out and Despain had pulled the pirogue up on the bank, Simone reached into her reticule and drew forth some bills. She took several of them and handed them to the small man, who stared at them in surprise.

"Why, this is too much!"

"No, it's worth every penny, and we thank you so much."

"I'll be coming back when I get on my feet," Bayard said. "Can you take me back?"

"Certainement!"

Robert called out, "Good to see you, Mr. Bayard!"

"Good to see you, Robert. As a matter of fact, it's good to see anyone." He stepped slowly into the carriage and slumped into the seat. Simone got in, sat across from him, and closed the door. She saw that Bayard was still not himself. His face was pale, and he was trembling.

"Shall I go home, Miss?" Robert called.

Simone suddenly remembered that Bayard no longer lived at the house, but the altercation with her father seemed to have happened a long time ago. "Will you go home with me, Bayard?"

Bayard nodded. "Yes. Take me home, sister. I have a great deal of fence-mending to do. I don't know what I'll say to Father."

Simone took Bayard's hand in both of hers. "Tell him what happened, and tell him that you are a new man. That's what Fleur and her mother said, isn't it?"

"Yes, it is." Bayard squeezed Simone's hand and nodded. "I can do that because it's the truth."

CHAPTER FIFTEEN

As soon as Louis heard the door open, he leaped up and ran out of the parlor. He was closely followed by Renee, and when the two of them saw Bayard, they rushed to him, crying out his name.

Bayard was nearly knocked off balance when his parents grabbed him. Something about the way his father and mother clung to him struck him hard, almost as hard as the snake itself! His mother was weeping, and Bayard could see tears in his father's eyes.

"We've almost been out of our minds, Bayard," Louis whispered hoarsely.

"Yes, we thought the most dreadful things, son."

"All of you come into the parlor. Bayard needs to sit down," Simone said. She noted that neither of her parents let go of Bayard but held him as they moved out of the foyer, down the hall, and into the parlor. They sat down on the sofa, and Simone stood back, watching them. Something about the scene made her want to weep herself. She did not speak as she watched her parents, their arms around Bayard as though he would rise and flee away from them.

"What happened, son?" Renee whispered. "Tell us everything."

Bayard took a deep breath and then began at the very beginning, not sparing himself. He spoke about how he had awakened after a night of carousing and left his boarding-house, then told how he had, in order to raise money, gone to the swamp to paint. His relating how the snake had struck him caused Renee's face to go pale, and his father shook his head in disbelief. "It's a miracle you're alive, son."

"That's what Fleur and Gabrielle both said," Bayard answered.

"Who are they? How did they find you?" Louis asked.

Simone listened to the story, and she saw her parents drinking it in. When Bayard told about calling on God just before he passed out, she saw her mother's face grow radiant. Renee and Louis shared a faith in God, and it had been a grievance to them that their children practiced no faith at all.

"And so that's the way it was. I want you

251

to meet them," he said, "both of them. Gabrielle, unfortunately, is dying."

"Dying!" Louis said. "Surely not."

"I'm afraid she's very ill. Both of them are convinced that God has told them He will call her out of this world very soon."

"The poor child!" Renee exclaimed. "She will be left all alone."

"We'll have to do something to help," Simone said. "They're such wonderful people. So different from anyone I've ever met."

"They are wonderful," Bayard agreed quietly. "We will have to find a way to help them." He took his parents' hands and said, "I'll find a way to say this better later on, but right now I want to tell you both: just before I passed out I realized what a rotten life I've led, and I thought of you two. I've been a terrible son." He paused and bowed his head for a moment, then lifted it and looked at his mother. "Mother, I hope you believe me when I say I'm going to be a different kind of man."

"Of course I believe you, son!"

Looking at his father, Bayard swallowed hard. "You did exactly right in putting me out of the house. It took all this to wake me up. But if you'll give me a chance, Father, I hope to show you something in my life —

something more than just talk."

Louis d'Or was overcome. He put his arm around his son's shoulder and squeezed him. "Of course," he said quietly. "We'll see great things."

"And now you must go to bed," Simone said. The three stood up. Simone stood on tiptoe to kiss Bayard's face. "I believe what Fleur and Gabrielle said. God's given you back to us, and now we'll see a different man."

They all climbed the stairs, and Bayard went into his room and closed the door. Simone said, "He's going to be all right." She felt the tears in her eyes and suddenly threw her arms around her mother. "He's going to be all right, Mother. I *know* he is."

"Yes, he is. I believe it," Louis said. He patted her shoulder and said, "I guess we'd all better try to get some sleep."

Simone went to her room and made ready for bed, but even after she lay down, she could not sleep. What had transpired had shaken her more than anything else ever had. As she lay in the darkness under the mosquito netting, she began to think of her own life. Somehow it was a rebuke to her.

All this time Bayard has been drinking and running with a low crowd, but I've been no better. I haven't paid any more attention to

God than Bayard did. I may have looked bet-
ter to the world, but I'm not.

On impulse she swung her feet over the bed and walked over to the bookshelf. She found the Bible there that she had rarely read and sat down beside the lamp. She thumbed through the New Testament for a time. She looked for something, and finally her eyes fell on a passage in the seventh chapter of Luke's Gospel. She read it aloud: "And, behold, a woman in the city, which was a sinner, when she knew that Jesus sat at meat in the Pharisee's house, brought an alabaster box of ointment, and stood at his feet behind him weeping, and began to wash his feet with tears, and did wipe them with the hairs of her head, and kissed his feet, and anointed them with the ointment."

Suddenly the words struck Simone with power and force. She seemed to see the fallen woman as she wept and knelt and wiped the tears that fell on the feet of Jesus. It was so vivid that she sat stock-still, closing her eyes, and thinking of what it all implied. Simone was a woman of great emotional potential, but she rarely wept, and never had anything from the Bible touched her like this. She bowed her head and tears came to her eyes. They ran down her cheeks, and she wiped them away with her hands. "That poor woman!" she whispered. "How she loved Jesus!"

She began to pray, "Lord, I am worse than that woman. I have been proud and arrogant, and I have been unfeeling and thoughtless. I would love, if I could, to do what she has done: embrace Your feet and wet them with my tears and then wipe them with my hair. Since I cannot do that, I want, dear Lord, to be like her. I want to be humble in spirit. I want my heart to be soft and receptive. Take away this stony heart of mine, and give me a heart of flesh."

Finally she stopped praying and just sat, her face in her hands. After a long time she went back to bed. She lay down and closed her eyes. A strange sense of peace enveloped her. She didn't understand it, but she knew it was of God. She remembered suddenly the peace that was in the eyes of the dying woman, Gabrielle Avenall. She had not been able to understand how a woman facing death could be so calm and so filled with contentment and even joy. But she felt now, in the silent darkness, that she had touched on the secret of God. "It's all in giving up what we are and letting Him do what He wants," she whispered, and then she drifted off to sleep.

As Bayard worked in his studio, he thought about how strange the past week had been. He had regained his strength almost completely, although he still had some numbness in his arm. It might always be there, the doctor had said. But aside from that, everything else was different. He got up each day and read the Scripture and then had breakfast. There was a change in his family that they could all sense.

As he stood painting, he heard the door open and turned to see his father.

"Can I come in, or am I disturbing you?"

"Certainly. Come on in, Father, and see what I'm doing."

Louis d'Or walked over and looked at the canvas. He gasped and said, "Why, Bayard, it's your mother!"

"I thought for a while," Bayard said, "of doing one of the two of you together. Maybe I will, but I wanted one of her and then one of you and then one of Simone."

"I can't believe it. It's her to the letter!" He stood admiring the painting, a glow on his face. He shook his head. "I said some pretty hard things about your career as a painter. I take them all back now. If you can do this, you can do *anything!*"

Bayard laughed and shook his head. "It's not really that good, Father."

"Certainly it is!"

"Well, it is for you, but the real aficionados would see a lot of faults in it. I have a long way to go, but I'm going to make you proud of me."

"I'm already proud of you, son. This week has been wonderful for our family."

"It's been that way for me."

"Let me ask you: have you felt any temptation to go out and do the things you used to do?"

"Oh, once or twice it's come to me, but I wouldn't go back to what I was for anything in the world."

"That's good to hear, son."

"I have been thinking about the Avenalls, though."

"So have I," Louis said. "We have to do something for them."

"Well, I suppose they could use some financial help, but that doesn't seem to be a problem with them. What I need to do is go back and spend some time with them. Maybe take them a gift — not money."

"Why don't you do a painting for them?"

"Why, that's a great idea! Why didn't I think of it?"

"Paint a picture of that girl. From all you've said, I'd like to see her. I may make a trip in that little boat, but I don't think your mother is up to that."

"Perhaps we can get her to come in. No, I don't suppose so. She can't leave her mother. But I will do the painting if she will pose for me."

Louis d'Or smiled. "I have an idea that she will. Anyway," he said, "we're all going out tonight."

"Going out to eat?"

"Yes. We're going to the opera afterward."

"I hear it's taken New Orleans by storm. The most successful opera they ever had."

"So I'm told. Simone has already been to see it three or four times. She's fascinated by it, so she persuaded your mother and me to go, and we want you to go along."

"All right. We'll see what all the fuss is about."

The opera was everything Simone had told her parents it would be. Louis d'Or was not a fan of that style of music, but he was enthralled. He leaned over once and said, "It helps to know the story. He's followed Shakespeare pretty closely. I can't understand a word of what they say, but I know what's happening."

"Yes, it is wonderful," Renee whispered. "I never heard such a voice as Mr. Seymour has — or should I call him Lord Beaufort?"

"I don't think he takes a great deal of pleasure in his title," Simone said.

"That's strange," Bayard said. "Most men would."

The four of them spoke no more, but after the final curtain and many curtain calls, they made their way backstage. Admirers surrounded Colin, but when he saw them, he excused himself and came over. "It's good to see you, Miss d'Or," he said.

"My parents and my brother had to come. I've told them so much about it." She introduced them, and Louis said, "Indeed, I am not knowledgeable in music, but I was strongly moved by this opera."

"The credit goes to my father. He's the one who created it."

"But it takes you and the others to make it come to life," Simone said, smiling, "and it always does."

"I insist that you have dinner with us. You don't perform on Sunday, do you?"

"No, we do not."

"Sunday night then. Will you come?"

Colin hesitated, but Bayard urged warmly, "It would be a great pleasure to all of us, sir. I remember what you did for me, and I hope you will come."

"Then I will. I will see you Sunday night."

Colin arrived early at the d'Or house, and
Simone greeted him and took him at once
away from her parents. "You've got to see
Bayard's work. Come along." Bayard followed the pair up to the third floor to his
study, and Simone stood back as the two
men looked at the paintings. She could tell
that Colin was impressed. Indeed, he said
so most enthusiastically.

"Why, these are very fine, Bayard," he
said. "I had no idea that you had such talent."

"Well, I'm really a beginner, and I've
wasted a lot of years," Bayard shrugged.
"You've heard about what happened to me."

"Only the outline of it. I want to hear the
rest."

"It's a wonderful story, my lord," Simone
said with evident pride in her younger
brother.

"Please don't call me that. Colin is fine."

"All right then. Colin," Simone said, "I
think you would like the young woman who
saved Bayard's life. She and her mother are
extraordinary people."

"Is that so?"

"Yes, fervent Christians, both of them. I've

never seen two people closer to God," Bayard said.

Colin's thoughts immediately returned to his promise to the marquis. He felt a tugging at his soul that he could not ignore.

The three stood talking until Agnes appeared and said, "Please, it's time for dinner."

"We'll be right there, Agnes."

Simone led the way out, and the two men followed. When they entered the dining room, Colin said, "I'm sorry you had to call us, but it was interesting to see the work your son is doing."

"Isn't he talented?" Renee smiled.

"You have to forgive Mother. She gets overenthusiastic about my humble abilities."

"I'm not sure that's true, Bayard," Colin said with a smile.

"Well, come sit down. I'm starved. And you can tell us about your opera. I know very little."

The evening was a tremendous success. Colin, after much prompting, talked a great deal about the music and the opera — not just the one he was performing in, but others. All of them were impressed at how much work went into the production.

"Why don't they translate it into English, Colin?" Louis asked. "It would make it easier to understand."

"Well, they do translate some, but the translations are almost always bad."

"Why is that?" Simone asked.

"Well, you see, it's very difficult to translate a thought from one language to another, especially if the language doesn't have a word for the thought you want to express. And in opera, every syllable is matched with a musical note. What might take twenty syllables in one language might take forty in another, and that would upset all of the music."

They went to the parlor, where Colin played the piano and sang several songs. They all felt the power of his voice. Finally Louis and his wife stood to retire. He said, "I haven't expressed my thanks to you, Colin, for what you did for my daughter and son."

"Why, it was nothing."

"That's not so," Simone said at once. And Bayard chimed in, "It certainly wasn't. I was in bad shape, and I'll never forget it."

"None of us ever will, Colin," Renee said. She put her hand out. He took it, and she squeezed his with both of hers. "Thank you so much for what you've done for our family."

Bayard said, "I'm turning in. Good night, Colin."

After they had left, Colin was left alone with Simone, and both of them felt some constraint. "I must be going," he said.

"I thank you for coming. It meant a great deal to Bayard and to my parents and to me."

"It was my pleasure." Colin looked at her. He had borne a resentment for the woman for so long, but now as he looked at her, he felt as a man feels who looks on beauty and knows that it will never be for him. He saw that quick breathing disturbed her breast, and color ran freshly across her cheeks. "Is something wrong?" he asked.

"I've been trying to think of some way to say something to you, and I've been afraid."

"Why, there's no need of that, Simone."

"All right. I'll say it then." She took a deep breath and said quietly, "I treated you abominably and — and Armand even worse! I'm so ashamed, Colin, of the way I acted!"

It was the sort of statement that Colin never thought he would hear from Simone d'Or. He knew her temperament could swing to extremes of laughter and softness and anger, and he knew there was a tremendous capacity for emotion in her. He had not thought that she would be able to overcome her pride and admit what she had done.

"I must confess I had uncharitable thoughts toward you, Simone."

"I should not blame you."

As he looked into her eyes, Colin saw something he had never seen before. An emotion strongly worked in her and left its fugitive expression on her face. He saw it in her eyes and on her lips, and then something happened that he could never explain to himself or to anyone else. All of the anger and bitterness he felt for the woman left, and he was aware only of a vulnerability he had never dreamed of. He saw grief in her eyes and knew that her words were not empty, and with this knowledge came something entirely different. A vague, restless desire that had been in him suddenly stirred, and he knew what it was to long for her in a way that shocked him.

She held his glance, and he studied her beauty. She was near enough to be touched, and he wanted to touch her, for her nearness sharpened a long-felt hunger. She had a woman's fire and spirit, and he saw a sweetness in her that had not been destroyed, and somehow it gave her a faint fragrance and a powerful desirability.

Recklessness came over him, and knowing

he was doing the wrong thing, he reached out and pulled her to him. To his surprise, she did not pull away. He lowered his head and kissed her, and her lips were soft beneath his own, and he felt a rush of inexpressive things. *This is not right,* he thought. He was still waiting for her to pull away, but she did not, and when she put her arms around his neck and pulled him closer, a shock ran through him.

As for Simone, she had seen desire in his eyes, and when he had pulled her into his arms, she had gone to him, not knowing why. And then when he kissed her, she thought, *Something old and something new has come!* A wild sweetness was there and immense shock and the feeling of a deep need satisfied. She felt it pass between them, and somehow it took a loneliness out of her and incompleteness out of him.

She stepped back then, putting her hand on his chest, and faint color stained her cheeks. She couldn't believe what had happened, and yet her glance was half-possessive. For a moment they stood like that, something whirling rashly between them and swaying both of them in its violent compulsions.

"I shouldn't have done that, Simone."

She smiled. "I can't believe it happened."

Colin stood, his eyes fixed on her, and then he turned his head slightly to one side. "I'd better go now."

"Will I see you again?"

Colin stared at her. "Yes," he said quietly. "You'll see me again. Good night." He turned and left the room. She stood still until the door closed, then raised her hands to her cheeks. "Why did I let him do that?" she whispered. But she knew that she would do it again, and the thought both troubled and thrilled her.

CHAPTER SIXTEEN

Rosa Calabria stood in the wings, watching as the company performed the opera that had come to mean so much to her. She had been in poor condition and facing a bleak future when almost, out of nowhere, Colin Seymour had appeared and offered her work. Now as she watched him singing, her heart grew warm, and she turned to Marie Devois, who stood beside her, awaiting her entrance.

"I've never heard a more beautiful voice, Marie."

"No, I haven't either." Marie turned. She was wearing the simple dress for her role of Juliet, and there was a beauty about her that could not be denied. "If ever a man had everything, Colin's the one."

The two women listened as Colin's voice rose and filled the opera house with power, volume, and sweetness. Marie tilted her head to one side, and a smile turned the

267

corners of her lips upward. "The way the women chase Colin is a shame, but I can't complain, because I'm doing the same."

"Why, it's your role in the opera, Marie."

"That's only part of it." Marie laughed and ran her hand over her hair. She turned to face Rosa and said with a sudden intensity, "I'm going to have him, Rosa."

"What do you mean?" Rosa asked, although she had little doubt.

"I mean he's a man any woman would want, and I'm going to get him. He likes me a great deal already."

"That's a different thing from what you're talking about, Marie."

"Oh, come on. You've been around for a long time. You know what it's like with a man and a woman. You've had lovers enough."

"Don't remind me of it," Rosa said, shaking her head with an air of sorrow. "I wish I could go back and erase some of the things I've done in my life."

"You can't live in the past. I'm not going to. This chance has come my way. I'm going up in the world with the help that Colin can give. He'll be going to New York after this is over, I expect, and then Europe. I want to go with him, and I want to be more to him than just the singer in the operas."

The aria that Colin was singing was winding down, and Marie smoothed her dress and prepared to make her entrance.

"Why don't you leave him alone?" Rosa said.

"Why would you say that? He needs a woman. Every man does."

"He needs more than just a woman. He needs someone who loves him."

"I can make him love me. I want him, and that's enough."

With those words Marie moved out of the wings with confidence. Rosa watched sadly. "She wants him — and she'll probably get him too. Men are such fools!"

After the usual visitors had left from backstage, Marie dressed quickly in street clothes. She stepped out of her dressing room and waited until Colin left his. She said to him, "Well, it was a good performance tonight."

Colin smiled at her and nodded. "It was, wasn't it? You did exceptionally well with the aria."

"Why, thank you, sir. Kind words, indeed, from the master. You know, I'm starving tonight. Let's go get something to eat."

"That sounds good. Any special place in mind?"

"Most places are closed, but Luigi's will be open. Let's go get spaghetti, and they have the best wine there."

The two left the theater and walked to Luigi's, which was only three blocks away. Luigi Pastrimi greeted them fulsomely. "Come in — come in, the stars of the great opera. An honor to have you in my place."

"We're late, Luigi," Colin smiled. "Could you scrape up something for us?"

"For you, only the best. Come, I have a table over here. It will be very nice."

The two followed the short, chunky Italian to the table. He seated them and took their order personally. He scurried off, and Marie said, "You must feel very good about the way the opera is going. A full house every night, with no end in sight."

Colin put his hands flat on the table and studied them before he answered. He was tired. Singing for hours at a time was as depleting as digging a trench. "I am happy," he said, "but mostly for Armand."

"You miss him a great deal, don't you?"

"Yes, I do. I think of him every day."

Marie covered his hand with hers. "That's very sweet. I know he would have been very proud of you."

"I hope so. He did more for me than anyone in this world ever has."

Marie squeezed his hand. "You've brought honor to his name." She leaned back as Luigi brought a bottle of wine and poured for them.

"You'll like this wine. It is the very best, my lord."

"You know I'm not a wine drinker."

"Oh, come on," Marie smiled. "You'll hurt Luigi's feelings." She lifted the glass and held it out. He picked up his own and clinked her glass with it. She said, "A toast to the best tenor in the world."

Colin laughed. "I can't drink to that, but I'm glad you think so." He merely sipped the wine and put it down. He listened while Marie did most of the talking. She was excited, he could tell from the way her eyes danced and the way she moved her hands in eloquent gestures. He had been rather proud of his choice, for she had blossomed as the opera had progressed.

Finally he said, "You know, Marie, you're one of those singers who just gets better all the time."

Marie looked down, then back at Colin. "Thank you, Colin. You don't know how much your approval means to me."

"Well, you certainly have it."

When the meal came, they ate hungrily and lingered over it until finally Colin said,

"It's getting late. We have a rehearsal tomorrow at ten. I'd better get you home."

The two rose, Colin paid the bill, and they left the restaurant. In the carriage, all the way to Marie's apartment, Colin seemed to be deep in thought. She finally asked, "What are you thinking about?"

"Thinking about? Oh, I don't know, Marie. I'm just tired, I suppose."

"You're working too hard. You need something to relax you."

He laughed. "I'll relax when I get too old to sing."

"I don't think that will ever happen."

The carriage stopped before Marie's hotel. She had taken a much nicer place than the one she occupied when she first started the opera, for she was well paid. She turned to Colin and said, "Come up with me."

Colin was taken off guard. "It's very late, Marie."

Marie put her hand on his arm. "I'm lonely tonight," she whispered. "Please come, Colin."

The invitation in Marie's eyes was clear. Colin had seen a great deal of such flirtation since his success. Women sought him out, but he had kept his distance, using his work as an excuse. But as he sat in the carriage, he was aware of Marie as a woman and not as a singer. She had a challenge in her eyes, making her a more complex and unfathomable woman than the one to whom he was accustomed. Indeed, she was beautiful and robust, with a woman's spirit and fire. There was no curtain of reserve in her eyes so that her invitation struck him hard. He was a man with all of the hungers and desires of a healthy man in the prime of life, and at that instant he felt vulnerable. The urge to go with her and to take what she was offering became stronger, and he struggled against it. There was the impulse to satisfy the rich, racy current of vitality within this woman, and he knew that he could not conceal this from her.

She leaned forward and put her hand on his cheek. All the curves of her healthy, supple body were plain to him, and the desire in her eyes stirred him. Her lips, very red, broke into a quick smile, and she whispered, "I like you very much, Colin, and I have the feeling that you like me too."

"I do like you, but —"

"What's wrong? Why don't you take what you can find in this life? It's short enough." She leaned in farther and kissed him. At that instant he was aware only of the warmth of her lips, the fragrance of her perfume, and the softness of her form as she lay against him.

"Come with me," she whispered.

With almost a physical surge of strength, Colin shook his head. He again felt that tug in his soul. "It wouldn't be good, Marie. I'm not in love with you, nor you with me."

"That can come," she said. But she saw that his shoulders stiffened and knew that she had lost. "Don't think less of me, Colin. I'm just lonely."

"I don't think less of you, Marie. We're both tired and worn out. You go get a good night's sleep. I'll see you at rehearsal in the morning."

"Yes. Good night," she said.

Colin watched as she descended from the cab and walked toward the door. He knew that most men would have taken what she offered, but something held him back. He felt like a fool and struggled with his faith in God and his human aspirations and desires. Finally he snapped, "All right, driver, you can go now." Settling back in the seat, he felt the strain of the moment that she had brought about, and suddenly he knew that he had escaped somehow from something that he did not fully understand. Taking a deep breath, he whispered, "A close call, Colin, old boy. You'd better be careful. There may be more of them."

Colin had stepped offstage, leaving the second tenor who played Mercutio to sing the solo that always brought large applause. He stood beside Rosa Calabria. "He brings the house down with that every night."

"He's good. Not as good as you, of course."

"You always make me feel appreciated, Rosa."

As Colin listened to the tenor with pleasure, he felt a touch on his arm and turned to find Rosa looking at him with concern in her face. "What is it, Rosa? Something wrong?"

"Not with me, but I have to tell you something, Colin. You've been such a good friend to me, so kind, and I'm worried."

"About what?"

"About you."

"Why, there's nothing wrong with me."

"You'll probably hate me when I tell you this and think I'm just a jealous woman, but be careful of Marie."

Colin nodded and said almost grimly, "I know."

"You do?"

"Yes, but thanks for being concerned."

"Men can be very weak where women are

concerned. I wouldn't want anything bad to happen to you, Colin. You're too good a man to be ruined by a woman."

"Marie's all right."

"She's hungry for success. She'll do anything to get it. You'd be her ticket."

"Do you dislike her so much?"

"No, not at all. I was just like her. That's the reason I know what she's got on her mind."

"I think I've already found that out, but I haven't been a fool, and I won't be. Not with her. Probably in many other ways. There's my cue."

The second tenor finished his solo, and Colin reentered the stage. It was the scene where he and Mercutio talked about love, and as he spoke, Colin glanced at the audience and saw Simone sitting in the third row. Instantly everything else seemed to fade out. By the look on her face, he knew she was remembering how he had kissed her. He himself had been thinking of the embrace and knew that it would stay with him a long time.

Finally the curtain closed, there were the usual curtain calls, and afterward the visitors went backstage. To Colin it seemed that at times, handling the visitors diplomatically, always with a smile, and thanking them for coming, was more taxing than performing the opera. He was glad to see Bayard and Simone together, and when they complimented him, he took it as gracefully as he could.

"I suppose you get tired of people telling you how wonderful you are," Bayard smiled.

"Oh no, that's always good to hear, but I don't ever know what to say."

"What do you mean?" Bayard, looking puzzled.

"Well, I mean someone says you have a beautiful voice. What do you say, Bayard? Do you say 'Oh yes, I do'?" He saw them smile at this and shrugged. "Or do you say, 'Oh no, I don't,' in which case you sound like you're asking for more praise?"

"What do you say?" Simone asked.

"I say, 'Thank you.' "

"Probably best," Bayard said, nodding. "Look, old man, we're going out to eat, Simone and I. If you don't have another engagement, perhaps you'd go with us."

Simone saw that Colin hesitated, and she wondered what it meant. *Perhaps I've scared him off,* she thought. *Half the women in New Orleans are after him, and the way I kissed him, I suppose he thinks I'm another of them.* Her cheeks reddened at the thought as she saw he was watching her. "You're probably busy. I know you get many invitations," she said.

"No, as a matter of fact, I have no engagements. Let me change, and we'll go out someplace."

The restaurant that they finally found open was a small place, full of the rich scents of meat sauce, crab boil, sautéed shrimp, cheese, and salami. The fried oysters and sliced tomatoes and onions they ordered as a first course were delicious. Simone had deep-fried, soft-shelled crab and shrimp salad with a small bowl of *étouffee.* The men ordered shrimp gumbo and oysters on the half shell. Accompanying the meal were rolls, sausages, and cheese. All were liberally dosed with sauce piquant. During the meal Simone relaxed, and the men got along famously. Bayard was an entertaining speaker and kept them both laughing with stories of the year he had spent in Paris studying painting.

They were only halfway through the meal when Bayard glanced up to see a party entering the restaurant. He straightened in his chair when Leon Manville, from Claude Vernay's circle, came in with three friends Bayard knew slightly. Simone saw Leon at the same time.

"Who is that?" Colin inquired.

"Oh, just a fellow that used to be a friend of mine, of sorts."

Colin picked up on the distaste in Bayard's voice and studied the man carefully. He remembered seeing him then. He had been with Claude Vernay at the duel in which Armand had been shot. His eyes narrowed, and at that instant the anger and bitterness that he had managed to put away for a while came back. "I remember him," he said.

"I hope he doesn't come over here. I never liked the fellow," Bayard said quietly.

But he was disappointed, for Manville approached the party and said, "Well, hello, Bayard. How are you, Simone?"

"Hello, Leon," Bayard said rather shortly. "How have you been?"

"Fine as silk. Aren't you going to introduce me to your friend?"

Colin looked up at the man. He was tall and muscular with dark brown hair that fell across his forehead. He had strange, hazel-colored eyes, and there was no warmth in them.

"This is Lord Beaufort. My lord, this is Leon Manville."

"I remember him," Colin said coldly.

"I remember you too. There wasn't any

'lord' about it the last time I saw you. You're the singer, aren't you?"

"Among other things," Colin said.

Simone felt the tension and said, "Excuse us, will you, Leon?"

Manville looked irritated. "You're getting too good to speak to your old friends?"

"I'll have to ask you to leave, Leon," Bayard said quietly, standing as he spoke.

Leon Manville glared at Bayard, then turned his attention back to Simone. "You always were a proud one. I don't see anything to be that proud of."

"Do I have to ask the manager to speak to you?"

"Why don't you speak to me yourself, Bayard? We've been drunk together enough. You remember that woman we fought over in Algiers at Mamie's Place?"

"I don't want to discuss that."

"I'll bet you don't. I haven't seen you lately. Have you gotten too holy to speak to your old friends?" Manville's voice had grown louder, and his companions looked uncomfortable. Simone said, "Please, Leon, go to your table. We don't want any trouble."

Manville leered. "You'd give a man trouble, Simone. I always thought there was something under that manner of yours. You're no different from any other woman.

All you need is a strong man to bring it out of you. Maybe me."

Colin saw the color rise in Simone's cheeks. He jumped to his feet and said, "That will be enough. Leave us alone now."

"And what'll you do if I don't? You opera singers are a bunch of ladies, from what I hear." Manville stepped behind Simone and put his hand on her shoulder. He squeezed it, and she tried to move away, but he gripped her too firmly. "Why don't you come with me, Simone? I'll show you a better time than these two."

Bayard shouted, "Take your hands off her, Leon!" He moved forward, but Leon, a strong, powerful man despite a beer belly, struck him in the chest. The blow drove Bayard backwards, and at that instant Colin stepped forward.

Colin saw triumph in Manville's eyes and knew that this was what the scene was all about. It was directed at him, not at Simone or Bayard. "Turn her loose," he said, but instead of doing that, Manville swung his hand to slap Colin in the face. Colin moved out of the path of the blow and grabbed Manville's wrist. He gave it a twist that brought a sudden cry of pain. Colin kept the pressure on and swung Leon around, and when he was standing free of Simone, he released the wrist and stepped between Manville and Simone and Bayard. "I said, that will be enough."

But Manville surged forward, anger flickering in his hazel eyes. He raised his hand to strike, but Colin was much faster. He drove a blow straight into Manville's face, right in the mouth. The force of it nearly forced Manville off his feet. Blood seeped out of his lips, and he reached up and touched it. "You all saw it," he said loudly. "He hit me! You can get away with that in France, but not here. I'll have my second call on you."

Colin stared at him, his eyes cold. "I have delegated all that sort of fighting to my dog, Manville."

Manville cursed. "You'll fight," he said. "You may be handy with your fist, but I'll have you with a sword or a pistol. You can take your pick."

"My choice is to throw you out of here if you don't leave now."

The blood was dripping off Manville's chin, and he wiped it with his hand. Hatred was like venom in his voice. "I'll drive you out of New Orleans, Seymour. You won't be able to leave your hotel room."

At that instant the manager appeared, saying, "I must ask you to leave, or I will send for the police."

"I'm leaving," Manville said. "My lord, you'll fight, or I'll give you no peace." He turned and left with his friends.

Bayard stood beside Colin. "It was my fight," he said. "It just happened so quickly I couldn't handle it. She's my sister."

"No, it's me they're after."

"But she's my sister."

"He's not doing this on his own, Bayard."

Suddenly Simone understood. She knew that Leon Manville was nothing but a crony of Claude Vernay's. As clearly as if it were written out, she knew that it was Vernay who had sent him. "Let's leave," she said.

Colin nodded. "I think it's time."

Simone felt afraid. She knew that Claude Vernay was a merciless man. She couldn't say anything, but she feared for Colin. The three paid their bill and left the restaurant.

The manager said to his chief waiter, "That is a bad thing. He means blood."

"But would he be permitted to fight a member of the nobility, a famous man like Lord Beaufort?"

"When a man wants blood," the manager said, "he will do whatever he has to to see it."

Simone heard two days later about the

persecution that Leon Manville was exacting on Colin. Bayard told her, "Manville's really out to make him fight. He was at the opera night before last. He shouted that Colin was a coward and made such a scene they had to throw him out."

"Couldn't the police do anything?"

"You know how they are about this dueling business. They see it as kind of a game." Bayard's voice was bitter. "Leon even went into the barbershop where Colin was getting his hair cut and cursed him. Colin held himself in, so I hear, but he can't forever. Something's got to be done. I just don't know what."

All of this disturbed Simone terribly. She knew that Leon Manville was a bully, and his reputation as a duelist was well known to everyone in New Orleans. Finally she sent for Claude, asking him to meet her at Jackson Square. She did not want to have him in her home.

When he arrived, he smiled and said, "Well, my stock must be going up in the world. You're speaking to me again."

Simone had made up her mind what to say. "Claude, you must stop this terrible thing you're doing to Colin."

"I'm not doing a thing to Colin. It's Leon."

"Leon never had a thought in his head that you didn't put there."

"I tell you I have nothing to do with it."

"Don't lie to me, Claude! I know you better than that."

Claude's face grew pale. "If you were a man, I would have you out for calling me a liar."

"I'm sure you would. That's what you do."

"You're falling for this singer, aren't you?"

"Don't be ridiculous. Claude, you're going to get into serious trouble if you fight this man. No matter how it turns out, you'll lose."

Claude Vernay seemed not to have heard. "You're in love with him," he said, "but I'll tell you this." He lowered his voice, and his lips twisted in a cruel expression. "He'll never have you. I promise you that."

Vernay turned and walked away, his back straight, and Simone knew that she had made a mistake even talking to him about the matter.

Chapter Seventeen

"We've got to do something, Bayard," Simone said. "Things can't go on like this."

Bayard looked up from his painting and saw the distress on Simone's face. For a time, she had sat silently watching him, but then she burst out with concern for their friend. He put his brush down. Fresh, pale sunlight streamed through the windows, illuminating the study, and from outside a mockingbird filled the air with music. It was Thursday, September the eighteenth, and a week had passed since the encounter with Manville in the cafe.

"I don't know exactly what we can do."

"I went to Claude. He's behind all this, you know."

"I wasn't sure you understood that."

"Of course I do. Leon didn't think up a thing like this. He had no quarrel with you or with Colin, but Claude hates him."

"It's because of you, isn't it? He wants

you to marry him, and you've refused him."

"I was never serious about Claude. Oh, well, maybe I was." Simone sighed. "I was younger and impressionable, and he was better in those days."

"He was always a cruel man. I knew it, and I was surprised you didn't see it. I should have said something." His face lit up with an idea. "Maybe I ought to call Leon out myself."

"No, you mustn't do that! Neither of you needs to fight Leon. That's what he wants. He's nothing but a butcher."

"That's about what it amounts to. You remember poor Fred Graham? He displeased Leon, and Leon insulted him. It wound up in a duel, and Leon cut poor Fred to pieces. He's an expert swordsman. Better than anyone except Claude."

"I'm going to go talk to Colin," Simone said.

"You can talk to him, but what can he do? Leon's following him around the streets. No man can take those insults without breaking."

"Anything would be better than getting maimed or killed," Simone said. "I've got to try."

"You can try, but Colin's a pretty stubborn fellow. I doubt if he'll listen to you."

■ ■ ■ ■

Simone found out that Bayard was right about Colin. She had called on him at his hotel, and he had come down to the lobby and taken her to the restaurant where they drank café au lait. Simone studied him carefully and saw little sign of strain on his face. He did not mention Leon, so finally she brought up the subject.

"I've heard about all the awful things that Leon is doing to you, Colin."

"He has become quite a pest." Colin lifted the small cup, sipped from it, and shrugged. "I can't put up with it much longer."

Simone felt a quick surge of fear. "You mustn't fight him, Colin. He's deadly with a sword. And it's beneath you."

Even though Colin had set out for revenge, his return to New Orleans had awakened his faith and had stirred uncharted, romantic feelings in him for the first time. Still, he could not ignore Leon's proddings any longer. "It's not my choice, Simone. I'd be glad to walk away from it, but it seems he won't permit that."

Simone said, "It's not Leon. It's Claude. He's the one who hates you."

"Because of you."

Simone was startled. She had not expected him to say — or to know — that. "He's been in love with me for a long time — at least as much as a man like him can be in love. I was flattered by his attentions when I was younger. He started coming around when I was only seventeen. He was handsome and rich, and so many of the younger men, like Bayard, admired him. He's an expert with a sword or pistol. That was exciting to me." Her lips twisted bitterly, and she said, "I should have known better."

"This dueling code is a bad thing. I think it got started somewhere in Europe, this code-of-honor business. I wish men had never heard of it," Colin said.

"So do I. They use the word 'honor' like the chorus of a song. They look for any excuse to cut someone down. And quarrels among the Creoles hardly ever end in fist-fights," Simone said. "There is some sort of unwritten law that absolutely forbids the striking of a blow, and anybody who forgets it is barred from the so-called privilege of the duello. These men feel as if they've been insulted if they are refused a meeting."

The two drank their coffee. Simone added, "I don't understand it, Colin. The least breach of etiquette, any sort of impolite-ness, even awkwardness can create a challenge, and nobody dares refuse."

"I understand that sometimes duels are fought between two young men who simply want to fight, with no problem at all between them."

"Bayard told me about one of those. He said there were six young Creoles who were promenading the streets one night. One of them said, 'Oh, what a beautiful night. What splendid level ground for a joust. Suppose we pair off and draw our swords and make this night memorable by spontaneous display of bravery and skill.' Isn't that foolish?"

"What happened, Simone?"

"Well, the idiots fought until two of their number lay dead in the field."

"It's all foolishness," he said, "but I'm going to have to do something about Manville."

"Oh, please, you mustn't fight him! It's not right. It will be like Armand."

Colin looked at her. "You still think about that?"

"Of course I do. The older I get, the more I think of what a fool I was. A brainless girl!"

"Actually, I don't think there was much you could have done. Armand was a strong-willed man, and he felt he had been insulted. He was caught up in this duello thing, the only irresponsible impulse I ever saw in him."

Simone felt miserable at the memory. "You think of it, too, don't you? You must have hated all of us after it happened."

Colin said quietly, "For years, I brooded over it. Armand, at the last when he was dying, begged me to forgive Claude, but I was never able to do it."

"You must have hated me also."

"Armand was the most important person in my life, the one who had been kind to me above all others, so I loathed everthing about New Orleans, especially Claude and the stupid duello code." He smiled. "But I find that I don't have that in my heart anymore. I don't want to fight anyone."

"I'm glad to hear that, and I'm glad you no longer feel hatred for me."

Colin reached over and took her free hand. "I see a difference in you, Simone. You're not the same as you were. You've always been beautiful, but now I see beauty on the inside."

Simone met his eyes and saw the honesty and truth there. "Then you won't fight him," she said.

"I think sooner or later I'll have to or leave town."

Simone wanted to plead with him, but she saw the firmness of his lips, the steadfastness of his eyes, and knew that it was useless. He removed his hand, and she said, "I'll pray for you, that it will never happen."

Colin did not answer. He knew that Leon Manville would never stop. He had made up his mind even before Simone's visit that it would have to come to a halt, and he had a plan. He knew that Simone was afraid that he would be cut down like Armand, but he knew that this would be different.

Colin did not have to wait long to put his plan into operation. The very next day Leon accosted him as he got out of the carriage to go into the opera house. Manville rushed forward, his face red, and shouted curses at him. "You coward! You filthy coward!" Manville raved. "Why don't you put on a skirt? You're nothing, you hear me? Nothing!"

Colin turned and faced Manville. He said, "I'm tired of your yapping, Manville."

"Then why don't you fight?"

"I think I will." Colin was aware that a crowd had gathered around the two. The quarrel was known throughout New Orleans, and he knew there were odds offered on whether or not he would fight. He smiled. Before Leon could move, he cracked him across the face, staggering the man. "There. That's what I think of you."

Leon stared at Colin, hatred blazing in his hazel eyes. "My man will call on you, sir. I'm looking forward to our engagement."

"I hope you'll enjoy yourself now, because you won't afterwards," Colin said.

Manville laughed, and two of the men who had accompanied him laughed also. "You hear the rooster crow, my fellows? Since I'm the challenged one, I have the choice of weapons. It will be pistols, and I guarantee it won't be a flesh wound. You'll have a hole right between your eyes."

Colin shrugged and said, "Have your man call. I'll be glad to see him."

Bayard entered the house with his shoulders drooping. Simone was passing through the foyer on the way to the study when she saw him. "What's wrong, Bayard?"

"It's Colin. He's accepted a challenge, and he's asked me to be his second."

"Oh no, that can't be!"

Bayard shook his head angrily. He ran his hands through his hair and said, "I've tried everything I can think of to stop him, but he won't. He says he can't live under those conditions any longer."

"He'll be killed," Simone whispered.

"That's what Manville will try for. You know, in many of these duels they just aim to draw a little blood, but Manville's serious about this. Claude's got him worked up, and he'll kill Colin if he can."

"Can't we do anything?"

"I've tried to think of something, but I can't find a solution."

"Why can't we call the authorities? Dueling is against the law."

Bayard laughed bitterly. "You know how much attention the police pay to this. Why, they're making bets along with everybody else. They always manage to get there after the duel is over."

Simone said nothing. In her heart she was crying out, *Oh, Colin, don't do it. Don't let yourself be destroyed.*

The duel was set for seven o'clock in the morning on a Saturday. The first frost had already touched the city, but as Colin traveled to the spot selected for the duel, he noticed that the sky was absolutely blue and cloudless, without an imperfection in it. Robins had filled the trees along the bayous, and camellias that appeared fashioned from crepe paper still bloomed with all the colors of summer even though winter was on its way.

The air was cool as he approached the spot that smelled of wet trees and torn leaves blowing in the wind. Colin saw that a large crowd had gathered. The whole thing disgusted him, but he could see no way to solve the problem except by the means he had chosen.

Bayard approached him. His face was white and drawn. "There's still time to fix this thing, Colin."

"I don't think so." Colin looked across the field and saw that Claude Vernay was standing with Leon. "I see Vernay's here," he said.

"Yes, he's Leon's second."

"Well, let's get to it."

"We go over, and the two seconds are supposed to try to work out some sort of apology. It never happens, though."

The two walked over to Vernay and Manville. Bayard began to speak of the possibility of an apology, but Colin glared into the eyes of Claude Vernay. It was a handsome face, but there was no mercy there. The eyes were opaque. It was as if they were a flat surface with nothing behind them. Colin listened as Bayard spoke, but he knew that it was a waste of time.

"My man is ready," Vernay said flatly.

Bayard shook his head and turned to Colin. "I am ready also, sir." Bayard could hardly restrain himself. He said bitterly,

"Claude, I can't believe you were my friend once."

"I'm still your friend, Bayard."

"No, you're not." He would have said more, but Colin interrupted. "Let the thing proceed," he said.

"Good." Manville grinned ruthlessly. He was enjoying himself, anticipating an easy victory. "Will you examine the weapons?"

"I've seen to the loading," Bayard said.

Colin picked up the two pistols and seemed to be weighing them.

"Choose whichever you want," Manville said with a sneer. "I can kill you with either one of them."

Colin held a pistol in each hand. He casually stuck them in the band of his trousers.

"What are you doing?" Manville demanded.

"Just testing, if you don't mind, to be sure they're true." He reached into his pocket and drew out some coins. He selected two, held them up, and said, "These should do."

"Do for what? What is this nonsense?" Vernay asked angrily.

"Surely you don't mind if I test the accuracy of the weapons."

In Paris, Colin had often performed a trick. After years of steady practice, he had grown to be deadly accurate. He took the two coins and without another word flung them high into the air. The early morning sun caught the glittering coins. Colin leisurely pulled the two pistols, fired with his right hand then his left. The two coins disappeared, and a cry of admiration went out over the crowd.

"I think these will do. Tell me, Manville, would you prefer to be shot in your left eye or your right?"

Manville's face had grown still. He shot a quick glance at Claude Vernay and said hoarsely, "I've changed my mind. It'll be swords."

"That's fine with me," Colin said.

"I brought the blades just in case," Vernay said. He retrieved the weapons and presented them to the duelists. He told Colin, "Take your pick."

Colin took both swords, held them, and said, "You know, I'm one of those strange fellows. I'm ambidextrous."

"What does that mean?" Manville demanded.

"It means I can kill you with either hand, right or left, it makes no difference. When my right arm gets tired, I simply swap to my left. I have a great advantage, you see."

Vernay said, "You're a boaster, but Leon has never been beaten except by me."

"Let's just see how good he is," Colin said coolly.

Vernay said, "Step back, everyone." He himself backed up, and Manville took the sword, making a few passes with it that made swishing sounds in the air.

Colin took his position, his left foot forward, his right foot back, and extended his left hand out of the way. The world seemed to fade then, and he saw only the face and the blade of his adversary. It was another advantage he had. He had always been able to focus solely on the man who faced him with a foil. His teacher, François Morell, had often commented on what a blessing this was. "Men sometimes get confused and disconcerted by something other than their opponents. You never have that problem, my lord."

As he expected, Manville came forward thrusting and slashing. At once Colin saw that Manville depended on physical strength and intimidation. Coolly he thwarted the first blow and did not back up. Manville thrust his foil upward, and with a quick gesture, Colin moved his blade to match Manville's guard. He shoved with all the strength in his arm and Manville reeled backwards. He tripped and fell but scrambled to his feet. His eyes were wide with shock, and Colin said, "That was rather clumsy, Manville. Come, you can do better."

Colin waited as the man approached him again, this time more carefully. He was a good swordsman but nothing like the master from whom Colin had learned. The two circled each other, and Colin quite easily parried. He made no attempt to carry the fight to Manville. He kept his guard up, and knowing that the grass was wet and slippery, he moved carefully.

The clashing of the blades and the heavy breathing of Manville were the only sounds until Manville tried for a killing move. A cry rose from the crowd.

"I thought you were an expert swordsman," Colin said. "But I see you are just an amateur." His remark excited the rage of Manville, who tried even harder. The fight went on and on, and finally Colin saw that his opponent was growing weary. He said, "My arm's a little tired. I think I'll use my left." He switched to his left hand and began to put more pressure on Manville. He moved forward, feeling strong. He drove Manville back, and finally, when Manville ran toward him, he parried the blow, and his blade shot out and slashed Manville's tie. Part of the tie fell to the ground, and

Colin said, "You have to be more careful of your attire, sir. It wouldn't do for a great swordsman like you to be dressed in anything but the best."

The crowd laughed. For Colin the duel had become silly. Manville was exhausted, and Colin could have killed him at any time. He had no plan to do that, however. Then finally he saw his chance. Manville's right arm was trembling with fatigue, and he meekly held up his left to protect himself. Colin lunged forward. He felt the jar as the tip of his sword struck Manville's hand, penetrating it, and he twisted the blade as Manville screamed.

Withdrawing the blade with one smooth motion, Colin stepped back and lowered the tip. "I think this duel is over."

"My hand! You've ruined my hand!"

Manville had dropped his sword and was clutching his hand. Blood poured through his fingers.

The surgeon came forward at once and looked at the hand. "You've got some tendons sliced there. I don't think this hand's going to be much use for things like dueling," he said.

Colin turned to Claude, who was shocked into silence. "Why don't we finish this now, Vernay? I think everyone here knows you've been hiding behind your man."

"I don't know what you're talking about," Vernay said quickly.

"I'm not sure about all the rules, but perhaps this will give you a good reason for fighting." He reached forward and slapped Vernay lightly on the cheek. "That provocation enough for a challenge?"

Vernay glared at Colin. He was thinking how easily the man before him had shot the two coins out of the air and how he had toyed with Manville as if he were a child. "You're safe. You know I will not challenge you."

"I rather thought you wouldn't. Well, this is the end of it, as far as I'm concerned."

Claude Vernay wheeled and walked stiff-legged away from the crowd. Rage flowed through him. He knew that he had no chance with the man with a sword and very little chance with a pistol — Colin was simply more skilled than he, to his surprise. As he walked away, however, he already had begun to think. *He may beat Leon, but there is one he cannot beat.* He thought of Jean Paul Compier, who was known as the best swordsman in France. The two had been companions, and now the plan formed in his mind. *I will send for Jean Paul. He will take care of this popinjay! He will put a sword through his heart!*

CHAPTER EIGHTEEN

New Orleans had buzzed with talk about the duel between Colin, the famous star of the opera, and Leon Manville. Many had actually congratulated Colin, something that displeased him and to which he barely responded. The news had come out that Manville's hand had been badly mangled so that he lost partial use of it. No one had seemed particularly upset about that, for he was widely known as a bully, and he had no powerful friends.

Simone was tremendously relieved when the affair was over, and she had thrown herself into helping Bayard, who had scheduled his first show. He had worked hard and accumulated a good stock of paintings, and the show was well advertised throughout the city.

The day of the show, Simone traveled to Fanair Hall, which was often used for such things. The hall was a very old building but well preserved, and the reception area was adequate for such a show. Simone had hung decorations and arranged for refreshments, and she was delighted when the citizens of New Orleans filed in. Many of them came out of curiosity, she knew, but the d'Or family had many friends, and Simone was busy greeting and showing people around.

She worked all day, but the high moment of the show came for her when Colin arrived late that night, after the opera. She met him at once and said, "It's going so well, Colin. We've already sold six paintings. Isn't it marvelous?"

"Yes, it is. I must go congratulate Bayard, but he seems rather busy right now."

"I think this show proves that he has the talent to be a successful artist."

"I agree. Well, perhaps you'll show me around."

"Oh yes, of course. Come along."

Colin followed Simone as she showed him various paintings. He stopped before the one of her and said, "That's new, isn't it?"

"Yes. Colin decided to paint one of each member of the family."

"How much is it?"

"Oh, it's not for sale. I just wanted to put it up so they could see how well he's done."

"He's done very well indeed."

Simone protested, "I don't really look that good."

"I think you'll have to let others be the judge of that. As for me, I think you do." He turned to her and would have said more, but at that moment Bayard approached and greeted Colin warmly. "I'm so glad you came, Colin. Has Simone told you how well we're doing?"

"Yes, I'm very pleased, Bayard. I'd like to buy that one, but she tells me it's not for sale."

"Maybe I can convince her to pose again and paint one just for you."

"I'll commission you to do that. How much would you charge me?"

"Charge you! Don't be foolish! For you it will be a pleasure."

Colin was truly happy for Bayard. He knew a little bit about how far down in the world he had gone and now was pleased to see the glow of health in Bayard's cheeks and the pride in his eyes.

They stood talking until Bayard's parents came up. They greeted Colin, then Bayard said, "Now that I have a little money, there's something I must do."

"What is that, son?" Louis said. The success of the show had stunned and pleased him. Painting had always seemed a frivolous thing for a grown man's occupation, but he saw the leaders of the city, powerful men and women, who had come to the show and bought his son's work. This dissolved Louis's whole objection, and he gazed at Bayard fondly. "I suppose you're going to buy a fancy racehorse now."

"Not at all. I've thought a great deal," he said, "about Fleur and her mother. I haven't had any way to help them, but now I do."

"Are you going out to their place?" Simone asked.

"Yes. I'm going to take tomorrow off."

"Anything they need, I'll be glad to help with," Louis said quickly.

"Thank you, Father, but this is something I would like to use my own money for. I owe those two a great deal."

The rains had passed away, and as Bayard approached the cabin, he felt extraordinarily well. The light had washed the sky, and the wind had blown through the cane fields as he had ridden his stallion to the cabin. He had discovered that it was not necessary to go by boat. If one had a horse, there was a rather roundabout way. He had to stop twice to make inquiries, but the day was beautiful, and he was happy about his plan.

Mimosa trees stood in front of the house. He could smell the damp earth as he called, "Hello, the house!" and quickly dismounted. The door opened, and he smiled as Fleur stepped out. She was wearing the same outfit that he had seen her in the last time. He took off his hat and said, "Good morning, Fleur. I've come for a visit."

"I'm glad to see you, Bayard. Tie up your horse, and come in."

Bayard tied his stallion to a sapling and entered the cabin. She waved toward one of the chairs at the table. "Sit down. Perhaps you are hungry."

"No, but I could use some of that good, strong coffee that you make so well."

"I have some ready. I just browned the coffee beans yesterday and ground them. It will be ver' fresh."

Bayard had a strange feeling. He glanced over toward the bed and saw where he had lain for almost a week, totally out of the world. He shook his head. "I think about my time here so often."

Fleur said, "I think about it, too." She obtained two cups and said, "I have fresh milk."

"That's the best way to drink coffee," he said. She poured the cup half full with the black, thick coffee and then added milk.

307

Giving him a spoon, she sat down opposite him. "What have you been doing?" she asked. "How is your family?"

"I've been doing better than I ever have in my life," Bayard said. He leaned forward and began to describe the work that he had done, and with great excitement he told her of the show and how he had sold many paintings.

Fleur listened to him silently, and Bayard was puzzled. She had always been so filled with life, her eyes gleaming and dancing as she spoke. But she was very quiet now, until finally she said, "Oh, I'm happy your paintings are sold. Are you still walking with God?"

"Yes, I am, as best I know how. I owe that to you and your mother." He looked toward the door and said, "How is your mother, Fleur?"

Fleur looked down at her coffee cup, picked it up, and moved it around in a circle on the tabletop. When she looked up, her eyes were dark. "*Ma mere,* she go to be with God a week ago."

"Oh, Fleur, I wish I had known. I would have come."

"It was time for her," Fleur said simply. "The night before she die, we talked a long time. She seemed ver' well. She tell me things about herself I had never known, and then she kiss me, and then she blessed me. When I go to her the next morning, she had gone."

"I'm so sorry." Bayard reached across the table and took her hand.

"It is not to be sorry. She is with her Lord now."

"What will you do now?"

"I will stay here, I suppose."

"Fleur, that's not good. You need to be with people."

"I have friends. I do not see them ver' often, but they came to the funeral."

"You are cut off out here." A sudden impulse moved Bayard, and he said, "You must come and stay with my family for a while."

Fleur looked up, her eyes widening with surprise. "Stay with you, Bayard?"

"Yes. You are all alone here. There's nothing to think of but your loss. I want you to come."

"But I do not know your family, and they do not know me."

"They will love you as I do."

The words struck Fleur. She stared at him in surprise. "I do not know what to do. It is lonely here. *Ma mere,* we had each other, and now I have no one."

Suddenly Fleur got up and walked to the window and stared out. She had made no sound, but her shoulders were drawn tensely together. Bayard got up and walked over to her. He turned her around, and when she looked up at him, he said, "You have done so much for me, and my family's so grateful. I want you to come at least for a visit." He gave her no chance to object but smiled and said, "They will be very glad to see you. Now, you get your things together."

"Is it right for me to do this?"

"It's very right."

New life seemed to flow into Fleur's face. "Maybe the good Lord send you to bring comfort to my heart. I think I was ready to give *ma mere* up, but I am ver' lonely."

"It's not good to be alone."

Fleur smiled up at him. "That is what the Bible says. God say it to Adam. He say, 'It is not good for man to be alone,' and He made Eve for him."

"Well, I certainly agree with the Lord."

"I will have to stop and tell Lonnie to take care of the livestock."

"We can do that. Come, I'm anxious for you to meet my family."

■ ■ ■ ■

PART FOUR:
1838
FLEUR

■ ■ ■ ■

CHAPTER NINETEEN

All the way from Fleur's cabin into town, Bayard had talked steadily. Fleur rode her mare, and the two traveled at a fast clip. As they neared the city, Bayard saw that the girl was frightened.

Once in New Orleans, she looked around carefully at everything. "I have never see such a big place. How you ever find your way?"

"The same way you find your way in the bayou, I expect. By going over it and over it. Come. Our home isn't far from here."

When they arrived at the house, Fleur admired its size and said, "This is your house?"

"My family's house. The stable is in back. We'll have our driver take care of the animals."

They rode to the back, and Robert met them. "Robert, this is Miss Fleur Avenall. She's going to be staying with us. I want you to take good care of her mare. Grain her, and rub her down."

"Yes, sir. Good to see you, Miss Fleur."

"Your name is Robert? I am glad to know you."

"Come along. Simone will be so happy. She talks about you a lot."

Fleur grew tense when they entered the house. She looked around and saw the wallpaper with bright colors, the shining cypress floor, the light streaming through the high windows. "I've never been in a place like this."

"Fleur, you've come to visit!" Simone had come down the hall, and she hurried forward with a smile on her face. She put out her hand, and when they had shaken hands, she put her arm around Fleur and said, "What a delightful surprise!"

"I have some bad news, Simone," Bayard said quickly. "Fleur's mother passed away last week."

"Oh, I'm so sorry, Fleur. I wish you had gotten word to us so we could have come."

"I did not really think of it."

"But you're here now, I hope for a long visit."

"She certainly is — as long as we can persuade her. I want you to take her upstairs and let her have the green room. I'll have

Robert bring her things up."

"Of course. Come along, Fleur." Simone led the way up the stairs and down the hall. She opened the door and said, "This will be your room. I hope you'll like it. It's always been one of my favorites."

Fleur stepped inside and then stopped dead still. "I have never see such a room," she whispered. The room was wallpapered with green-and-gold flocked wallpaper all the way up to the high, white ceiling. The dark wooden floor was covered with a very large brown, green, and beige carpet with designs of flowers, leaves, and birds on it, and two tall windows were covered with dark green velvet curtains that were now pulled back to admit the day's light. The furniture was all quite large and made of mahogany, with the bed dominating the middle of the room with its tall posts and covered canopy. Many pictures decorated the walls, all in ornate gold frames, and a beautifully carved mirror hung over the washstand holding a fine porcelain basin and pitcher.

"I think is too fine for me."

"No, it's just right for you." Simone put her arm around the girl. "I'm so sorry about your mother, but I want you to stay with us for a long, long time. I've always wanted a sister, and now I have one."

When Fleur looked up, Simone saw tears in her eyes. "I am too ignorant. I would not know what to say to your family or your friends."

Simone said, "That's foolishness. Why, you know a lot more about many things than any of my friends."

"What could I know that a fine lady like you would not know?"

"Well, I don't know how to skin a coon or dress a 'gator."

Fleur smiled. It was not a full smile, but she no longer looked sad. "I will teach you how when you come and visit with me."

"That's a bargain."

The two talked until Robert brought her things up, and when Simone saw the pitiful clothing, only one faded dress, she said, "I know what we will do first thing. I need some new things, and we'll both go out and buy new dresses."

"But I have no money."

"Oh, that's not necessary. Papa is always generous. You are so pretty, and we'll fix you up fine."

Bayard saw during the evening meal that Fleur was overwhelmed by the world into which he had thrust her. His parents had welcomed her fulsomely, and Simone had made much of her. Still Fleur looked with panic, he saw, on the table that was set with china and a full set of tableware. *Why, she doesn't know which fork to use or even how to eat in a place like this,* he thought. *It must be terrible for her.*

The others saw the girl's embarrassment and tried to set her at ease, but Fleur ate very little and finally whispered in a voice barely audible, "I would like to go to my room, if you don't mind."

"Why, of course," Simone said. "You must be tired. Shall I go with you?"

"No, thank you. I can find it."

As soon as Fleur left, Simone said, "She's frightened by all of this."

"Well, she might be," Renee said. "From what you told me, she has absolutely nothing. Think how out of place we'd be if we were put in a cabin in the middle of a bayou."

"Well, she will learn," Louis said quickly. "She's a fine girl, and I can see that she's very intelligent."

"We must be careful of her feelings," Simone said. "I'll spend every moment I can with her. I'm going to take her shopping tomorrow, Father. She doesn't have a thing to wear. I must have some money."

"Buy her whatever she needs, my dear."

Bayard was troubled, for he had wanted things to be different. After everyone had gone to their rooms, he found he could not sleep. Finally he made up his mind: *I've got to do something!*

He went to the room assigned to Fleur and tapped on the door lightly. "Fleur, are you awake?"

There was a long silence, and then the door opened. Fleur had not dressed for bed. He realized she probably had nothing to wear. "Are you sleepy?" Bayard asked.

"No, I'm not."

"Come downstairs with me. I want to show you something."

"You mean now?"

"Yes, now. Come along." She stepped outside, giving him a strange look. He turned and walked down the stairs, and she accompanied him. "Let's just go outside." Once outdoors, he said, "Come around over here, out from under the trees." He led her to an open spot and said, "There's what I wanted to show you." He gestured at the stars and said, "I've never seen as many stars in my life. You remember we talked about that out at your home."

Fleur looked up. The moonlight bathed her face with a silver light. She seemed small and fragile, but her eyes lit up as she looked at the sky. "They are ver' beautiful. I remember I tell you God named each one of them."

"Well, I know a few. There's Arcturis right up there. You see?"

"Arcturis? That is his name?"

"That's what the astronomers call it. And over there, that's Sirius. They call it the Dog Star." He continued to name off the few stars he knew, and she watched quietly.

Suddenly Fleur said, "I must go home. I do not fit in this place."

Bayard saw that her face was drawn tight. He could not help but notice how lovely her skin was. The summer darkness lay over it, but her shirt fell away from her throat, showing the smooth olive shading beneath. Her black hair lay rolled and heavy on her head, a dense black that shone under the moonlight. The pale light revealed the soft lines of her body. Bayard remembered then how she had saved his life, nursed him back to health, and a great desire to do her good stirred in him. He asked suddenly, "Did you weep when your mother died?"

She held her head up, and he saw the tears glittering in her eyes. "No," she whispered, "I did not."

He saw the tremor in her body, and then the tears overflowed. He reached out and pulled her close, holding her head against his chest. "Maybe I can help," he whispered. Her body continued to tremble, and he heard her quiet sobs. He made no attempt to speak, but he held her firmly until the weeping stopped. She straightened up and put her hands on his chest. "Is the first time I have cry."

"We all need to cry, Fleur, even me."

She looked at him shyly.

Bayard reached down, took her hand, and kissed it. "I learned so much from you and your mother. Maybe now you can learn a little bit from me and from my family. You must stay here and become a part of us. It will be exciting," he said.

Her face seemed to glow then. She looked up at him and said, "Maybe I will stay for a little while, me."

CHAPTER TWENTY

As Simone walked down the street into Jackson Square, she paused for a moment to look at the paintings and drawings of the sidewalk artists who had set up their easels along the piked fence surrounding the park. One of them was painting a picture of the St. Louis Cathedral, which was very poorly executed, according to her judgment. She thought, *Bayard could do so much better than that.* The artist, a short, greasy-faced man with bloodshot gray eyes, stared at her. "You want to buy?" he demanded.

"No, thank you."

The artist gave Simone a look of contempt, then turned and continued to splash paint on the canvas almost carelessly.

The wind was refreshing coming off the river, and the bright sun threw its warm beams down on the banana and myrtle trees inside the square. Simone had always liked to walk the Quarter in the morning, when the streets were fresh and before the din of shoppers began, and now the sight of it pleased her. She could smell the coffee and fresh baked bread in the small grocery stores, and from the alleyways came the cool, dank smell of old brick.

For some time she wandered around, looking occasionally through the scrolled iron doors of the brick alleyways. Once she saw a courtyard of a building lit by the sun. Purple wisteria and climbing yellow roses decorated the wall, and the ivy rooted in the mortar clung to it determinedly while four-o'clocks bloomed in the shade, and a green garden of spearmint erupted against the sunlit stucco walls. She turned to leave the square when someone spoke.

"Hello, Simone."

Turning, Simone saw Colin, who took off his hat. The wind blew his auburn hair, and his eyes looked bluer than any she had ever seen. The color reminded her of cornflowers that grew in the open fields. "Hello, Colin," she said. "What are you doing here?"

"Just getting away from things. Would you like some coffee?"

Simone nodded. "That would be nice."

"We could go in the Cafe du Monde. They have great coffee there."

He escorted her into the cafe. He ordered

beignets and café au lait. The two nibbled at the delicacies and sipped the coffee. Simone asked about the performance the previous evening, and he spoke of it almost with disinterest. Then he asked, "How is Fleur doing?"

"Why, she's been with us for only three days, but she's doing very well. Of course everything is a little strange to her. All she's ever known is a cabin out in a bayou."

Something seemed to be troubling Colin. He swirled the milky coffee in his cup and stared down at it intently, as if it had some great meaning. Simone finally asked, "What's wrong?"

Looking in her eyes, Colin said, "It's a dangerous thing to experiment with lives, Simone."

"I don't know what you're talking about."

"You can change the color of a dress, or you can change a hat you're wearing — but it's more difficult to change people."

"You sound as if you don't approve of our bringing her in to stay with us. I'm surprised at you."

"Maybe I'm wrong, but has she been happy?"

His question made Simone uncomfortable for some reason, and she shifted in her chair and glanced down at the table. She picked up a spoon and stirred her coffee without answering for a time. Indeed, she had been somewhat disappointed at Fleur's behavior. It had seemed so *right* that Bayard should bring her there. After all, they owed her a tremendous debt, and now there was a chance to pay it back. And Simone had thrown herself into helping Fleur with all of the energy that she possessed. Thinking about it, however, she realized that Fleur had not responded as well as she might have liked. She had seemed to withdraw into herself and spend as much time in her room as possible, coming out only when Simone and Bayard insisted on it.

"It will just take time," she said finally.

"I hope you're right. But —" He broke off and shook his head doubtfully. "It's going to be more difficult than you think."

The stubborn streak that lay beneath the surface of Simone d'Or's personality arose. She had been accustomed to having her own way, and now being challenged, she responded by saying stiffly, "I don't agree with you. What do you know about it, anyway?"

"It happened to me, Simone. When I went to France, I couldn't speak French. I didn't know anything. I was ignorant, and there I was right in the middle of the highest form of French society. I remember when Armand took me to the parties and balls and the meetings with his artistic friends, I felt more stupid than you can imagine." He smiled wryly at her, and she noticed tiny crinkles at the edges of his eyes. "I would have cried, but I was too old for that. But I wanted to."

"You turned out all right. You adjusted."

"It took a long time, and it was a painful thing. I think you'd better be prepared for Fleur to want to go back to her old life."

"She's free to go if she wants, but Bayard and my whole family want to help her."

"Sometimes the wrong kind of help can be harmful. And sometimes people don't need help."

"I'm telling you, Colin, you don't know what you're talking about. She's a beautiful young woman. All she needs is a little training, a little help with her speech, a few tips on how to dress. She'll fit right in."

"You're talking about a girl who has lived next to a swamp all of her life. She's been out hunting alligators and fishing and trapping wild animals, and you're pushing her into Creole high society, which, if I may say so, is not the most enviable one, in my judgment."

Simone grew angry. "I see there's no point

in our talking about it, Colin. You're wrong, and that's all there is to it." She rose, saying, "I must go now. Good day."

She left the Cafe du Monde, walking as rapidly as she could. She did not look back, and by the time she reached the spot where Robert was waiting for her with the carriage, she had decided that Lord Beaufort had gotten too wise for his own good. After all, he was nothing but a fisherman! What could he know about people? she thought. She snapped at Robert, "Take me home at once!"

"Yes, ma'am," Robert said carefully. He had learned to recognize the storm signals that rose sometimes, transforming Simone d'Or from a pleasant, smiling woman to a determined, hardheaded one. *I don't know what set her off, but it don't take much!* he thought casually, and then spoke to his horses, "Get up, Nell. Get up, Betsy."

As soon as Simone stepped into the house, she asked Agnes, "Where is Miss Fleur?"

"She's upstairs in her room, Miss. She's been there all morning. Don't know why she wants to stay inside on such a beautiful day."

Simone nodded and moved down the hall toward the stairs. As she ascended the carpeted steps, her head was full of the program that she had decided on for Fleur. The conversation with Colin Seymour had increased her determination, and she muttered, "All Fleur needs is a little help — and I'm going to see that she gets it!"

Knocking on the door, she waited until Fleur invited her to enter. The young woman was sitting on a chair beside a window. The sunlight touched her glossy black hair.

"What are you doing up in your room alone, Fleur?"

"Just thinking."

"Well, you've thought enough." Simone smiled and went over to her. "You have the most beautiful hair I've ever seen. We're going to do something with it."

"What you do with it?" Fleur asked with a frightened look.

"I'm going to take you to a woman who fixes my hair, and we're going to go to some stores and buy you some new clothes."

"You already buy me new dress. See, it fits fine. I don't need no more."

Simone laughed. "We only bought you two dresses. We're going to the reception tomorrow, and you need a new gown. Come now, we'll have all afternoon to shop."

"I think I rather stay here, Simone."

"Don't be foolish. It'll be fun. I'll tell you what: we'll go shopping, and then we'll get a fine meal at Antoine's. Then we'll go to the opera. Would you like that?"

"I don't know. I never go to no opera."

"Well, you'll like it, I'm sure. Come along now. You better wear that coat that we bought. It's getting brisk out there, and it'll be cold when we get back tonight."

"This is Francisco's. They have the finest ladies' fashions in New Orleans. Come along. We have a lot to do."

Fleur hung back. She had accompanied Simone reluctantly, and now the sight of the store with its bright lights throwing a glow over the selections of dresses and shoes and other ladies' accessories intimidated her. She longed to be back in her room, or even back in her cabin on the bayou — though she had enjoyed being with Bayard and watching him paint. And she enjoyed the family. But once outside the house meeting strangers, she became frightened and felt ill at ease.

"Good afternoon, Mademoiselle d'Or. It is good to see you." The speaker was a petite woman wearing a gray dress and an elaborate hairstyle. She had bright brown eyes and a smile to match. "What can I do for you today?"

"Eleanor, this is Fleur Avenall, a very special friend of mine. We're going to the reception for the new lieutenant governor tomorrow, and Miss Avenall needs a new outfit."

"That will be a pleasure. If you will come this way, Miss Avenall, I will show you what we have."

Fleur followed but paid little heed to the woman's talk. Everywhere she looked she saw well-dressed women wearing flashing jewelry, with their hair done in fashions she could not quite understand. They were talking and laughing, and Simone kept up a running conversation with the woman named Eleanor. Fleur said almost nothing, and for the next hour she simply did as she was bidden. She tried on half a dozen dresses as well as shoes, bonnets, and gloves.

"These shoes, they are too tight," she complained. After wearing moccasins most of her life, she felt the leather shoes bite into her flesh. "They hurt."

"Oh, they're not too small, I'm sure," Lucille said. "You will get used to them. New shoes take breaking in."

"Moccasins don't take no breaking in. You make them and put them on, and they feel good right off."

Simone laughed. "Well, you can't wear moccasins to the reception. Those will look very pretty. Now, which of the dresses did you like? I thought the green one was very nice indeed." Simone waited, but Fleur seemed confused. "Of course, the white brings out your hair and your eyes."

"The white is ver' pretty, but the green is nice also, Eleanor said."

"Very well. We'll take them both," Simone said. "Now, you'll need a cloak to wear. What do you have, Eleanor?"

"We have some fine wool cloaks just imported. It is merino wool, the very finest." Eleanor brought out a cloak and draped it across Fleur's shoulders. "It would look just right with either dress, and it is so warm."

"Do you like this, Fleur?"

"Yes, I like him, but what keep him from falling off?" The coat had no buttons and simply draped over the shoulders.

"It's supposed to be like that, Mademoiselle Avenall," Eleanor answered. "It allows the beautiful dress to be seen."

"We'll take it," Simone said firmly. "Now, let's see, is there anything else?"

"I think is enough, Simone," Fleur said quickly. "Too much for me."

"Certainly it's not too much! You must

look beautiful for the reception." She paid her bill, and the pair left for home.

Fleur stood in the middle of the room while Simone's maid, Lucy, moved about her, touching her hair with a brush, adding a hairpin to keep it in place. Fleur did not like the way her hair was fixed, all curled and tied up. Always she had let it simply hang down her back, tied with a thong. She felt awkward in the new clothes. When Lucy said, "Now you are perfect," she looked in the mirror. The white dress brought out her dark hair and eyes, as Simone had said, but she reached up and tried to tug the dress upward. "This shows too much of me," she said.

"Oh no, it's very modest!" Lucy said.

"I don't think so, me! I wish I had a sweater, something to cover myself up."

Lucy restrained a laugh. "Wait until you see some of the other ladies' dresses! They are cut much lower than this."

"Then they should stay home!"

Simone entered the room, smiling. "Let me see you. Turn around — oh, it's perfect!"

"This dress shows too much of me. I want to put a shawl or something over my chest."

"Why, it's just right," Simone said with surprise.

"I never wear nothing that show me like this. Maybe I could wear a shirt or something *under* the dress."

"I've tried to tell her it's very modest. See, Miss Simone's dress is much lower than that."

Fleur looked at Simone's maroon dress that was indeed even more revealing than her own. "Don't you feel funny, letting your skin show like that?"

Simone exchanged smiles with Lucy. "It's all the fashion. You've just never worn a ballroom dress. Now come along. It's time to go."

Fleur followed Simone down the stairs and found Bayard waiting. His eyes lit up, and he said, "Well, the two most beautiful women in New Orleans are here. Let me look at that new dress, Fleur."

Fleur flushed. "I don't like it," she said in a low voice.

"You don't like the dress?"

"No, it show too much of me."

Bayard was surprised. He was accustomed to such fashions himself, but he saw that Fleur was indeed troubled. "I know it's different from anything you've worn out at the bayou, but when you go to dances out there with the Cajuns, don't they wear anything like this?"

"No. Women wear their dresses up to their neck. This is not nice."

Bayard chewed his lip and said, "Well, I think you'll find that things are a little different at these receptions."

"It'll be fine," Simone said. "You look lovely."

"Yes, every young blade in New Orleans will be pestering you for dances."

"I can't dance, me," Fleur said. "Just the zydeco is all I can do. I bet you don't do that where we going."

"I don't think so." Simone was taken aback. She assumed that every young lady could dance. She looked at her brother. "Bayard, you'll have to stay with her."

"We don't have to dance," Bayard said. "We can just walk around and sample the food and meet people. Come along now, we don't want to be late."

Colin had arranged for the company to have a night off. They had worked hard, and except for Sunday nights, they had performed regularly. He was stepping downstairs from his room when he saw Rosa crossing the lobby. He called out to her, and she turned to smile at him.

"Hello, Colin. Where are you going?"

"I'm trying to decide whether to go to that

reception for the lieutenant governor. I don't like such things usually, but I suppose I ought to go."

"It should be fun," Rosa said.

"I'm a little bit worried about the young woman I told you about — the one who's staying with Simone and Bayard."

"The one named Fleur, who rescued Bayard? I'd like to meet her."

"Well, here's your chance." Colin made up his mind suddenly. "You go with me. I'm afraid Fleur's going to feel out of place. She's never been to a thing like this. She's just a country girl, really."

Rosa offered, "You want me to go with you?"

"Yes. Let's go to the blasted thing. We can make her feel at home."

"All right. Let me stop at home to put on a different dress, and I'll be ready."

The ballroom was filled, for the new lieutenant governor of Louisiana was already a power in the state. Everyone knew that he would be the next governor and was anxious to show him respect.

As Bayard and Simone arrived with Fleur, they were greeted on every hand, but Fleur could only look at the magnificence of the ballroom.

The room was large and oval-shaped, with domed ceilings and pictures of gilded angels and clouds painted throughout. The walls were painted a brilliant white, and the floor was highly polished marble of white with gold flecks. Large, round columns encircled the room about ten feet in from the outer walls, and upholstered chairs of gold and blue silk damask and tables covered with fine white linen, china, and crystal lay behind the columns. Floor-length windows around the room were covered with heavy blue velvet curtains and crystal chandeliers seemed to be everywhere, lit with hundreds of candles.

Fleur felt terribly uncomfortable, and her face was pale, but neither Simone nor Bayard noticed. They were too busy greeting people. Finally two men came up, and the shorter one was introduced as Governor Taylor while the tall man beside him was Jeffrey Williams, the incoming lieutenant governor.

"Are your parents here, Miss d'Or?" Governor Taylor asked.

"They will be here later, sir."

"You've met the new lieutenant governor, Mr. Jeffrey Williams?"

"I have not. Glad to know you, sir. This is my sister, Simone, and our good friend Miss

Avenall," Bayard said.

The lieutenant governor's eyes were fastened on Fleur. He stepped forward and bowed from the waist. "Happy to know you, Miss Avenall. Perhaps you'll honor me with a dance?"

"No, I don't dance."

Both the governor and the lieutenant governor looked shocked.

Bayard said quickly, "She is new to our city and hasn't yet picked up our ways."

"Well, if you ever learn, I'll be first in line." Williams smiled, and the two men wandered off.

"I don't think this a good idea," Fleur said.

"Now, don't be foolish. Come along, let's just walk around," Bayard said. He took her lightly by the arm and steered her toward the refreshment table. They were sampling the food when George Ahern, the mayor, came up. Bayard introduced him to Fleur, and Ahern asked, "You're new to our city?"

"Yes."

"Where are you from, may I ask?"

"Whiskey Bay."

Ahern's eyes flew open. Whiskey Bay was one of the many spots deep in bayou country. "Well," he said, "we're glad to have you here tonight."

Several others had been within hearing

distance, and one of them, a tall, fashionable woman remarked, "Whiskey Bay — nothing there but alligators and moccasins."

Instantly Bayard turned and glared at her. She met his eyes and then reddened. She turned and walked away, and Bayard said, "Don't mind them, Fleur. There are people with bad manners everywhere."

"Please, Bayard, take me from this place!"

"We won't stay long," he promised. He realized that bringing her had been a mistake, but he couldn't leave so early in the evening. He saw Colin speaking with Simone and another woman he recognized from the opera. "Look, there are some friendly people you should meet."

He led Fleur over and introduced her. Colin smiled. "Hello, Miss Avenall. May I introduce my friend, Miss Rosa Calabria."

Rosa smiled and stepped forward. "You look lovely. I'm so happy to meet you."

"I am glad to meet you. I heard you sing last night."

"Did you like the opera?" Colin asked.

"Yes. It was loud."

Colin laughed, and the others joined him. "It was indeed loud. Operas may be good or bad, but they are all loud."

Fleur looked around with alarm. "Did I say something wrong, Bayard?"

"No, of course you didn't. I think all of us agree that operas are hard on the ears."

Colin said, "I thought I might ask you to dance, Miss Fleur."

"I can't do that."

Silence ensued, and Simone said quickly, "I'm going to have Fleur start taking dancing lessons at once." She was upset and saw that Colin was looking at the girl with pity in his eyes. "It won't take long for her to learn," she said.

"I'm sure it won't," Colin said quietly.

Simone watched as Colin and Rosa spoke with the girl. Bayard stepped close to Simone and whispered, "We were wrong to bring her here."

"No, we weren't," Simone said. She was still determined to prove that Colin was mistaken. "It's just a small thing. Anybody can learn to dance."

"I don't know. It's more than that."

At that moment Claude Vernay strode across the room. He stood before Fleur and said, "Bayard, would you introduce me to your friend?"

Colin turned to face Vernay. "It wouldn't be proper, Vernay."

Vernay turned pale, and the people within hearing distance were watching carefully. New Orleans loved its drama, and the townspeople knew the antagonism that existed between the two. Vernay shot a venomous glance at Colin, then turned and walked away, his back stiff.

"Why is that man so mad at you?" Fleur asked.

"Just a disagreement. Come on, let me get you something to drink."

"I already have something to drink. I didn't like it."

"It's not very good," Bayard agreed, "but I'm sure we'll have some entertainment. Did they ask you to sing, Colin?"

"No, they didn't, and I'm glad of it. I'm about sung out."

Simone hailed three of her friends across the room. She introduced them to Fleur, who said little, but the reaction of Simone's friends was obvious. They were amused at the young woman. One of them said in a bright voice, "What a delightful friend you have, Simone. She's so — so exotic."

Her tone was such that everyone who heard knew she had insulted Fleur. Simone was furious. "Yes, she is, Mary. She is unspoiled and has a sweetness in her that I don't find in any of my other friends." She turned around and said, "Come, Fleur."

Bayard accompanied them, and Fleur reached up and put her hand on his arm.

"Please, Bayard, take me home."

"Yes, I will. Simone, I'm taking Fleur home."

Simone started to argue, but Bayard shook his head and led Fleur out of the room. The music was playing, and Colin asked, "Would you care to dance?"

Simone turned and looked at him. She was thinking of the conversation when he had warned her against the difficulty of bringing Fleur into a world she did not know. "She just needs more training, Colin," she said firmly, "and I'm going to see that she gets it."

Colin replied, "Lots of luck. I think you'll need it." He turned and walked to Rosa, and the two left at once. Simone knew that he had come for Fleur's sake, and a feeling of disappointment filled her. Still she thought, *It'll work. I can make her into a society woman. Colin's wrong about this!*

Chapter
Twenty-One

Simone put down her pen, flexed her fingers, and sat looking at the words she had written in her journal. *Nothing is working out with Fleur. I don't know what to do, but I will not give up.*

A knock on the door startled her. "Come in, Lucy."

Her maid entered the room, her eyes big. "Lord Beaufort is here to see you, Miss."

Simone rose and said, "Very well. I'll come down."

"Is he really a lord like they say?"

"Of course he is, Lucy. That's why they call him Lord Beaufort. What a silly goose you are!"

She descended the stairs and found that Colin was waiting for her in the foyer. He was wearing a pair of worn brown trousers, a green-and-white checkered shirt, and a short wool coat that came down to his fingers and was open at the front. His boots were heavy and had thick soles. "I came without an invitation, Simone," he said, and his eyes were dancing with some kind of excitement.

"Well, come into the parlor." They had parted on icy terms at the ball, and she wasn't sure whether she was glad to see him or not.

"No, I've come to take you for an outing."

"An outing? What sort?"

"I bought a small boat some time ago. I've been meaning to ask you to come for a sail with me."

"But Colin, it's freezing out there!" Indeed, the first of November had just passed, and New Orleans had been held in extremely cold weather, which was very unusual for the city.

"Don't be so picky, Simone. It'll be something new for you. I imagine you haven't been out on many small sailing crafts."

"No, and I'm not sure I'll like it," Simone said. "I can't swim."

"You won't have to. I can pull you out, but we won't capsize. Come on. I need your company."

Simone had been upset with Colin for his advice about Fleur Avenall, but at the moment, she was tired of balls and parties and the formal manners of her world. So she sighed and asked, "What does a lady wear on a boat like this?"

"The oldest clothes you have. Good boots and warm socks and warm underwear."

Simone was surprised. No man had ever mentioned underwear in her presence, and she saw that he was waiting for her to complain. Instead she fell into his mood. "All right. Give me a few minutes. You might as well go back to the kitchen. They'll give you something to warm you up."

"I'll wait for you there."

Upstairs Simone searched her closet for something suitable. Lucy asked, "What are you looking for?"

"Some winter clothes. The warmest I have." She picked out a wool dress that she had not worn for years.

"Why, you can't wear that old thing. I don't know why you keep it."

"It'll do. Now, find me two sets of the warmest underwear I've got."

As Simone stepped out of the carriage, the breeze off the river cut into her like a knife, despite two sets of underwear and her heavy woolen coat. She gasped, but Colin did not seem to be troubled. He did not even bother to button his coat. "There she is, right over there," he said, pointing. "Isn't she a beauty?"

Simone walked with him to the pier, where the boat was bobbing up and down. "It's so small," she said.

"Twenty feet long and plenty of room. She's got a good wide beam and a deep draft too." A man was working on it, a short, tub-shaped fellow with a red face and blue lips. "A bit rough out today, Cap'n."

"Just right for sailing, Frank."

"Well, sir, she's all ready." He offered his hand and said, "Let me help you in, Miss."

Simone stepped gingerly into the boat, and Colin said, "Take that seat up in the bow."

Simone obeyed and sat down. While Colin spoke with the man and then boarded, she looked out over the river. Few boats were on the water, only a few paddle wheelers headed for the docks of New Orleans. The wind bit at her, and she shivered and wished she had put on *three* sets of underwear. She was glad she had worn a pair of furlined leather gloves.

"All set?" Colin asked cheerfully.

"I suppose so. I still think this is insane."

"Anybody can go sailing in the spring or summer. It's good to have a challenge." He began to loose the ropes and cast them off, and the man took them and rolled them up. Colin moved quickly, pulling at a rope that raised a sail, and at once the stiff breeze caught the vessel and pulled it sideways. Simone watched as he leaped back to the tiller and cried out, "Well, here we go!"

"Be careful of them waves, sir," Frank called out. "They can turn you over before you know it."

"I'll watch 'em, Frank."

The small craft moved swiftly through the water, and Simone saw Colin smile. *He's really enjoying this. I don't know why anybody would!*

As the boat moved along, Colin spoke about how he had found her and restored her with Frank's help. "She's a real traveler. Someday I'd like to have a bigger boat. I miss the sea."

The wind whipped about Simone, seeming to wrap her in its coldness. The sail was stiff with the breeze as the craft drove through the gray water, and from time to time she saw Colin adjust the tiller. He was jolly, seeming not to feel the cold weather, and he began to speak of the time when he was a fisherman. "I never thought I'd miss those days," he said. "It was a hard life, but there were some good things about it."

By the time they neared the Gulf, Simone

felt that she was frozen. It was impossible to keep her face warm, and her lips were numb so that she had difficulty responding to Colin. Her eyes watered, and she beat her hands together from time to time and stamped her feet to get the blood going.

Finally the Gulf opened up before them, and the waves made the small craft bob up and down like a cork. Once a wave smashed into their side, and the small craft listed alarmingly.

"Colin," Simone said, "this is enough! I'm freezing to death!"

"Why, this isn't too bad. I can take you down and show you some islands that we might even explore a little bit."

"No, I want to go home." At that moment the wind rose, and the craft bobbed some more. "Please, Colin, I'm afraid!"

Colin looked at her, then shrugged. "Well, fishermen pay no attention to this sort of weather, but we'll go back." He put the sail around, then grabbed the tiller and straightened the vessel. They ran before the wind all the way back down the river. Simone was as miserable as she had ever been in her life. Her world was comfort and warmth and someone looking out for her. She thought as she watched Colin maneuver the boat back toward the dock how hard his fisherman's life must have been. Just the thought of putting her hand in that cold water was painful.

Colin pulled up to the dock and said, "I guess Frank went to get something to eat." They had been gone for two hours, and he leaped out and quickly secured the boat fore and aft. Then he reached for her and said, "Come along. I'll help you out."

Simone had trouble when she got to her feet. She had no feeling in them and was afraid she would twist her ankle. She took his hand and stepped on the dock, shivering. She repeated, "I'm freezing!"

"It's not that bad. I've been out when ice was on the water. Look, there's Frank's shack up there. Let's go see if we can get something to warm us up."

He held her arm firmly until they reached the small shack. When he knocked, no one answered. "He must have gone to get a drink. Come along."

"We can't go into his house."

"He won't mind. Come inside."

Simone stepped into the shack, which was no more than twelve feet square. A stove was throwing out waves of heat, and she went over to it at once and held her hands out. Great tremors ran through her, and she had to clamp her teeth together and force herself to be still.

Colin soon had water boiling, and by the time Simone was fairly comfortable, the coffee was ready. He took two unmatched cups, poured them full, and said, "No fancy trimmings. Just black and hot."

Simone took it and sipped it cautiously. "It's good," she said. She drank the coffee gratefully and looked up to see Colin smiling at her. "What are you grinning about?" she asked.

"You didn't have a very good time."

"Of course I didn't. It's miserable out there. I can't think why'd you ask me to go."

Colin sipped his coffee, swirled it in the cup, and stared down into it. Finally he lifted his eyes. "Not your kind of a world, is it?"

"No, it certainly isn't."

"I could teach you to live in it."

"I don't want to live in it. I like my own world."

He seemed not to have heard her. "It would take a long time, but you would learn."

"I have no interest at all in joining that kind of world."

Colin moved closer, reached out, seized her arm, and squeezed it. His voice was level, and his eyes were direct as he said, "Neither does Fleur want your world, Simone. She was as miserable at that fancy ball as you were out in that boat. Fleur could learn to live in your world, but it was as cruel of you and Bayard to throw her into that place with no preparation as it was for me to take you out in an icy, rough sea."

Simone felt the pressure of his hand squeezing her arm and of the intensity of his bright blue eyes. She understood then why he had taken her out there. "You did this to teach me a lesson."

"Sure I did. You don't learn easily, Simone. Sometimes I don't think you learn at all. You've got your little plans all put together, and everybody has to fit into them. But life's not like that. You were wrong about Fleur. Why don't you admit it?"

Simone was furious. She put the cup down on the table next to her and lifted her hand to slap him, but the cold slowed her movements. Colin caught her wrist and held it. "You can't slap everyone who offends you."

"Let me go!"

"Do you really want me to?"

"Yes! Take your hands off me!"

Colin pulled her to her feet and held her by her forearms. "I don't think so, Simone.

I think you like it when I hold you."

"Don't be ridiculous! I don't like to be handled!"

"When I kissed you, you didn't fight much."

Simone didn't answer. She was embarrassed when she saw that he had not forgotten her surrender to his embrace. She had many times wondered why she had given in to him. "I'm ashamed of what I did."

"Ashamed of what? Being a woman and feeling something for a man?"

The room was close about them, and she could feel the strength of his hands pressing into her arms. She looked up and wanted to break away, but he was too strong — and she was not sure that she actually wanted to. "Let me go. You confuse me!"

"I'm not a complicated man, Simone. Your life is complicated, and your emotions too. You keep them in a little box and trot them out on occasion, expecting them to behave exactly as you want. But love isn't like that."

"Love? What are you talking about?"

"I'm talking about a man and a woman. You know I hated you once, but I don't any more. You're spoiled to the bone, but I feel something for you that I've never felt for another woman." He pulled her forward, and she cried out, "Let me go, Colin!"

"I won't do it." He pulled her closer. He knew his hunger for Simone would never lessen — and would never be satisfied. There was a beauty in her that made him feel strong enough to take on the world. He knew it was foolish and that she was still often selfish, but that did not change what he felt. He knew she wanted to be touched, and he wanted to touch her. He lowered his head and put his lips against hers, and at first he felt resistance. Ignoring it, he held her close, and then her lips softened and he felt a tremulous warmth in them. He held her tightly and kissed her until finally he felt an eagerness in her lips. It was like falling into some sort of gentle softness.

Simone seemed to have lost all her power to think. She wanted to fight, to resist, but something in her would not permit it. She knew that they were both on the near edge of rashness, that he was struggling with his impulses. She knew that any gesture on her part would sway him, and it frightened her somehow. She lifted her arms to his shoulders and looked into his eyes. "Please," she whispered, "let me go, Colin!"

Colin did not release her, however. Instead he said, "Men see beauty in different places. My tough luck is that I see it only in you, Simone." He reached out and put his hands on her face. "Do you think you could ever learn to care for me?"

Simone could not believe what she was hearing. "I — I don't know."

Colin smiled. "Well, that's good. You're blunt — and mean enough to say so at once if you didn't care at all for me."

"I am not mean!" she exclaimed.

"No, not on the inside. Just on the outside. But inside you, Simone, there's a loving, generous woman, beneath that veneer that society has put on you. And I'm going to make sure that woman gets out."

"I want to go home," Simone whispered. She was frightened now, not of him but of herself. "Please, Colin, take me home!"

"Of course." He stepped back, moved to the door, and opened it, and she walked outside. The cold air hit her again, and as he took her to a carriage, neither of them spoke. He handed her in, followed her inside, and spoke to the driver. Colin was silent for several minutes, then said, "I'd like to take you out on the Gulf sometime when the sun's shining and the water's warm. Would you go?"

Simone was shaken by what had taken place. "I think maybe," she said finally, "I see what you mean about Fleur."

"She's a sweet young girl, but it's going to

take a lot of care to make her into what you want. And I'm not sure that's wise. Make sure she wants it."

Simone could not respond. As the horses moved along the streets, she knew that she would not forget that day. It was the second time he had kissed her, and both times all of her defenses had collapsed. *What kind of a woman am I? I might have given in to him.* The thought frightened her, and she pulled the cloak tighter about her and said no more.

Fleur had put on her oldest clothes and gone out to the stables. She was grooming her mare, and when that was finished, she started mucking out the stalls. Robert walked in and stopped, shocked. "Miss, you shouldn't do that!"

"Why not?"

"That ain't no job for a lady."

"Oh, I'm no lady, Robert."

"Beggin' your pardon, Miss Fleur, but you're mighty wrong about that."

"I can't do none of the things fine ladies can do, Robert." She leaned against the wall, holding the rake in her hand. "I go to that ball, and it was terrible. I couldn't even talk right."

"Well, I've been around these so-called

ladies quite a bit. Most of them ain't got no more feeling than a snake. They don't care for nobody but themselves."

"Well, what is a lady, you think?"

"I don't rightly know, Miss," Robert said, shaking his head. "It's got somethin' to do with how you treat other people."

Just then Bayard appeared. "I've been looking for you, Fleur."

"I thought I'd come down and groom my horse."

"That's good. Robert, Miss Fleur and I are going on a little ride."

"A ride? You mean around town?" Fleur asked with surprise.

"No, I thought we'd go out to your place. I've had our cook pack a lunch. We can stay all day."

Bayard was surprised at the sudden life that came into the girl. Her eyes flashed, and she grabbed his arm. "Do you mean it? Can we really go?"

"That's what my plan is. Are you ready now?"

"Oh yes, let's go, Bayard!"

Ever since the two had arrived at the cabin, Fleur had been very quiet. Bayard had watched her carefully and been quieter himself than was usual. He understood then how her staying at his home had been hard on her. She walked around the cabin, touching things, and finally went outside, braving the sharp bite of the wind. He followed her to the edge of the water. The swamp was still now, broken only when a fish came to the surface and sent concentric circles outward. Once a heron flew slowly overhead and settled somewhere deep in the bayou.

"It's good to be here, Bayard. Thank you for bringing me." She turned to him, and at that moment he saw something in her eyes he could not identify. He had no idea what her life had been as far as men were concerned. He knew she was shy and suspected she knew nothing of romance. He reached out and took her hand and found it cold. He held it, feeling the roughness of her palm. Then he said what he had brought her to say. "Fleur, I've become very fond of you."

Startled, Fleur tried to read his face. "Fond of me?"

"As a man gets fond of a woman."

"I don't know about things like that," she said quickly.

"I've fallen in love with you."

His words shocked her, and she tried to pull her hand back, but he would not release it. "Nothing can come of that," she said.

"Why not?"

She gave up her struggle and let him hold her hand. Her face was troubled. "I can't live in the city, me, and you can't live in the bayou."

Suddenly Bayard felt a great sense of need to protect the young woman. He dropped her hand and put his arm around her. As she came against him, he was aware of the softness of her body and saw that her lips were trembling. "People change sometimes, for love. I can change, and so can you. I've never felt like this about any woman, Fleur."

Fleur was trembling. She did not know how to answer him, but in all truth he was like no man she had ever met. A sense of longing had been in her since she had saved his life, but it had been something she had kept very secret. Now she said, "Your family would never agree, even if I did."

"You won't be married to my family. You would be marrying me."

"You want me to marry with you?"

"Yes, I do." He pulled her close and kissed her on the lips, then put his cheek next to hers. She seemed to resist for a moment, and then she put her head down against his chest.

"I don't know what to say. I am afraid."

"Don't be afraid, Fleur," Bayard said.

"I've been afraid most of my life, but ever since I met you, there's been something different. Part of it is you, part your faith in God, which has touched me."

Fleur felt tears come to her eyes. "I don't know how to answer you."

"Come, let's go back in the cabin. You're cold." He led her back inside, and when the door closed, she turned to face him. He stood waiting.

Fleur said, "I think I love you, Bayard. I have never loved any man, so I'm not sure."

Bayard laughed. He took her hands and kissed them. "Well, be very sure," he said. "Don't be afraid of anything."

"There's a man to see you, sir. He wouldn't give his name."

Vernay looked up at the butler and asked, "What does he look like?"

"He looks foreign somehow, Mr. Vernay."

"Bring him in, Dennis."

Vernay stood, and as soon as the man entered the room, he smiled. "Hello, Jean Paul."

"Hello, Claude." The man who entered the room was not large. He was somewhat less than average height, but he had a neatness and trimness and strength in his body, and he wore a careful expression. The two men shook hands, and Vernay said, "Sit down. You must be hungry."

"No, I ate before I came."

"How long have you been in New Orleans?"

"I just got in yesterday."

"Did anyone see you come?"

"No."

"Well, that's good. I'll fix us a drink." Vernay went over to the cabinet and poured two drinks. He brought them back and sat down and handed one to Jean Paul Compier. "You have a good trip?"

"It was all right."

The two talked for a few moments, and finally Compier asked, "Why have you sent for me, Claude?"

"I have a problem. I need some help."

Jean Paul Compier made a sour face. "I have a problem too."

"I guess yours is financial. I know you've been having difficulty."

"I gave up gambling, but it was too late. I have lost nearly everything."

"What about your idea of an academy to teach fencing? A fitness academy for young men."

"That's what I want to do, but it takes money." Compier had dark brown eyes, studious and calm. "What about this problem that you have?"

Claude hesitated, then said, "I have to go back to tell you about it." He described how he had wanted to marry Simone d'Or and been frustrated. He spoke of Armand, the former Marquis of Beaufort, and saw Compier's gaze grow intense as he described the duel. "I didn't mean to hit him in the back. He whirled around for some reason. It was an accident, but it was the worst thing I could have done. He was a popular man."

"He was a very fine musician. I admired his work greatly. But he's dead."

"But the man who now bears the title is not." Vernay went on to speak of how Colin Seymour had shamed him. "He's a curse to me, Jean Paul. I want him finished."

Compier sat absolutely still. "I am not a murderer, Claude."

Claude Vernay did not answer immediately. "How bad do you want to start this new academy? Very bad indeed, I think — and you've wanted it for a long time."

"You know I have."

"Do this thing for me, and I will become your silent partner. I'll put up all of the money. We'll split the profits. You're famous in France. Young men will flock to you."

"What is the man's name? The man you want me to fight, it's Lord Beaufort?"

"That's him. I despise the fellow."

Compier stared at the glass in his hand. His voice was soft as he said, "I have heard him sing several times. He is a great singer."

"It's up to you, Jean Paul. I can't force you to do anything you don't want to. If you don't want the job, I'll pay your expenses back to France. I might add," he said, "that Seymour is a master with a sword and pistol. It may not be as easy as you think."

"My friend François Morell, his teacher, has spoken of him."

"What did he say?"

"He said, 'I would bet no more than even money on you, Jean Paul, if you had to fight my pupil Colin. He can use either arm for swordplay.' "

"That's the truth. I've seen it for myself." Claude Vernay knew that there was no point in arguing with Jean Paul Compier. The man had been famous for years as the best blade not only in France, but in Europe. His weakness had been gambling, and knowing this, Vernay thought him a likely ally.

Compier looked at him bitterly. "Yes, I will do as you ask."

"You will? That's good news."

"No. It's bad news, Claude. I despise

myself for what I have become. Nothing but a murderer! But I'm getting older, and this is my one chance."

"The challenge must not be connected with me. You must provoke him and leave me out of it."

"I will find a way, Claude — and may God have mercy on my soul!"

CHAPTER
TWENTY-TWO

Simone smiled but shook her head, saying patiently, "The way to pronounce the word *very* sounds like this: *ver — ree.*"

"Am I not say that, Simone?"

"Not really. You usually leave off the *ree* and just say *ver.*"

"Me, I am not know I say it like that. *Veree.* Is right?"

"Exactly right."

"Then you tell me every time I say him wrong."

"Of course I will. You are learning so fast — and by the way, words are referred to by *it,* not *him.* I know in French every word has to be masculine or feminine, but in English inanimate objects are just referred to as *it.*"

"What is an — what you call it, 'object'?"

"Don't worry about it. Read some more. It'll all become clear to you after awhile."

Fleur began to read aloud again from the book that Simone had given her. It had become a daily practice for the two of them to go to Simone's room and work on Fleur's English and accent. When Fleur and Bayard returned from their trip to the cabin, the young woman had shown a devoted interest in becoming more of a lady who would fit into Bayard's world. Simone was thrilled and threw herself into teaching. She was glad Fleur had made clear that she wanted these changes. Colin had been right. It would have been wrong to force city ways on her if she didn't truly want to be part of it. She had started teaching Fleur to dance. She found out that Fleur had a natural rhythm and learned very quickly. As a matter of fact, she learned everything very quickly.

Finally she said, "You're doing well. You are going to speak English much better than I speak French."

Fleur shook her head, and her black hair tumbled as she did so. "Me, I not think so." She was quiet for a moment and finally said, "I have a question for you."

"What is it?"

"I not know how to ask it."

"Just ask it right out."

Fleur said, "Bayard has said that he — that he cares for me."

"I'm not surprised, and I'm very happy

about it."

"You would not mind having me in your family?"

"Why, of course not. I can think of nothing that would please me more."

"Your parents, they might not find it so pleasing."

"Of course they would. They are very fond of you, Fleur."

"But I'm not the kind of woman that would fit in here."

"That's what we're doing now. You're studying and working and making marvelous progress."

"It can never be," Fleur said simply. "I can never be like you."

"You don't need to be like me. You need to be like yourself. All of these other things, the speech and the dancing and the clothes, these are just surface issues. Who you are is much more important." Simone took Fleur's hand. She was surprised to hear herself saying this, for she was well aware that she had had different goals once. "Look, Fleur, if you love Bayard, and he loves you, you must not pass up the miracle."

"The miracle? What is that you mean?"

Simone released her hand and stood and walked to the window. She stared outside.

The weather was cold; it was now mid-December. She was surprised to see a robin hopping along, pecking at the hard ground. It was past the time for robins, and she wondered what the bird was doing there that time of the year. She turned then and said, "I think it's always a miracle when two people find each other and love each other. Just think, Fleur, out of all the millions of people in the world, for a man and a woman to find each other out of all these: it *is* a miracle."

Fleur laughed. "I think you are right, but I do not know much about love. You must teach me, Simone."

Simone suddenly flushed. "I'm not the one to ask. I'm certainly no expert."

"But you have had many lovers."

"No, don't say that. It's not nice."

"It's not nice? Why?"

"Because 'lovers' — well — that refers to two people who have become — um, intimate."

Fleur looked at her knowingly, "Ah, I understand. What are these men that come after you as I see them? They are not your lovers, what are they?"

"Oh, I suppose *suitors* is the word."

"Suitors. I'm think a suitor was one that made suits." Fleur spoke so earnestly, with her eyes so wide, that Simone was amused. She chuckled and said, "No, that's another thing entirely."

"But have you loved none of these men?"

"I thought I was in love with one once, but he . . ." She thought of Claude Vernay and how she had been flattered by his attention and fancied herself in love. Now that he had shown himself in his true colors, she was disgusted to think that she could once have felt so strongly about him. Shaking her head firmly, she said, "No, I didn't love any of them."

"But then how will you know when the right one comes along?"

"As I say, I'm the wrong one to ask. I've read many romantic novels about love, but they all seem foolish to me now."

"I wish I understand more about love. I care for Bayard. He is so good to me, and I think that I can never be happy if he were not around."

"Why, Fleur, I think that's as close to defining love as I ever heard! Someone you can't be happy without."

"I do not know how it is between a man and a woman when they marry. Several men have kissed me and tried to have me, but I always fight them off."

"I'm glad you did, Fleur. That's a good

thing. You'll come to your husband a pure woman, and that's good. We'll talk about this again, but right now, we'll work on your grammar."

"My grammar? What is this — my grammar?"

"Oh, basically it's the way you put words together to make sentences."

"My grammar, she is bad?"

"Your grammar, *it* is not too bad. Just a few little things that we need to work on . . ."

Jean Paul sat at the back of the opera house. He had been to see *Juliet* three times, each time growing more impressed with the power and the sweet tone of Colin Seymour's voice. As the last tragic scene unfolded, the scene in which Romeo died, he listened to the final song. Despite himself, he felt moved by the story and by the singer. He shook himself slightly, suddenly angry. "You fool," he said, "it is only a song, and this is only a made-up story."

He started to leave and stumbled over the feet of the man next to him, who gave him a harsh look. He left the theater and stepped out into the cold night air. The streetlights made greenish dots in the darkness as he made his way along the street. He pulled his cloak around him more closely and gripped the sword cane. During his stay in New Orleans, he had concentrated totally on the task that he had agreed to do. He had not gambled, for he knew bitterly that it had caused his ruination. He had not drunk a great deal either, only at night when he could not sleep. He knew that the thing he was about to do was wrong, and Jean Paul Compier was aware of a shame that seemed to be with him constantly.

As he approached the rooming house where he stayed in the French Quarter, he saw a buggy outside and recognized it. Walking closer, he spoke to the man sitting inside. "You are here, Claude."

Claude Vernay started, for he had not heard Jean Paul's footsteps. "Don't sneak up on a man like that," he snapped.

"I was not sneaking. What is it you want at this time of the night?"

"Get in the carriage. We need to talk."

Jean Paul walked around the carriage, opened the door, and climbed in. He sat down, and Vernay pulled out a flask. "Have a drink," he said. "Cold as the poles in here."

"Not now."

Vernay took a drink but did not put the flask away. In the darkness Compier could make out only the outlines of his face. "Where have you been?" he asked.

"What difference does it make?"

"It makes a great deal of difference."

"I have been to the opera."

"Ah, did you speak to Seymour? Did you —"

"No, I did not. I merely went and watched the opera."

"What good does that do?"

"It does no good at all, but then I am not supposed to do him good, am I?"

"I can't understand," Vernay complained. "You've been here long enough, but you haven't even approached the man. Haven't even spoken to him."

"If you want to call this thing off, I am willing."

"Wait a minute, Jean Paul. Don't be so touchy." Vernay knew there was no way to force him.

Compier said, "This is not something that can be done twice. The challenge must be complete the first time, and the approach must not be crude. Now, tell me more about this man."

"Why do you want to know about him?"

"Everything I hear about him is helpful. Why can I not just puncture him in the arm?"

"What good would that do me?"

"What good will it do you to kill him?"

"He and his adoptive father have kept me from what I want."

"From the woman? If she loves you, this man would not be a problem. And I can't understand why you do not fight him yourself."

Vernay did not answer for a time. He drank again from the flask, then said, "That's none of your business. I'll be paying you a lot of money. What good is money if it won't buy a man what he wants?"

"We are a fine pair, you and I, and I am the worst. You want to kill the man because he stands between you and a woman. And I am nothing but your lackey."

"Come on, Jean Paul, it's just a business matter. For you it's not personal. You've killed men before."

"I am not proud of it, and those were not intentional. They were both accidents in dueling. I overestimated the skill of those men to fight me. And I am not proud of what I am doing now."

"Are you going to back out then?"

A long silence ensued, and then Compier said, "I would like to, but I must have money. Tell me again about him. I need to know as much as I can before I make my approach."

Compier listened as Vernay talked. Finally he said, "It will be soon. I will find a way. Have the money ready."

"Of course. You know I'm good for it."

Compier stepped out of the carriage, but he looked through the window and added, "Yes, my friend, you will be good for it, or it will be a sad day for you." He turned and walked toward the rooming house, leaving Vernay staring after him. "I'll have to pay him. He'd kill me if I didn't."

For the next two days Jean Paul Compier drank steadily. His thinking processes seemed to be impaired, but he knew well it was the distaste he had for the job that troubled him. Finally he came up with a scheme and sought Vernay late at night, when no one saw him.

"This man doesn't go out to a public place very often. I can't very well jump on the stage and start an argument with him." Compier held back his actual plan of attack.

"That's no problem," Vernay said quickly. "He's being honored at a dinner the day after tomorrow. It'll be a fancy affair. There'll be a meal, and afterwards there'll be drinking and a great deal of talk."

"Can you get me an invitation?"

"Certainly."

"Do it."

"All right. And I must be there when the duel takes place. I want to see him wallowing in his own blood!"

The dinner was well attended by the cream of New Orleans society. The mayor, George Ahern, was master of ceremonies, and there were several speakers. The party was composed entirely of men. Jean Paul Compier had given his invitation and taken his seat silently. He spoke to no one during the dinner and ate practically nothing. Finally, after the speeches, the mayor said, "Some of you may need to leave, but our guest of honor will be here for a short time in case any of you haven't met him."

Compier watched as some of the men filed out. Most remained, however, talking and laughing. The cigar smoke made a purple haze in the room, and Compier watched carefully as a group of men congregated around Colin Seymour. He studied Seymour's face as he had ever since he had come to New Orleans. He was impressed by the clean good looks of the man and more by his simplicity of manners. *It would be easier if he were a bully or a bore,* he thought but then forced the idea out of his mind. He stood and crossed the room to the circle of men. Slowly he worked himself forward, and finally he and Colin were face-to-face.

"How do you do, sir?" Colin said. "I don't believe we have met."

"No, we have not," Compier said. "But I knew your adoptive father."

"Did you really? I don't remember meeting you."

"We would not have met. I knew Lord Beaufort when he was a younger man, and I must tell you, sir, he was a man I despised. He had no honor at all in him."

Compier had spoken loudly enough so that the group immediately fell silent and stared at him. The silence seemed to spread outward, and the other men, seeing something was happening, stopped speaking, and some moved forward so they could hear better.

"You are mistaken, sir. My father was incapable of doing a dishonorable thing."

"You are innocent, perhaps, my lord, but the man you call your father brought shame and disgrace on my sister. He got her with child and cast her out. She died a derelict."

"You are a liar!"

A gasp went around the room, and Compier felt a sense of grim satisfaction. *At least,* he thought, *I have done part of what I came to do.* "I will overlook your insult, my lord. You do not know me."

"I know you are a liar, and I will prove it any way you choose."

Compier smiled. "My name is Jean Paul Compier. If you lived in France, you should know that name."

Claude Vernay had been standing back on the outer circle. He moved forward and faced Compier briefly, then turned to say, "Lord Beaufort, I am no friend of yours, but I warn you: have nothing to do with this man. He is the deadliest swordsman in Europe. It would be suicide."

Colin ignored Vernay's words and studied Compier's face. "I don't know what your motive is, sir. Perhaps it's mistaken identity, but —"

"It is not mistaken identity, my lord. The marquis was a vicious man."

Colin stood silent. He felt no fear, but a great prejudice against the code duello had been settling in him, and he had resolved that he would never again take part in such a thing. He said so now. "I will not fight you, Compier. I despise this whole business of dueling. It's foolish." His voice rose, and he said, "A man's honor is not in his trigger finger or in his agility with a sword. The worst villain in the world may possess these qualities."

Compier smiled thinly. "Those are the words of a coward — as Armand de Cuvier was. I called him out when he disgraced my sister, and he refused to meet me. Instead he sent hired assassins to kill me, and they almost did."

"That's another lie!"

"Though you are not the true son of the man you call your father, you are the same sort of coward he was."

"You are a liar, and I will proclaim it anywhere in this city." He hesitated. "But if it takes some sort of senseless duel, I will fight you." A slight smile came to Colin's face, although he was paler than usual. "If you wish to fight, fine. We will stand three feet apart with loaded pistols pointed at one another's hearts. On the count of three, we will fire."

Compier stared at him. "It is not the code duello, my lord, and I am the challenged party. I would be a fool to commit suicide. You may place no value on your own life, but I value my own. We will fight with swords. I have the choice of weapons."

Colin asked, "Why should I fight you with weapons that you have spent a lifetime mastering? I will meet you with bowie knives or with axes or with clubs, or as I said, with pistols at a distance of three feet. I will not let you kill me simply because you are an accomplished butcher. Good day, sir."

He turned and walked out, and Compier said as he left the room, "You will fight me, my lord, or be branded a coward."

Bayard, who was also in attendance, was momentarily shocked into silence by Compier's sudden appearance and his words. His face reddened. "I think you are the coward, Frenchman. You will not fight unless you are certain to win."

Compier's mind worked quickly. He knew about Bayard and that the two had become good friends. "You are brash, sir, and young. Shut your mouth, or I will shut it for you."

"I'll speak what I think, and I think you are a scoundrel!"

"You are his friend, then, the friend of Lord Beaufort?"

"Yes."

"Then you are the friend of a villain. He is like his adoptive father, a man with no shame, and you should feel shame at being the companion of such a man."

Bayard stepped forward and slapped Compier's face. Compier could have dodged the blow easily, but he said, "Don't be a fool. Get away, boy."

Bayard repeated, "I think you are the coward." He slapped him again, and the mayor said, "Stop this, Bayard."

"I'll meet you with any kind of weapon, Compier."

"With the blade, then," Compier said. "I will ask my friend to call on you."

Compier left the room. Vernay stayed long enough to hear almost all the men telling Bayard d'Or that he must not meet the man. Bayard was adamant, and Vernay left feeling a grim satisfaction.

He waited until night and went to Compier's room. "You did well," he said. "I see exactly what you're doing. You think Seymour will not allow his young friend to fight."

"He is a man of honor — unlike me and unlike you. Yes, I think he will do all he can to dissuade young d'Or, but d'Or is like I was at his age. But I won't have to fight him. You understand that."

"I don't think it'll be necessary. Seymour will come to his rescue. Then he will die."

"Perhaps not. He may kill me. That would be a great economy for you."

"Don't be foolish. He can't stand in front of you. No one can. I've got the money ready. It'll be in cash. After the duel, I'll pay you."

CHAPTER
TWENTY-THREE

Simone opened the door to see Colin. His face was drawn tight, and he said merely, "Hello, Simone."

"Colin, come in." Simone stepped back, and Colin entered the house. She saw that she was stiff and tense.

"I just heard about Bayard's challenging Compier. I came right over to talk to him."

"It's — it's terrible, Colin." Simone's voice was barely above a whisper. She clasped her hands, and he saw that they were trembling. She pressed her lips together in an attempt to gain control and said, "Father's talking to him now, and I've tried everything. He just won't listen. Has he lost his mind?"

"Could we go into the parlor? I'd like to wait until he gets through talking with your father."

"Oh, of course, come in. It's cold out here in the foyer." Simone led him to the parlor.

A fire crackled in the fireplace, and she picked up a poker and jabbed at the logs. They settled and hissed, sending a storm of golden sparks up the chimney. Putting the poker back in the holder, Simone turned to Colin, and her eyes mirrored the fright she felt. "He'll be killed, Colin. I know he will."

"We mustn't let him do it, Simone. I feel responsible. I should have taken up Compier's challenge."

"I heard that he was deadly with any sort of weapon."

"That's true. Armand spoke of him often. He didn't admire him, but everyone knew about him. I think all he's ever done is fight with a sword."

"What's he doing over here?"

Colin shook his head and said, "He claims he wants to start a fencing academy here in New Orleans — at least that's what I heard."

The two stood silent for a moment. Simone walked over to the window and stared out. Colin went to stand beside her. "You mustn't let this destroy you, Simone."

"We've never had anything like this happen. Now I know how you felt when Claude challenged Armand. I was unmoved by it. Oh, what a terrible beast I was!"

Colin put his hand on her shoulder. "You've changed since then."

"I'm glad you think so, but I can hardly speak. I didn't realize what a terrible thing fear was. It's worse than being physically ill. Oh, Colin, what are we going to do?"

"We have to talk sense to Bayard. He's fallen into this 'honor' business again. All of this is part of that stupid code duello mentality. Why can't people see that it's brutal and cruel? How many good men have died because of some mistaken idea of honor?" He took her arm and led her over to the sofa in front of the fire. "Here, sit down," he said.

"I'm too frightened even to pray. That's silly, isn't it? When we're afraid, that's when we need to go to God."

"You're right about that. Well, we'll agree to pray for Bayard, that he'll come out of this safely."

"Son, don't you see how foolish this is? The man's nothing but an assassin."

"I'm sorry that we don't agree on this, Father, but I don't see any way I can refuse to meet him."

Louis d'Or paced the floor in his study. His voice was tight with anxiety. "Bayard, God has just come into your life. We all see it, son. Something happened to you when you nearly died out in the bayou. You've become a different sort of person, and a great future lies before you. Are you going to throw it all away because of your foolish pride?"

Bayard listened, and although he desperately wanted to please his father, he had stubbornly set himself to do the thing. Finally his father threw up his hands and said, "I can't believe you're going to do this. I thought you had more sense." He turned and walked out of the room.

As soon as he left, Bayard sat down in a chair beside the bookcase. His nerves were on edge, and he started when the door opened. Seeing Fleur come in, he stood up at once, and when she put out her hands, he took them.

"Your father, he talk to you about this fight. I hope you listen to him."

"I'd like to, Fleur, but I can't."

A steadfastness in her gaze held him. "I think you are wrong."

"Everyone thinks I'm wrong."

"And that don't tell you nothing? Your father, your sister, your mother, and me. And I hear that everyone who is talking about say you are crazy to fight this man. He is a butcher!"

Bayard released her hands and turned away. He could not bear to meet the accusation in her eyes. He walked over to the desk, stared down at it, then turned quickly. "You don't understand, Fleur. No one does. All my life I've done nothing but take the easy way out. I became a weak lowlife, and this is the one chance I have to prove that I have some metal in me."

"No, it proves you have pride in you!"

"Well, pride is a good thing, isn't it?"

"No, not the kind you have. The Bible say that God loves humility. I remember a verse my *ma mere* say over and over to me. It is in the Proverbs, I think. It says, 'By humility and the fear of the LORD are riches, and honour, and life.' And that is what you are giving up because of your pride. Not riches or honor, for there is no honor involved in this. Only pride! So you are giving up your life for a worthless thing."

She went to him and put her arms around him. She put her head down on his chest and whispered, "Don't you see, my Bayard? What does it matter what people say as long as you know you are doing the wise and right thing?"

Bayard stood absolutely still. Finally he gave a short laugh. He put his hands on Fleur's shoulders and said, "All right. I'll apologize to the man. It goes against the grain, but I will do it because you say so."

Fleur's face lit up. She put her hand on his cheek and said, "That is a fine thing. God will honor you for this. Bayard, you must do it as soon as possible."

"It will have to be in public. I'll look him up tomorrow."

"Come. We must tell your parents and your family. They are so worried about you!"

Bayard slept little that night. He practiced the speech that he planned to make to Compier until it became bitter in his thoughts. His family had been ecstatic when he told them that he would apologize, as had Colin. Colin had grasped his hand and said, "That's the mark of true wisdom there, Bayard. You wouldn't make anyone happy getting yourself killed."

Bayard waited until midafternoon, and then he stood outside the saloon he had heard from Byron Mayhew that Compier frequented. Taking a deep breath, he muttered, "I'd almost rather be shot than do this." Nevertheless, he straightened his shoulders and walked in. As soon as he entered the room, men began to mutter. When he started for the table where Jean Paul Compier sat playing poker, a silence ensued.

Compier was aware of him. He put his

cards down and turned to face Bayard. He said nothing, and Bayard could not read what was in his eyes. But he had a chore to do, and he said quickly, "I have come to speak with you, sir."

"Well, speak on."

The words were like acid in Bayard's mouth. "I have come to apologize. I behaved in a most ungentlemanly way, and I must ask you to overlook my words."

Jean Paul's eyes changed. Something flickered in them, but his voice was harsh. "So you insult me in public, and now you think by a few words you can wipe it out? I refuse your apology. If you are not a coward, I will meet you at the appointed time."

Bayard knew then that the matter was hopeless. He nodded, saying quietly, "Very well, sir." He turned and left the room and went home. He knew that the news would frighten his family, but he felt fenced in — trapped. "There's no other way for it."

Vernay was ecstatic. As Compier started to leave the saloon, he grabbed his arm. He said, "You've got him now! I know Seymour. He'll never permit that boy to fight. He'll come rushing in to save him, and then you can kill him out of hand."

Jean Paul Compier struck Vernay's hand

away from his arm. "Never touch me again," he said. He glared at Vernay until Claude felt a touch of fear. He knew the deadliness of the man. "What's wrong with you? It's going just as we planned."

Compier said bitterly, "You are a dog, and I am worse for what I am doing. Get out of my sight, Vernay!"

Vernay at once backed away. "We have an agreement," he whispered.

"If you do not leave, you will not be in any condition to know anything about our deal, for I will kill you."

Compier watched as Vernay's face turned pale. Then as he turned and strode out of the saloon, Compier thought, *I thought I had sunk low, but never as low as this.*

Colin went again to the d'Or house and found Bayard in his studio. He was not painting but simply standing beside a window, looking out on the frozen earth. When Colin entered, he said, "It's a cold night for you to be out."

"I just heard about what happened at the saloon." He put his hand on Bayard's shoulder. "You can't do this to yourself."

"I don't have any option."

"Yes, you do. It's not your fight. Vernay is behind all this. He's out to destroy me, and he's using you."

"Talking won't do any good."

"I look on you as a friend, Bayard. I might as well tell you that I love your sister, and I'm going to marry her if I can."

"That is good news, Colin. I've watched her. She cares for you very deeply, and she needs a man like you."

"That's good to hear from you, but this thing you're going to do is not wise. Speaking of love, I have the feeling you care for Fleur. She's going to need all the help she can get, and a dead man can't help her."

"I've got to do it, Colin. I failed at everything I ever tried. I always gave up when things got tough, but I'm not going to give up on this!"

Colin argued strenuously, but finally, when he left the house that night, he shook his head, saying, "He's so young and so foolish. Something has to be done!"

CHAPTER
TWENTY-FOUR

Hearing the knock on her door, Fleur opened it to find a pale Simone. "Colin is here." Fleur saw Colin standing behind her and said, "Come in, please."

The two stepped into her room, and Fleur said, "This duel must not happen!"

"We've all tried our best to talk to Bayard, but he won't listen."

"I know. I have try everything." Tears came into her eyes, and she said, "I have not known Bayard long, but I know that I care for him. He must not throw his life away!"

Colin threw up his hands in despair. "I have tried everything I can think of. He won't listen to reason."

"Well, I have prayed, and I think God has give me an answer."

"What is it?" Simone cried. "What is it, Fleur?"

"Listen and I will tell you. First thing we

must do . . ."

Bayard put on his best suit, even though it seemed foolish as he finished fastening his tie. *I'm going to be dead, so what difference does it make what I wear?* He looked at himself in the mirror and saw a stranger. *You're a fool, Bayard d'Or. Everyone thinks so. Your stupid pride's going to get you killed, and then what will this so-called honor matter?* He turned quickly away from the mirror and left his room. It was early morning, and the winter darkness lingered. Bayard felt numb, and his mind would not function properly. It was as if he had willed himself not to think but simply to go through with the terrible act.

As he stepped outside the house and headed for the stable, suddenly a figure appeared. He started, then relaxed. "Fleur, it's you. You startled me."

Fleur came closer. She was wearing a heavy, wool coat against the cold, but she wore no gloves on her hands. She reached out, put her hands on his chest, and said, "I have come to beg you not to go."

"I must do it, Fleur. Please don't say anything else. I've had a hard enough time saying good-bye to my family."

"I thought you love me."

"I *do* love you, but I couldn't face myself in the mirror if I let Colin risk his life for me."

"You are throwing everything good away."

"I can't help myself."

"You won't change your mind?" Fleur said. "Are you sure, Bayard?"

"I must do it."

Fleur stood very still, then dropped her hands to her sides, and her eyes glittered strangely. "Then I must stop you."

"Fleur, don't interfere."

Fleur said, "Ansel!"

Bayard caught a movement, a man coming out of the stable. He was a big man accompanied by another, also large. Instantly Bayard stiffened. "Who are you? What do you want?"

"I am Ansel Guidry, and this is my friend Chapin Billaud."

Bayard faced them cautiously. "What are you two men doing here? What do you want?"

"What do we want?" Ansel said. "We want you should do as Fleur asks. She is our friend, as was her *mere*."

"These are some good friends of mine from the bayou," Fleur explained.

"We Cajuns have to stick together." Ansel grinned wolfishly. "The little one, she ask you to do something for her, and she says you will not do it. So, we have come to help her."

Bayard turned and asked, "What does this mean, Fleur? Did you ask these men to come here?"

Fleur said evenly, "If you will not listen to reason, then I will have to use force. You are *not* going to that fight!"

"Oh yes, I am!" Bayard said. He shoved his way around the men to get to his horse, but Fleur called out, "Ansel, stop him!"

Ansel whirled quickly for a big man and grabbed Bayard's left arm. The other man took his right. "Take your hands off of me!" Bayard cried. He struggled but was powerless as a child in their hands.

"Don't hurt him, Ansel!"

"No, *chéri,* we treat him like a baby."

"Bring him into the stable."

Bayard tried to escape the men's grasp, but it was useless. As soon as they were inside, Fleur said, "Tie him up, Chapin."

Chapin produced a short length of rope. "We tie you here, I think, Monsieur. Be content."

Bayard protested, "Fleur, you can't do this to me!" He lifted his voice and called, "Robert, where are you?"

"Robert has gone home. There is no one

here but us. Tie him to that pillar," Fleur said quietly.

The two men backed Bayard to one of the posts that held up the roof, put his hands behind it, and tied him firmly. "I am sorry to have to do this, Monsieur, but sometimes a man, he won't listen to reason."

Bayard stared at Fleur's friends. They had no animosity in them. The one called Ansel asked, "Can we do anything else for you, *chéri?*"

"No, thank you, Ansel, and you, too, Chapin."

"We go now." Ansel Guidry smiled then at Bayard and said, "Do not be angry, Monsieur. This is the wise thing. We must help the little one. She has lost her *mere,* who was our good friend. She can't lose anyone else. If you ever need us, Fleur, you come at any time."

"Thank you," Fleur said again. She watched as the two men left and then stood in front of Bayard, who stared at her in disbelief. "It's going to be a long wait," she said. She got a blanket and put it behind his feet. "Let yourself down. You will be more comfortable."

Bayard exclaimed, "Turn me loose, Fleur! This is crazy!"

"No, it is not." She put her hands on his

face, pulled his head down, and kissed him. "You can beat me when this is over," she said with a smile.

"This won't do any good. I'll find Compier as soon as you turn me loose."

"No, you will not. Colin has gone to fight him, and God will give him the victory over that man."

Bayard struggled, pulling against the ropes, but an expert had tied them. "I can't let Colin fight my battles for me."

"It is not Colin. I have prayed, and I think this is what God wants. Please do not hate me, Bayard, because I do this." She put her arms around him and lay her head on his chest. He smelled the fragrance of her hair, and her voice was so soft he could barely hear it. "One day after we are married, I may get very sick or have trouble, and I know you will take care of me. And now I must take care of you." She lifted her head and put her hands on his cheeks. "Now sit down." She pulled at him until finally he sat down. She got another blanket, pulled it around the two of them, and said, "Now, my English must be ver' good to be your wife. You teach me how to talk like a lady, Bayard."

Suddenly Bayard laughed. He could not help himself. "At a time like this, you want me to give you a grammar lesson?"

"Ah, but yes. I must live in your world. When this is all over, I will take you to my house. I will teach you how to catch a 'gator without having him bite your face off. Now, teach me how to talk."

Compier stood straight in the fast-fading light. A crowd had gathered, as he had known it would, when word spread that Colin would fight him after all. George Ahern, the mayor of New Orleans, stood before him. "Compier, I must speak with you."

"*Certainement,* Mr. Mayor."

"You see those two men over there?"

Compier looked to see two large men wearing bulky coats. "My vision is good," he said.

"They are officers of the law. If you kill Lord Beaufort, you will be arrested and charged with murder. Do you understand?"

Compier looked at Claude Vernay, who had heard the mayor's words. "With murder? But it is a duel!"

"Dueling is illegal," Ahern said. "We are fools in this city for permitting it to continue. It shouldn't have gone this far. Go ahead and have your duel. I think you're expert enough simply to pink the young man in the arm, but if you kill him, you will hang for it. You have my word on that, Compier!"

Compier stared into the mayor's face. Ahern was not a tall man. He was chunky and short, but there was a fierce light in his brown eyes. Compier was certain that Ahern meant exactly what he said. He had no time to think further, for suddenly Colin Seymour stood before him.

Colin said, "Compier, I know that your fight is with me, not with my friend Bayard d'Or. I refused your challenge once, but I will take it now."

Compier suddenly felt a flash of admiration. He well understood that Colin Seymour was not a fool. "You must know, sir, that you have no chance with me."

"That may be true, but it is something I must do. I can't permit those remarks about my father to go unchallenged." Colin added, "I don't understand you, sir."

"Why is that?" Compier asked.

"I have heard from my friend and teacher, François Morell, that you were two things: the best swordsman in Europe, and a man of honor. I can believe the first, sir, but not the second." Colin looked inquisitively at Compier. "And any man who makes himself the tool of another has sold his honor, and

I'm convinced that's what you have done."

The crowd waited to hear Compier's reply.

Compier suddenly smiled, and he stood straighter. "I have changed my mind about the weapon. We will use pistols."

"They are not really your weapon," Colin said. "They're mine."

Compier looked at Claude Vernay, and their gazes locked until Vernay had to drop his eyes. "I will have my honor back," he said. "Are you ready?"

"Yes," Colin said.

The two put themselves into position, and as Colin walked the ten paces, he was thinking. *This may be my last moment on earth.* At the count of ten, he turned quickly. He saw that Compier had already whirled but then was shocked when Compier lifted his pistol and fired it into the air.

"You may take your revenge now, my lord," Compier said in a strong, clear voice.

Colin stared at the man. He pointed his pistol in the air and fired it, then moved forward at once. "It's all over then, Compier?"

"No, it is not. I have two things to say." The spectators, who had watched the drama with fervent interest, moved forward so they would not miss a word. "The first thing I say is that I lied when I spoke of your father.

He was a man of honor. Everything I said about him was a lie, and I ask your pardon."

"I think I can guess why you said such a thing," Colin said.

"Indeed, I think you can." Compier turned and glared at Vernay. "The second thing I say is that Claude Vernay is a cowardly dog! He hired me to pick a quarrel with Lord Beaufort. I regret I ever agreed to do such a thing, and I hereby renounce him. You are a liar, a coward, and a cheat, Vernay! I hope you take exception. We can settle the matter right now. The weapons are here."

Claude Vernay glanced around wildly and saw that every man's face was set against him. He suddenly wheeled, shoved his way out of the crowd, and broke into a run.

"That man's finished in New Orleans," Ahern said with grim satisfaction. "If he doesn't leave, I'll have him run out." He walked away, leaving the two men together.

"Why did you do this, Monsieur Compier?" Colin asked quietly.

Compier looked at the ground. "Why does a man do that which he knows to be wrong? I'm getting older, and I wasted my life. I wanted one thing: to start an academy for young men to learn the sword. Vernay promised to furnish the money." He lifted his eyes and said, "I almost sold my soul, and I ask your pardon again."

Colin put out his hand. When Compier shook it, Colin said, "I like to see a man who can change. Come and visit me this week. We will see what can be done."

Compier gasped, "You mean it, my lord?"

"Try me."

Compier bit his lip. He cleared his throat and whispered, "Yes, I will come."

Simone was waiting, and when Colin rode up, she grabbed up her coat and ran outside. She saw Colin dismounting. She flew to him and cried, "Colin, you're safe!"

"I think God was with me."

"What happened?" she asked. She held onto him. "You're not harmed."

"It went off much better than I thought." He told her quickly what had happened and then asked, "Where's Bayard?"

"He is in the stable. He's probably frozen stiff. Fleur's friends tied him up a couple of hours ago."

"Well, we can go turn him loose now."

They walked around the side of the house. As soon as they entered the stable, Fleur jumped to her feet. "You're safe!" she cried. "I knew God would help us!"

Colin laughed and looked down at Bayard. "You've been treated roughly, my friend, but it's all right now." He waited until Fleur had pulled the knots loose, and Bayard got to his feet, rubbing his wrists.

"What about the duel?"

"There was no duel — or not much of one."

Bayard listened as Colin told him the story, then he reached out and pulled Fleur close. He looked down at her and said, "I never saw a woman who would have her fiancé tied up."

"I promise never to do it again," Fleur said. Her eyes were flashing, but her lips were trembling. She said, "And we must never quarrel again."

"I can't promise that, but please don't have me tied up when I disagree with you." He smiled.

"Come inside," Simone said. "It's freezing out here."

"And I'm hungry," Bayard said. "I haven't eaten anything all day."

"Neither have I," Colin confessed.

The four of them went inside, and soon they were seated around the table eating the rice and sandwiches that the d'Ors' cook put together. They all talked loudly, their faces flushed with happiness and excitement. Finally Fleur and Bayard left, and as soon as they did, Colin said, "I suppose I need to be going home, but I've got something to tell you."

Simone looked at him. "What is it?" He had grown quieter. He rose, and as the two walked down the hall toward the front door, he said, "I'm leaving for New York next week."

"New York? What for, Colin?"

"I'm meeting with the head of the New York Opera Company. They're interested in having me bring *Juliet* to New York."

They reached the door, and Colin put on his coat. Simone said, "I knew you'd be leaving — that New Orleans wouldn't hold you. How long will you be gone?"

"I am not sure." He took his hat from the rack but did not put it on.

"I was terrified when you went to fight that man."

Colin did not answer. He was looking at her in a peculiar way. He suddenly moved forward, and Simone felt that he was going to embrace her. But instead he took her hand, kissed it, and said, "I'll see you again before I leave." He turned quickly and left. The parting had been formal, and after the victory in the duel, she could not understand it. She went back into the kitchen, where she poured herself another cup of coffee.

She sat for a long time in silence. Then Fleur entered the room and said, "Isn't it wonderful? It's all over now."

"Yes, it is."

"What did Colin say?"

"Nothing really. That he was going to New York to see about putting on the opera there."

Fleur looked intently into her face. "Did he say he loved you, Simone?"

"No."

Fleur heard the shortness of Simone's answer and said quietly, "I thought he would."

"So did I, Fleur — but he didn't."

CHAPTER
TWENTY-FIVE

Christmas Eve had come to New Orleans with a most unusual phenomenon: a light snow arrived that December afternoon and coated the ground with white. Snow was a rare thing in the Crescent City, and in the residential areas the children were out trying to make snowmen from the thin layer of snow. Very few succeeded in this, but there were snowball fights, and those who had traveled from the northern parts of the country were gathering up enough to make snow cream.

At the home of Louis d'Or, the carriages that had come for a Christmas Eve dinner created tracks in the snow, and the coachmen beat their hands together as they waited outside. After a time, Agnes the maid invited them into the kitchen for some "Christmas cheer," and they gladly accepted.

Inside the large dining room, extra places

had been set so that twenty-five people were wedged into the room. The chandelier overhead threw its sparkling light down on the excited faces, reflecting off of the silverware and the fine china, and the servers were bringing in the food: turkey and dressing and a huge ham.

Louise d'Or and his wife, Renee, sat at opposite ends of the table. They beamed at each other from time to time, their glances often going to Bayard and Fleur, who sat together midway at the long table. Louis d'Or was more jovial than anyone had ever seen him. His eyes flashed, and he yielded the knife that sliced the turkey with a flourish.

Fleur was wearing a new gown that she had picked out herself. It was a pale blue that fitted her form extremely well, and from her ears two green stones flashed and caught the light overhead. Often she put her hand on Bayard's arm, as if seeking reassurance. Once she whispered, "I never seen so much food."

"Well, I have an engagement party only once, so Father and Mother went all out."

Suddenly the talk died down, for Louis had risen from his chair. "I will interrupt the festivities only long enough to make an extended, boring speech."

"No, Louis," Renee said. "No speeches, please."

"Well, you see what honor I have in my own house. My own dear wife can't bear my speaking. Very well. It will be a short speech then." He grew serious and looked around the table, his eyes finally coming to rest on Bayard and Fleur. "This is the time of Christmas. Usually we think about giving and receiving presents. Tonight I want you to meet the person who has given my wife and me such a great gift. My daughter-in-law-to-be, Miss Fleur Avenall, who gave us back our son."

Applause rose from the company, and Fleur colored but managed to smile. She kept her hold on Bayard's arm, and he reached over and enclosed her hand in his.

Louis smiled at this and continued, "She gave us our son by saving his life, and I'll be glad to tell that story, although you've all heard it, but we are giving her a great gift, too: our only son. So, at this time of Christmas, I propose a toast to my son, Bayard d'Or, and to his bride, Miss Fleur Avenall."

The voices rang out, "Hear, hear!"

"Now we need to hear from the bride and groom. Bayard, what do you have to say for yourself?"

Bayard did not rise or release Fleur's

hand. "Thank you, Father. You left out a great deal about what a prodigal son I was. I would be out there yet, I suppose, if it were not for this woman beside me. She not only saved my life physically, but she and her dear mother, bless her soul, taught me to love God and to trust in Him." He turned to Fleur and smiled gently. "Soon we will stand up and make our vows, but I'll make you one just now, Fleur: I am yours as long as you will have me, to love you as long as we are on this earth."

"That is very beautiful," Fleur responded. Then humor twinkled in her eyes. "Still, maybe I will have to tie you up a few times when you misbehave."

Laughter exploded around the table, for everyone there, close friends and acquaintances, knew the story of how Fleur had managed to stop Bayard from a senseless duel only by tying him to a post.

Simone laughed with the others. She was glad for the couple, and after the dinner was over and the guests had gone, she went to Fleur and said, "I'm so happy for you."

"It is wonderful," Fleur said, her eyes dancing. "We have decided to have our honeymoon in my old cabin. But then your father and mother, they have given us a wonderful wedding present. We will spend six months, maybe longer, in London. Bayard will study his painting there, and I will learn to speak and act like a lady."

"It's like a storybook, isn't it?"

"Yes, it is." Fleur looked more closely at Simone and asked, "Have you heard from Colin?"

"Yes. The rehearsals are going fine. He had to train a whole new company for the production in New York."

"None of the old company will be in the new opera?"

"Just a few. Rosa Calabria will keep her role as the nurse, and a few others."

"What about Marie?"

"She was not asked."

Fleur hesitated, then said, "Does he say anything else in his letter, I mean?"

"Not really."

Fleur noted the sadness in Simone's face and hugged her. "I will pray for you, my sister."

The house was quiet. The guests had departed, and the family had gone to bed. Looking at the clock on her mantel over the small fireplace, Simone saw that it was after ten. She was listless, and for a while she sat trying to read, but the book made little sense to her. She tossed it aside and started to get ready for bed. Sitting down, she began to brush her hair, and her thoughts were happy as she thought of Bayard and Fleur. *They're going to be such a fine couple, and when they come back, Fleur will fit in perfectly.*

Her thoughts went then to herself. She felt restless and out of place and frustrated. She knew that it had to do with Colin. She could not understand him. He had left so abruptly, almost formally, and his letters had been the same. She had received only three, and they were all filled with information about how the preparation for the new opera was going. There was no personal warmth to them, and as she brushed her hair, Simone thought, *Something has happened to Colin. I know he cared for me, but he left so coldly. I have prayed for an answer, but I don't know what it is.*

Finally she put the brush down and started to remove her dress, but even as she loosened the first button at the back of her neck she heard a voice. She stood stock-still, then with a glad cry, she ran over to the window. She opened it with a bang and leaned out. There in the snow stood Colin. He was singing the love song of Romeo to Juliet. His voice rose and filled the air. He was smiling. Finally the song ended, and he asked, "Do you remember that from the opera?"

"Yes, of course."

"Well, in the opera Romeo climbed up to the balcony. I'm not sure I can climb up there, Simone. I might fall and break my neck."

"You wait. I'll come down."

Simone flew down the stairs and out the front door, forgetting even her coat. She ran to Colin, who caught her up in his arms and hugged her so tightly that she gasped. Then he put her down on the ground and kissed her. She held him tightly, and when he lifted his head, he said, "Our story is not going to end like the opera. I always hated the end of Romeo and Juliet."

"So did I." Simone looked up, and her eyes were sparkling. "It's so dreary."

"Well, our life isn't going to be like that."

Missing his statement, Simone asked, "Colin, why did you leave almost without a word?"

"I wanted to give us both a chance to think about this. I wasn't sure you'd have me. But I have thought about it, and now, sweetheart, I want to tell you." He kissed her again and then laughed. "Romeo's love for Juliet was nothing. Kid stuff. My love for you is the real thing."

Simone seemed to relax. "I thought you didn't want me."

"Not want you? I want you like a man wants air or water. So, will you have me?"

"Yes!"

They stood clinging to each other, and finally he said, "We'll be engaged then until the run of this is over in New York, and then we'll be married."

"Will it be a long time?"

"It will be long for me. One day would be long for me. But I haven't told you about our honeymoon."

"You've already got that planned, without even talking to me?"

"I think you'll like my plan."

"What is it, Colin?"

"After we're married, we'll get on a ship, and we'll have a honeymoon on board. Then we'll get to France, and we'll go to my estate."

Simone snuggled closer to him. "Is it a castle?"

"Not exactly, but with you there as queen, I'll feel like a king." He asked, "Do you remember I once told you about alchemy?"

"Yes, I have never forgotten it."

"I'm sure of it now. Scientists all failed to turn lead or iron into gold, but you have proven that there is an alchemy in the truest sense of the word. You are another woman from the one I first met. All that was cold and hard is gone — and nothing is left in you but warmth and gentleness and love."

Simone pulled his head down and kissed him, and then they began to dance around in the snow. Pulling him to a stop, Simone said, "God has answered our prayers, and it's going to be wonderful." She paused and added, "But my feet are freezing."

"You ought to be willing to suffer a little bit. You're getting me for a husband. Think how lucky you are."

"You are filled up with pride. I'll have to puncture that. But come inside. We must tell Father and Mother."

Suddenly a voice rang out. "You don't have to tell us anything!"

Simone looked up and saw her parents leaning out of their bedroom window. They were both beaming, and her father said, "I think everybody in the neighborhood heard your proposal, Colin. Now you can come inside and ask my permission to court my daughter."

Colin waved his right arm, his left around Simone. "I'll be right there, but I'm only taking yes for an answer."

The two walked toward the house, cling-

ing to one another, and the stars glittered
above them. Snow began to fall.

The employees of Thorndike Press hope you have enjoyed this Large Print book. All our Thorndike and Wheeler Large Print titles are designed for easy reading, and all our books are made to last. Other Thorndike Press Large Print books are available at your library, through selected bookstores, or directly from us.

For information about titles, please call:
(800) 223-1244

or visit our Web site at:
www.gale.com/thorndike
www.gale.com/wheeler

To share your comments, please write:
Publisher
Thorndike Press
295 Kennedy Memorial Drive
Waterville, ME 04901